THE BALLAD OF BEIJING

ALAN GOLDFEIN

to Ute

.

About the Author

Alan Goldfein has written for *Time, New York, The Village Voice, Commentary, Playboy, Oui, Satire, Beyond Baroque, Cimarron Review, Colorado Quarterly, Forum, Florida Quarterly*, and *The San Francisco Chronicle*. He is the author of *Heads*, and has been anthologized in a Random House Collection, *On the Job: Fiction About Work*. In the 1970s, Alan Goldfein received the Mark Twain Society Award and a New York State Council of the Arts award for fiction.

During an extended stay in Germany, the novels *Jews and Germans/Germans and Jews, Europe's Macadam/America's Tar, Let Us Now Praise America, The Black Wife*, and *The Guidance Counselor* were created.

Alan Goldfein has taught economics at the University of Maryland, history at Carnegie-Mellon-University, and writing at Berkeley. He has also written numerous episodes for television series, such as *Knots Landing, Perfect Couples, Bodies of Evidence*, and *Paradise*.

I

WHY WOULD I BE HERE?

2015. Beijing: The main question to ask, even of more immediate importance than why he, Arthur Becker, an American Jew, a writer yet, had killed the German man in Wiesbaden (really?—could there be any more important question to ask than why he'd committed murder?), a more important question had now butted-in: why he had fallen in love with the Chinese girl, Hung Huang, the intended of his (German) son Mick (Mick-ah-yell, in German), while all were together in that knotted-up Chinese city: A romantic love had set itself within him for Hung, a sensual love, not a bit paternal—as if this Hung Huang were the embodiment of the woman he'd wanted all his life. . . Moreso than his (German) wife Jutta. . . And he, a relatively bright fellow in his mid-forties, had just discovered that?

He'd gotten his tetanus and typhoid shots, plus a pneumonia booster and herpes zoster for shingles, which was purported to be widespread in China, and for which injection in Germany you had to fuss and finagle to scare-up (a journalist, he'd planned to investigate why this unhealthy hampering was the case—then, caught in the hectic business of leaving for The East, he let it go. . . No, he forgot.) The long flight from Frankfurt was, as expected (what else?) dull (except for two slambang slamscream aisle scraps between Chinese, one early-on, one near landing: "Chinks, they always do this shit on planes," said a nearby American, "they got no control, it's weird. Same reason they can't drive for shit."). Becker's prejudice was also burlesqued by this old Chinese man seated behind him in Economy: the fellow kept kicking Arthur's seat, getting him good in the right pelvis, as the pummeling was continuous, rhythmic, metronomic, for ten long hours. Throughout, Becker had come to liken those foot-jolts to some Chinese form of water-boarding, so finally, over Romania (or Bulgaria, or wherever) he had had enough and he spinned round to face the elderly kicking chink, who said nothing, not a word, while his wife, next to him, *admonished Arthur*: "He have the *Parkinson!*" Implication: 'It's *your* fault, American, for *your* look of admonishment, for *your* unsympathy! *Take* these kicks, *endure* them, for all you have done to us Chinese throughout the years! *Take* it, as you are *now* being forced to accept our poleaxing Chinese *GDP!*'

Becker took it.

Looking down then from that train-long monster double-decker Lufthansa Airbus 380 in landing approach, as it banked round and leveled-out, you saw Beijing suggest heaven and you saw it evidence an inky blotch of ballast. Skytowers distant from slow landing descent, some bronze-burnished in the light of late afternoon. Smokened valleys then, unverdant, under slated skirt-mine scars as the plane skimmed in descent over what was The Great Wall or a menacingly wriggling geo-fault (it appeared crumbling) (the pilot did announce—*"Der erst Super Eisene Forhang in Geshichts!"*[1]). Becker had off-kiltered from the plane, limping, tentatively flexing a knotted knee from so infinite a flight (Economy, as already reported); he had flown so long and far to "New Beijing" that his brain had even managed to acquit him of Professor Fritz Strobel's murder back in Heidelberg; and now this "New Beijing" was those skyscrapers mixed within a big bleak flattened fog—mushroom sombreros surrounding towers of silvered glass, an airpocalypse. In prep for going, Becker had dutifully read up (book-skimming, no Wikipedia): China: forty percent of the skyscrapers under construction in the world; drastic desperate industry: smells similar to a chemical spill on fire; levels of "fine particulate matter" fifty times the recommended exposure limit set by the WHO—Beijing kids younger than ten were being hospitalized with lung cancer, and life-expectancy was six years shorter than the modern normal, backslid to the Bible's three-score and ten. So this was his son Mick-ah-yell's Mecca?! Had Germany been so intolerable for Arthur Becker's boy?—half Jewish, though not really, as Mick's mom Jutta was no Jew, and the year was 2015. The kid chooses Peking U—they still called it by the old name—over Heidelberg or Stanford or Hopkins or an Ivy. Mick says, "China is the future, father, it is fever", and he opts for that gray density, for this stratospheric

---

[1] The first Super Iron Curtain in history!

glass-and-concrete with orange construction cranes like giant horseflies (one boasted a titanic sign that read FUTURE SPLENDID ARMS). Okay, yes, from the bus-limo into town Becker did observe the occasional curlicued pagoda, red-roofed or green, as if these relics were tourist lures planted among the megaliths—one such colossus was a giant egg, one was split-stance like a pair of pants. . . The limo driver didn't much give a shit; he let his unhooked safety belt hang lifeless, a dead dog's wag-less tail, as for the duration of the ride Arthur's young Brit seatmate, a buzz-cut type, clued him on "The New Byzantium": Cartier-van Cleef, Vuitton, Jaeger-LeCoultre, "eateries" Soho style, Kenny G broadcast all over the place ("A 'number' named "Going Home"), *Helen Keller* brand eyeglasses ("Comprehend *that* distaste, my man"), *weiwen* all over the place: spies, listeners, "spooks'n'snitchers". Arthur Becker looked round for *weiwen*, as between the fumes and foggy smog there came an orange-blackberry omelet sunset, an ancient-seeming dome, a soft agricultural sky ironically brought modern by today's steel-hard needs for industry. "Coal burn in the cocklight," explained the flippant Brit. . . Then, billboards, a juggernaut of marquees: A STRONG COMMUNIST PARTY MEANS HAPPINESS FOR THE CHINESE PEOPLE; SING A HARMONY SONG; THE CHINESE DREAM; and finally: a reclining thirty foot length Chinese woman in black lace bra and panties lofting a fifth of Jack Daniels and smiling in overstrong satisfaction. "Be wary," said the young Brit, in T-shirt and jeans, "the vagina which resideth in China." His grin was at once ironic and ferocious. "And wary yourself the Tibetans," he added:

"The Beijing Tibetans are not pure Dali Lamas, they're pickpockets, the Asian gypsies, if you will."

The limo-bus was now pulling over to the sidewalk to let some passengers; it just about grazed the bent body of an old man who must have been afflicted with osteoporosis—and the Chinese decrepit just accepted the close-shave, peacefully, a matter-of-course. Nor did anyone about make the slightest caring fuss. Not even the occasional few snugly wearing their smog-protectors: those whitish surgical masks. . . One of whom had earphones slung stylishly about his neck as if it were a stethoscope.

Arthur Becker hadn't come across stuff like this in the guide books.

The following email had appeared on Arthur's and Jutta's Heidelberg screens just five days previous. In English:

> Thema: Mein Liebling Hung Huang
>
> Date: 4 10 2015   05.55.42 OstAsiatische Zeit
>
> From: Mick-ah-yell@gmail.com
>
> To: JutArt@aol.com.
>
> Dear Mother and Father
> In my e-mails I have written to you frequently of
> Hung Huang, of the wonderful days that she and
> I have spent together as teacher and student of
> Mandarin Chinese, our method called Yinghua,
> which means English Chinese as there is not yet
> a German Chinese but should be coming—
> perhaps *I* will be its developer, I am joking. I
> have spoken too of our excursions, Hung and
> myself, of our together sightseeings and movies

and theatre and ballet; but I have not revealed to
you even on the telephone that Hung Huang is
The One, the love of my life. I have never felt in
my life the companionship of, and the mutual
understanding and respect with, another person
that I experience in concert to Hung Huang and
the utmost pleasure that it gives me just to
simple look upon her and the way she ingathers
at life with her soul so filled to fullest and so
many other aspects of our learning of each other
as if we are living *within* each other. I can say to
you, my parents, that I do now believe in Love
and I do now believe in Souls. In Chinese
Mandarin, we have *ganqing*. The Chinese, they
contain such words so gestalt, because that is
how the way they are, like Germans, to a portion.
This is why I have decided, along with Hung
deciding as well, and supporting, and agreeing,
that we shall be married, here in Beijing, in a
Han Chinese wedding ceremony that is
traditional. And this is *not* because there is so
much pressure in China to marry, although there
is that pressure still; but arranged marriage is
mostly now a black eye of the past, so mother
and father, you do not have to worry that we will
be "traditional Chinese" with all the old-
fashioned backward and unfair practices you
hear about those quaintish ancient ways. So,
also, our marriage is not to be what they now call
in China a "flash marriage", because there are so
many here now of that in new times. No, Hung
and mine is not impulsive, there will not to be,
what they have also now in China, a divorce
ceremony short quite upon the ceremony of
marriage—I am again being full of humor here.
And Hung's father, he is wise and he *knows*. He,
Jin Jianxin, he is not unfair nor ancient, he is a
great man, he is a help worker for the citizens in
all ways he can, so I admire him. I admire him so
much, as he has *wu wei*—the inner flow, he is a

Confucian, and the flow guides him, as he
organizes now a protest by taxi-men and truck
drivers and construction men and miners—all
which is very dangerous, as you may imagine.
My parents, I know that you believe I am too
young and inexperienced to extend myself so
deepful into such an overwhelming entrance into
the true life and its lasting ever, which is so
serious, but I know that I am ready, and I know
that Hung Huang is as well. We have Faith. Our
being together for so many hours for so many
days has taught us well and prepared us well;
and it is not that we are two different spirits
thrown together from opposing-situated worlds,
it is not that manner of childish passion, which
we decline. True dating I must say is new in
China, as at ours, the university level, but we
have helped ourselves to become mature, so that
we will hold our dignities and not fail in Uni or
in life, we will be not shirkers but contributors—
we can scantly wait. So Dear mother and father,
Hung and I wish that you might travel to Beijing
for what will be our wedding, but I know that
that is impossible, considering mother's duties at
Uni and yours, father, with your book research
and necessary consultations in New York. So I
will of course telephone to you as I have; but I
considered and thought that at first an e-mail
might be nonesuch, to fore-prepare I could say. I
have already mailed to you a large photograph of
Hung and myself together, embraced as you will
see. People make these portraits often in China
today, and they exchange them even as
friendship gifts, they are in *pinwei*—good taste,
for there is such good honest friendship here—
you will see. As we will all certainly cleave with
each other soon, in Beijing in the summer; or
after, even in Heidelberg.

And I did *not* mean speaking of YOU, my
parents, when I wrote above of the childishness

7

passion of two young people from two different worlds. I did *not*! Nothing was farther from my mind—until Hung Huang, who is sensitive and who I have told about you my parents and your history of German and Jewish, of your America and your Germany. Hung told it me that such describing as childish attraction might be unseemly and even slurry. Hung has read over this e-mail. More than once. Because such is representative of her conscientious deep-involving way, which is so imbued in her.

Your loving son, Michael.

My sole problem to this date is that I get *verstopft*[2] here.

So: this Chinese *Hung*, is it?—in the photo that arrived two days later she was just about swallowed-up by Mick, engulfed, and by the big-shouldered Beijing shadows—you saw a girl in plunged profile standing next to Mick and staring at him as if the boy were a pedestalized David who owned a pretty approximate take on the winding workings of the world (shy Mick, as far as Arthur knew, had never even tried to fake such take) and as you scrutinized that Hung face, you saw that it was so murkily joyful and side-angled you could not even tell that she was Chinese (or pretty)—unless you studied the image hard and made of it what you wished to make.

Wiseass Arthur Becker's first thought: "*Hung* is it?—for godsakes! What *is* this?—Who's on Hung? It's fucking Abbott and Cos*tello*!"

Even Arthur's wife Jutta, in Germany, knew Abbott and Costello.

---

[2] Constipated. Stopped-up.

'Irony is the last refuge of an impotent.' Arthur himself had written this in some book. Years before he had murdered that vilely offensive Professor Fritz Strobel in Heidelberg.

And then there was that Jin Jianxin, Hung's father. His name seemed to possess, already, this talismanic tonnage that Arthur couldn't deny—even to himself—was envy.

Mick-ah-yell was the German pronunciation of Michael—the boy had never appreciated Arthur's addressing him as Mike, or even Mick, so Arthur tried not to, but often failed, too often—"Mick" just seemed so natural for an American. And the boy did not look half German half Jewish, indeed there was barely a fraction of partition—Mick-ah-yell was German: His hair was a dirty blonde, his eyes a kind of aquamarine that at moments reflected deep perception and at others, deep repression, no sorrow no fear no, well (as far as father Arthur was concerned), soul; just hiddenness, or something needful-dodgy that reached-out but could not quite find their fathom. Arthur might look into Mick's eyes, searching for some relationship to himself, but what he found coming back at his own brown eyes (little beebee eyes really—he disliked his own eyes) was usually no mirror but a density, intelligence behind a handsome wall. Well, he usually found that in Mick's facing eyes, predictably (and sadly) found that in his son's fronting eyes—but no, no, not always—not *every* time. Sometimes, well, there *was* something, something, kindling that old paternal hope. The boy did have a rather long nose, but Mick's long nose was not a Jewish long nose—rather a Germanic long nose, knifesharp rather than inspectorial. And beyond all this there was just a certain strange mix in Mick's expression—or expressions—an opaque directness that hid that not-thereness so well.

Unsure Mick had set out with his group to Beijing shortly after his *Abitur* celebration for completing *Hochschule*, which had taken place all of three months before, and which had been ornamented, very un-Germanicly, by youngsters "twerking"—a new dance, America-formulated, which consisted of the tireless and extensively-bent-over pumping-out of one's rump to (what someone generous might call) music: again, thoroughly unlike any "dignified" Deutschlander Arthur had ever witnessed, young middle or old: He'd never forget it. Mick-ah-yell had prepped for China, in the Deutsch-intensive manner, by purchasing on Amazon a Mandarin primer, a language CD, a Mandarin-Deutsch-English *Lexikon* and a slender crib-book on *Street Mandarin for Today's Western Hipster*. Conscientious kid, Mick. The boy really had spent hours on Chinese-study—he'd enjoyed it, those harsh chop-vowels, meat-cleavers to Arthur's "tender" "racist" ear, especially when father heard son replicating and sharpening the cleaver as if that added experience and authority. There had even been those disorienting moments when Mick had begun to take on for Arthur a Sino-stiffened stance, even in the way he rode his bike. Yet: despite his naïve fear that his son's exploration of that distant Eastern land might prove to become his son's naïve relocation to that land, Arthur was in truth very proud of the boy: Mick set out to do something and then he went and he *did it*.

II

ACUTE MEET

Arthur Becker had chosen a hotel recommended in a guidebook as "Economical but Restful". As he had not earned a great deal from his writings in the past few years (or ever), the family living disproportionately off of Jutta's salary, the Jewish-American did not feel that he could justify luxury—so he'd opted for the Hotel Prince Gong.

In the hotel lobby a super-large mounted slimscreen showed wry Peter Faulk in his customary beige raincoat as *Columbo* (Arthur had seen the episode in Germany and in the U.S.), beneath the early Seventies show a news-crawl in Chinese characters. Then on the screen came another news-crawl—this time in English—explaining the Chinese news-crawl: its gist: a pastor had just been sentenced to fourteen years in prison for having erected a cross atop his church (The charge: corruption and inciting disturbance of the social order) . . . When Becker reached his room a pale blue uniformed young man (who said his name was Koon Poontang [or something]) was dragging out a large

11

plastic bag that smelled like nothing so much as shit. Not the greatest omen. He asked the boy what this was, and the boy said, matter-of-factly, as if what-else-could-it-be?—"shit". (Sure he knew that universal word—and to an illiterate Chinese kid it was just a word, no stinky-vile undertones). "Why?" asked Arthur, and the employee, registering that this here was one dumb Westerner, clued him: "No flush wipe-paper with your shit," he said. "Clogs. Place shit-white-paper in bag by bowl." Is he kidding? Maybe, Arthur considered, I should have sprung for a Five Star instead of this supposed Three. "Is it like this in all Beijing hotels?" he asked. "Like this in all. We protect Beijing pipes." Becker knew the lackey was lying but he just answered "Ah." He did not notice the red Do Not Drink The Water sign, waist-high on his hotel room door—the narrow hallway of this HOTEL PRINCE GONG had made him wearier than he was, due to its fuzzily decrepit air.

Becker's boy Mick would be arriving in a few hours, along with his fiancé Hung. Dromedarily swooped into a kookily camel-humped easy chair (which was curiously comfortable—despite that Becker could not remove its bizarro plastic cover—and the chair was hardly new! [like the well-worn ottoman, which was also plasti-covered]) Becker intended to review The Big Two: Chinese marriage; German murder. But that clotted choking air! He stood, took the long two-step to his room air filter, turned it on (the door sign had indeed said this was a FRIENDLY MUST—and it had read this in RED), then, being too lagged and bone-weary for reflection-and-review he'd hit the bed: sag moderate, bedspread frizzy, one long plush pillow (but way too narrow, way too) with a trio of embroidered throws. This Hotel Prince Gong was located in what Becker's guidebook (purchased in Heidelberg) described blithely as a "historical Hutong area" (the guidebook found it unnecessary to explain the derivation of "Hutong", and Becker had not yet troubled himself to purchase a Chinese-German [or English] lexicon.). Reclined and already homesick—for *Germany*!? no, for his wife, he called Jutta on his cell. She was just waking up, about to prepare herself for the pleasant walk downhill to teach and write at Heidelberg's "Uni". Jutta had not accompanied Arthur because she was so intensely scrupulous—she couldn't take off even half a school week. Her students needed her. Her secretary needed her. The faculty needed her. *She* needed her, that gluelike sacrament of being needed. (In addition to all of her established responsibilities she was also the newly installed [as newly-created] "Dean of Informatiks" [Don't ask: another unfortunate Deutsch misborrowing from admired English]). . . "I'm here safe," Arthur said. "What is China like? my expert," Jutta joked (and it was a joke as she had lectured in Shanghai and Beijing two years before [and it had taken the Chinese university system one full year to pay her the agreed-upon $10,000, approximate by yuan conversion]). "It's okay," Becker joked back to his wife. She asked if he had yet seen Mick-ah-yell. He said he would soon, in hours, and he told her that the scoop on Beijing's murderous environment, as horrendously unbelievable as it was, was the truth, not slander, not hyperbolic Western propaganda (as if she didn't know). Like a wonderstruck kid coming up the subway steps at

gleaming Times Square, a kid from, say, dustbowl
Tulsa in '33, he described the great skyscrapers ("so
glassy-reflective—makes it seem like there's even more
of them than there are—like you're seeing double,
triple") and then the dark cloud that smothered them so
that the towers had to poke through to show-off their
majesty (as if she didn't know). "Poor Mick," Jutta
said, Arthur replying with, "How can he even *think*
of—?" "You will have to listen to him," she interrupted
wisely—"listen close and understanding." "You're
implying," he said, "that I don't—usually?" She
laughed, genuine while forced. "Downtown here it's
like"—he'd been about to say 'a gas oven'; but even
with this Jew's own German wife he could not ever
bring himself to broach such implicating allusions—he
never had. Not even when he had first known her, back
in Berkeley, where she had been a visiting scholar.
Their conversation now ended with Jutta's emphasis,
"Do be understanding," and Becker promising to call
her the next day, once he had a take on "This Hung girl
and her Chink ways." "*Oh mein Gott, du blinder
Anhänger*"—Jutta's demi-droll reply, calling her
husband a bigot.

Jutta's voice: after that so long flight, her Germanic
lilts and dips, her humor, these so normal-daily marks
had him hearing them as not so normal-daily, as falling
away, unreachable: In this cruddy-cheap "Economy"
(and unsanitary?) Chinese room in *China* he was seeing
his wife, reaching for her. Already?

China did that?—you wimp. When he'd traveled to
New York he had not felt such *Heimweh* for Jutta. But
China rubbed at you, an immediate right-off-off-key
scrape, it suggested—what could he think?—"the slings

and arrows of outrageous" whatever—the door was familiar but the door's key didn't work—China's queerness-plus-familiarity said Earth was evolving away from you, fella, unsuperstitious schmuck who's now scrounging omens—and dear Jutta, she is Arthur's non-omen Earth. Now, truth: Jutta was not a sexy woman, she was not a sensual woman. She was a calm woman. Not-sexy, not-sensual, super-calm, a Cal Euro-Scholar, and Arthur the until-then hornball falls in love. *El amor brujo*—love the magician. And Arthur was not so benighted as to not be aware that Jutta reminded him of his mother Eva. Eva who had endured those horrid dark abandoned days like collapsing shadows after Arthur's dad Moe's suicide and come back to herself, a calm and generous woman—a woman who declared that she was "happy". . . Jutta had always reminded Arthur of his mother Eva. If this correspondence was Oedipal, so be it. Oedipal did not always mean desolate pathology, did it?—if you left out the literal poke-out of the eye. Oedipal could be a good thing. Hell, everyone couldn't but be Oedipal, Oedipal was how you grew. . . Arthur believed this, when he was not busy disbelieving and bemoaning (and making lame "self-blinding" jokes; and even blaming Oedipal for his murder of that old professor German Nazi who had been Jutta's be-and-end-all).

He extracted from his crack-skinned carry-on the large-but-obscuring color photograph that Mick had mailed: his son embracing that young Chinese girl. He honed-in, captivated by the fact that he could now discern that she had a sidewise pucker that intimated humor, a wry humor, and secret knowledge, though perhaps mistrust and secret fear. As far as Becker could now make out with his microscopic scrutiny of the shadowed photo-print there was no sign of submissiveness in the arrow-eyed stare of the girl, nor in the directly forward holding of her face, chin-up into a challenge or a dare—nor in demand of immediate love-forswearing, nor immediate anything that might come to her mind. Why Becker was on alert for signs of the cower—*or the govern*—was simply retrograde, embarrassing even to his solitaried self: Chinese rape of women—unpunished, even today; Chinese foot-binding of women—long practised. He knew, certainly, that such a painful-restrictive custom was long gone and there now was backlash, or bindinglash; but he had also read up that Chinese men (well, Manchu Chinese) had found those "pulverized" female feet a sexual turn-on— and such must still exist then in hidden warrens. *What species of grotesque crackpots would crave the mangled female paw? . . . And what species of grotesque crackpotesses would be so thrilled and aroused as to allow the mangle, to Submit?!—and then (now), to exact revenge? . . . On my (duped) Mick-ah-yell?*

Becker, what can you say?—he was a worrier and a vindictive one (such was also why he'd suffocated to death that damned German Strobel). And, face it, he found that he got a perverted kick now in imagining Mick binding a Hung foot, even if his kid fumbled at the job (He couldn't imagine Mick not fumbling). Even if the binding were fake and flimsy and ceremonial sex-play, and came apart as intended with a Hung simple twisting of her foot.

The jet lag. Sure, that's what's twisting Me.

No, more than that: I'm Me.

Becker was interrupted only once, not by Mick's arrival. This after about one hour by the insertion-and-strong slipslide under his door of two business cards. One was bright and yellow, the other plain and thin, like newsprint. The bright yellow:

THE HEAVEN IN BEIJING

CERTIFIED ADULT HEALTH PRODUCT
LATE NITE PAYABLE COMPANION
LOW REASON RENMINBI RATES OF PRICING
ALL WORLD RACES TO COME WELL

Not one but three telephone numbers (plus a fax) lined the card's bottom, and there was no address listed for any lightbulb spur-of-the-moment visitations. A real class act. Although Becker had not the remotest intention of making use of the sales promotion ("Be wary the vagina residin' in China"), he did not tear it up: he placed it in the mini-zipperable side compartment of his cracked carry-on, where he'd deposited his Heidelberg house keys, along with a bunch of paper euros, which he hadn't counted—and of course he mused over whether or not that bottom line—All World Races to Come Well—was a pun or a fortuitous combination. He then unzipped his bag, extracted the "offer" and lay the business card on the standard-stock nite-table next to the telephone, which was where he'd also placed his wallet and his watch, and the other card, which was a simple but hokey ad for *China Daily*, "The best English language scuttlebutter extendedly consumed in China". . . He looked about. Becker's room contained colorful vases of painted flowers and leaves; these pots couldn't have been antique, but they demonstrated a professional job of appearing pleasantly ancient. There was an enclosed courtyard below, which he could look down upon from his small third floor terrace—it contained one date tree and one persimmon-looking tree, but it was impossible to gaze beyond the courtyard to look out upon the city. So he closed the curtains—or rather tried. They would not budge, thus he received shards of fractured nitetime city light. There was no television. Weird. Very weird. Added to the fact that the hotel was piping into his room what else but "Going Home" by Kenny G: go to sleep music? Social engineering, but despite the Kenny Arthur could not doze-off. Just as well: Mick-ah-yell would soon arrive.

Tin phone-dingings. Mick told Becker that he was late because "we had to carry a coffin to a family". Becker did not go "Huh?". Not wishing to seem demanding or even overinquisitive at first reunion, Becker did not delve, and the coffin "explanation" was never explained. Becker told Mick he'd meet him down in the lobby in, say, five minutes—as he hadn't even undressed for his nap. Mick would understand his dad's probable flight-stink and rumpledness, but Arthur Becker would still take the time to splash water on his face and take a quick neck-crane-sniff at his armpits, then daub them good with Old Spice (He didn't care for the über-perfume of the German brands, even those of Nivea). "A nigger-shower," his dad Moe had tabbed this sloppy-sloshiness, his dad Moe who had pitched Minor League with many *"schwartzes"*—one rare Jew he was (and seldom spared anyone the boast)—but he'd never made the Majors, and that had bitched the hell out of him, his having felt that he was, easy, good enough and that therefore the world was unfair, "fucking goddamn unfair as shit". Dad Moe had duked-it-out with black teammates, son Arthur had killed a German. An old Nazi, true, unlike his son Mick-ah-yell, who was a good kid, a good German, despite his difficulties with being German and Jew, and his difficulties, for such reason, with his father. . . Sadly, true.

"Hung is with me," advised Mick, from the lobby.

"*Ten* minutes then," said Becker. "Let's double that five."

Silence: His son, being a guarded brooder German, did not find his dad's audible adjustment chuckle-worthy.

Arthur Becker doubled-up on his sloppy-sloshy "nigger shower", all the while imagining, first, this upcoming Chinese Hung girl at pretty much the same times as he pictured his Big-League-Failed father Moe who had committed suicide and had performed in his time many "nigger showers".

"Father, Hung. Hung, Mister, uh, Herr, uh, Arthur Becker. . . . My uh. . ."

Father! . . . Father! . . . Say that! Christ, Mick, you may not look like me except for the troubled-alert Jew eyes and the hesitant balkings—but Christ, damnit, Say That!—Father!—I'm your FATHER, Arthur.

"Arthur," Arthur said to Hung, extending a hand, an offer which the girl had some difficulty —she stared at the middle-aged cupped-up fingers and thumb as if they—what!?—were about to assay her tits, but then she took that Arthur hand and shook. Really, she pumped, a good one-two, as if her intended's father were really a reluctant wellspring in faroff, where? Chungking? Had Becker's hand-projection been too stark? Too quick-nervous out-shot? Too Western?

Hung smiled in a way Arthur saw as courtly-but-doubtful, and even painful; and she performed a graceful quarter-bow, uttering a deferential "Hung".

China: Face culture—Arthur's read-up.

And then, out of nowhere, and with these beautifully sorriful eyes, she addended a super American, "Gladtameetcha," and she laughed, a spontaneous honest one-caw-laugh, which Arthur loved. Hung's countrified Annie Oakley greeting fit well with her checkerboard plaid-pleated skirt, her "American" T-shirt (that no American would be caught dead wearing) that read BEHIND THE EIGHTBALL (showing a Chinese man gazing out tentatively from behind, indeed, an eight-ball—noggin-sized), her candy-striped socks rising from thick clogs. No, Hung was none too shabby—she might as well have been licking a fat round Lollipop and employing some word like lolligag. But, strange to say, sensitivity applied here too. Too much of it: Characteristics, deep ones, rose to just the rim of visible. Along with her first awkwardness on the handshake, you just sensed an inbuilt store, a fount of modesty. *Face culture.* Hung appeared to be slightly above average in height for what Arthur expected in a Chinese woman—she was maybe 5'6-7"; her figure seemed perfect, all the curves where men ideally desire curves (and fantasize curves); how did so many Asian women achieve these sexually utopian shoulders-breasts-hips-calves-asses-etc? for they sure seemed to—and brought to mind, Arthur couldn't help what was brought to mind, was a neologism derived from Philip Roth: preposterone: just now he was afflicted. But it was Hung's filaments of falling black hair which did supply the first direct attraction, as these arched about the sides of her broad face in the way that one sometimes sees in pictures the rounded openways to Chinese temples; they seemed primordial as they fronted (or guarded) the strands that swept behind them and round her head, meeting in what oldtime badass boys in America had sported: DAs—ducks' asses. As Arthur had noted in Mick's mailed photo, Hung's face leaned slightly forward at the base, which caused her lips to rest in a natural pout or pucker, which gave the enigmatic impression of an empathy that was demure, or of a disapproval that was nonetheless not non-pleasing (Becker could definitely see all that!—or want to see it). Hung's deeply-set black-brown eyes were however unnerving in their attentive eagerness and buoyance, and yet heaviness—3-D-ish deer eyes—oh you saw their compassion; and they took soundings, as if the person she had been called upon to face was rumored to be the imparter of great wisdoms, mind-altering, or devastations, or corruptions—or secrecies. Or attacks. Or humiliations. Beguiling shock compounds, staring straight at you (Becker recalled Bellow's Herzog thinking of a Japanese woman that her eyes rose from her cheeks just like how her breasts rose from her body)—you fought the itch to look away from that engaging, grasping directness, at least for a breather. Arthur Becker could bring to mind only one contemporary Chinese actress—and really she was American. She was sensual, mysterious, alluring, frightening when she wished to aim her eyes at the camera. Her name was Lucy Lu. This Hung Huang reminded Arthur Becker of Lucy Lu—and he expected that this resemblance was completely wrong.

Can't you just let Hung be finale of Hung!

"Hung's a genius," said Mick-ah-yell, flat-out.

Hung's features betrayed no quarrel with Mick's evaluation.

"In some ways," she said.

Taunting or modesty?

Arthur could not come out with what he had after all come way out here to come out with: 'Are you two sure of what you're doing? *Think!*' What father would blurt out such a caution-cloud on first meeting? He'd lay wait for a later time.

Hung asked proudly, "Did you, Herr Becker—I mean Mister—did you see our new *tuokouxiu* on your room TV? China now has many *tuokouxiu* for free opinion spreads and fast feedback."

"Tuokouxiu?"

Listening devices? He had read up but he'd missed that one.

"*Tuokouxiu*," explained Mick, "that is Chinese phonetic for Talk Show: *Tuok-ouxiu*. Hear it?—'Talk Show'. They're the new Beijing big thing."

"My room has no TV."

Politeness had Arthur balking that one out.

Hung's sympathetic deer eyes said she was sorry but also disbelieving.

Becker felt he'd hurt her by undermining her enthusiasm and Beijing hospitality.

Hung and Mick had worked-out "an interesting Beijing nite-route for nite-sights and dinner." They went hoofing and dodging beneath skyscraper shadowings through an old poor section, the Dongchung District, with an array of ratty-looking markets and stalls selling cheap clothes under wan streetlight but lurid neon and fluorescence, with cooked ducks dangling stretch-necked from hooks; also, small kitchen appliances, fruits and vegetables—and tons of smallish garlic bulbs in piles mountainous and visceral. "The garlic peasants," Hung shook her head in sympathy, "they estimated wrong and they held their crop too long, so now it is all bought cheap—and they will have to drive many kiloms with small yuan return. Many are Tibetans and Uighurs. My father Jin Jianxin is trying to teach to peasants markets—economics, but the government"—lowly she moaned the word—"it does not spread for them the information. . . Yet."

Even with the new tuokouxiu?

Arthur said, "I'm sorry." He wore the idiotic half-smile of The Foreigner mantling-up empty empathy. But, sadly, it was reassuring to him that this poor chaos still existed in great burgeoning China. A small man's great envy allayed.

"We in China yet require more *fuxing*."

Did I hear right?

It turned out *fuxing* meant rejuvenation.

The Dongchung street was so unintentional, a natural raucous boomtown jumble, a queer cinnamon-onion-sweetness with cigarette smoke and storefronts with Mao photo-ashtrays; it was all neon and noise: a forlorn calliope of centuries marred (*marred?*) by slow squidders of *Tai Chi*. They seemed like commentators, these mime-movers, a silent-dance Greek chorus: Hung said: "Man floats like goon-bird in his traffic." Mick said: "Hung jokes, giving a Tai Chi name, as all Tai Chi moves have names." Arthur said, "I know I know I know." These "floaters" were just beside a blocking beggar with gassed-out eyes who put out his cigarette butt with a filthy grinding unsocked big toe—you had to be a shake'n'bake halfback with super moves to keep yourself treading water in all this old Chinese jumble. Hung said, "China, it is still a rural land. Over one-hundred fifty million alive under per day one dollar."

Arthur reached for his idiotic half-smile empathy once more.

"The *hukou*," contributed Mick-ah-yell, facing his fiancé like a colleague, showing off his newfound expertise.

"The *hukou,*" said Hung, "it is a registration of where a person lives and must live and work. It limits people from traveling to better opportunes. So they stay with their small stalls and perhaps they starve."

Mick said, "We must end the *hukou*."

We?

But Arthur nodded.

Mick said: "Hung's father Jin was in youth a *zhinquing,* like your American VISTA peace corps in poor domestics, and he is working now to improve all this and liberalize it all, but it is like—as they say—'dancing in shackles'." Then, even more proudly: "Hung's father has received warnings from The China Society for the Elimination of Traitors."

Arthur had to smile at his son's new social gravity. Hadn't the boy come to Beijing to acquire an MBA and accumulate the-big-bucks? Mick-ah-yell had become captivated by Hung's belief-swollen eyes. . . Had his son and Hung slept together?—one might grasp why he felt envy, but, absurdly he felt even jealous.

Then, snap, a SOHO turn: a *Blade Runner* type strip mall with boutiques—La Di Da; BarStruck's; Carpe Diem; etc.; then a restaurant with a neon-lit sign reading BUDDHA'S (yes, Becker speculated about the rank inconceivability of an eatery in, say, Manhattan, being dubbed CHRIST'S or JEW'S); then came a large mural of a uniformed Hitler manifesting the Nazi salute in heroic mode as if he were Superman.

Hung got slapped hard at the restaurant; it wasn't hard to ascertain from the slapping woman's hemorrhaging face that she hated Hung. They'd gone to a dumpling "table-house" (attached alongside BUDDHA'S; Hung claimed it was "non-tourist") with low cane chairs and three long names in Chinese characters (and no English alongside) and waiters in T-shirts with Chinese messages—fortune T-shirts? The slapping woman had Prince Valiant hennaed hair, parrot green-yellow on its duck's ass in its rear, and stylish rectangular glasses, henna-ish as well, which about half the patrons here also wore. On leaving the woman had passed their table, hovered a moment as if working-up slap-nerve, said a ferocious few words in Han, turned back to hear people who sat a nearby table laughing loud, then backhanded Hung across the cheek, this while spitting on the tile floor (a number of the patrons here at BUDDHA'S seemed to floor-spit pro forma.) The woman had been holding in her non-slap hand the little hand of a cute child with a horrendous hairlip, who she carefully coaxed along as she left this dumpling annex of BUDDHA'S.

"What?"—Arthur.

"She said," said Mick, "that Hung was just buying soy sauce. It's an expression."

Mick had sure been a quick Han learner.

Arthur asked, "What does it mean?"

"It means," Hung said flatly, "I have no business here." Her look was undaunted; she did not touch her slap-reddened face.

"But what does that mean?" asked Arthur. " 'You have no business here'."

"It means, I have enemies."

Mick contributed, "*Hong yan bing*. Red eye disease. That woman harbored envy. Hung's father is on the *blacklist*. He has been in jail. His computer has been *hacked*. These are admirable."

"Per*haps*," said Hung (with what appeared to be disquiet at her fiance's endless reverence for her father), "that woman is a *yuanmin*, a person with a different grievance. Perhaps she had asked my father for help, for clinic or so for her child's poor lip, but my father he could not gain it.

"He is not perfect," added Hung, "my father.

"Many young here," Hung went on, "they think wrong-false things because they do not know what to think. They expect and they expect—they do not know how hard it is, my father's work—good work, and dangerous. This not-knowing, it makes them angry, the rejection-feel, so that they misconduct-out. And they cannot do such to my father. It is so easier with me."

In bed Becker downed his eagerly awaited Seconal, a hearty 20 milligramer. Big day tomorrow: the couple would be bringing along their best friend, they said, as he was "lonely as a bird lost from branches," and

"Nyemo, he could add especial perspection and dimension. He is a Tibetan."

Curiously, Hung spoke of this Nyemo with what Becker might have considered an admiring-intimidated air, as if the Tibetan were more daunting than, say, the woman who had gone and slapped her. Arthur considered that he even saw a kind of romance in Hung's inflated eyes for this Nyemo—it seemed beyond affection, and it was not an expression that she had shown for "her fiancé" Mick. . . Arthur got only three hours sleep, even by way of The Big Seconal. One of his dreams held onto Hung's face, its strength, its sympathies, its righteousness—and even the slanted humor in her eyes; he dreamed of his difficulties with his German son who, despite himself, despite his own warnings of twenty years, he thought of as his Jewish son—too much he thought this, he couldn't help it— and he dreamed of his murder of that old German, Professor Fritz Strobel. . . Because of Hung's expression when she had spoken of the Tibetan Nyemo—amorous? sexual? evaporating of Mick?— Arthur already disliked him.

III

THE PAST

Professor Fritz Strobel, Becker's victim, had been in his late eighties, conceivably he was ninety, maybe ninety two. He'd been the very picture of a model Hollywood German, posing imposing in those final years—full head of hair, far more salt than pepper sweeping with serious vain concern; Strobel was one of those lifelong rawbone svelters—he simply mocked you without trying to, just by the luck of his longtime slimline remnants, still garnished with much muscle. When Arthur had his encounters with Fritz Strobel he usually found himself thinking Max von Sydow—who of course was a Swede. Strobel had been Becker's wife Jutta's predecessor (and hirer) at Heidelberg in Informatiks, which was a branch of the Economics department. Communication was the keynote of the modern world, of global trade and global growth and global deception, and Informatiks proudly proclaimed here its measuring "sine qua nons", its clearing-ups— "words, words' intentions, word-quantity or lacks", "words monetaristic consequence". What a bunch of bull. On a few occasions Professor Strobel had been to the Becker family house for dinner, and on every one of those meetings he had not failed to express his iron-hard Informatiksish opinion that "those Jews, you cannot excuse them, they have taken too much, far too much, from the German economy *and* the flounderish Polish—and others." Which mostly meant "reparations billions to Israel" and "high-tech donations to that 'illegitimate nation', the only rich colonialists left on Earth." And: "A 'nation' built on false assumptions," these being that "that malignated word, the Holocaust", had accounted for no greater than, say, one million Jews, "a clever well-versed Informatiks emendable." "History's byword is after all exaggeration, or diminishment—that is ineluctable, its essence, and that essence comprises your Jews' making Germans absorb the bloody hands for, *acknowledge* it Arthur, what amounts to a history footnote." Silence had always followed those declarations; silence and young half-Jew Mick-ah-yell's hard-held gravitational staring down into his plate of food. . . If Professor Strobel had expressed such anti-Semitic Jean-Marie LePenn opinions at a Jew's house—or at a house half-Jew—it seemed safe to assume that he expressed them routinely and universally, if under the breath, if in the 'right' company. As Gunther Grass, the same age, had finally admitted to having been SS, Fritz Strobel might well have been the same. How could he not have been! . . . Then again, not infrequently when the professor expressed his opinions he did tend to add his provisos on the order of "Now, I am not *against* the Jewish peoples, individually or per se. You all have made your contributions, you have had *near*-geniuses." But, depending upon his audience, or his mood, he might then tend to add, "However, I myself, I do prefer the classicish way, the Greek: a rationalism that is lyric and is sensual—without its losing any grace."

Who the hell, at such moments, knew just what that pretentious bigot meant?

Although Becker did have his not infrequent fantasies of strangling Strobel, or at least battering the arrogant bastard, he still found himself tolerating the old bigot, his wife's onetime mentor. After all, it was rather difficult to put full stock in a belief that the old Professor, honored greatly in the German academic community (Strobel had "invented" Informatics), really meant what he said—unless he disliked Arthur so much, unless he was so concerned that the American was just not good enough for Jutta, that he was attempting to get The Jew's goat, perhaps even provoke the callow Californian into leaving Heidelberg and returning to callow California. Becker's Jewishness might not really have been the issue at all—Becker had certainly considered that; but as Jutta had been the proselyte of Fritz Strobel, Arthur Becker had been in a sense the proselyte of Moe Becker, ballplayer and brawler—and a man proud to be such as a Jew, as if tough-guy shtick made up for the general take on kike candyassery. And Arthur had such violence in him, he believed in its marinating inheritance, he'd always felt it, he'd always feared it. Still, it was not until he saw professor Fritz Strobel's full effect upon his own son (and his own *wife*?) that he conceived enactment, that he tried to convince himself he'd had to. Considering that he had an explosive character, he could rationalize, finally, after twenty-two years of this Strobel mind-cramped shit, that he had no choice. And considering that he was a writer (two novels, two pop-sociologies) he'd had enough of this, face it, Jewish shit of expressing his murderous moods merely with humor for himself, for, in a sense, his own smirky pleasure:

Ecrasez l'infame!

Stop being a fucking Jew and go kill the goddamn Jew-hater!

Sounds ludicrous, I know, it's crazy, but it's true.

Thus the humor portion went and flipped the page to fliptop reality when son Mick-ah-yell told his father one morning (interrupting Arthur's [failing] work) that he wished no longer to be considered Jewish, no not even *"teilweise"*. He admired *"uncle"* Fritz (who was no blood relation) and he revealed that he had worked-up his nerve and was now a member of The Pirates, a German youth group that, although Left, denied the Holocaust, and that he, Mick, resented being what he was not, i.e. Jewish; and then he told Arthur the following Pirate joke: "How do you get six thousand Jews into a VW Beatle?"

"How?" asked the Jewish father, awaiting detonation.

"You gas them and then you cremate."

Mick said that!

And with—well what could you call the kid's sly grin but shiteating? Arthur Becker's *German* son with his apprehensive searching Jewish eyes and broadish German shoulders and by now a lowering oboe-bassoon voice, a developing manly German tone that some—not Arthur, not till now—had labelled "the guttural hollow horror".

"Do you hate me?" Arthur had asked his Mick-ah-yell.

"No, father, no. The cre—the burning-up, it is Ancient History, so long ago. It does not entail cruel feelings."

My ass, you little fart.

Who I love.

Well hadn't there been a halting pause after the 'joke'-tell. A gap showing calibration of feelings. A resentment for the boy's embarrassments and concealments in Heidelberg during his twenty conscious years. Twice, to Arthur's recollection, Mick had been mockingly called Jew. Even in the recent nowadays, in 2005. And once Mick had joined in with a young crowd of devilish teenaged scum who had tormented a Jewish girl classmate: *"Judit die Jüdin!"* they had kept-up calling her until she'd cried and stayed away from school for a week, or maybe it was more. Or maybe Judit's parents had changed schools for her, that new Hebraische Academy opening in Heidelberg (out of the citizens' good hearts?)—how many students could it have had? No German goyim would have gone. Still, Judit could have switched to there for her well-being, her tiny camaraderie—the Arthur-forced apology by Mick to the girl would not have solved a thing. . . What then about Mick's well-being then?—his camaraderie. The boy enduring within his soul a chasm that required his closest calculations, no, calibrations, in order to venture bridging the busy autobahn of Johannes Q. Public. The boy in shadows even in the bright. *Sure, Mick exhibited the saddest complications and even self-torments—for Chrissakes now he's in school in CHINA, he's going to marry a chink. And, face it, you wanted Mick to marry Judit or some Judit among the German population, nowadays there were eighty thousand, whereas before the War there had been eight hundred thousand, but let's not get into that* . . . Anyway, to a man who had inherited fighting from the fighting Moe Becker, and the blaming too of baseball failure, old Fritz Strobel, more than Jewish Arthur Becker himself who had moved to Germany and shared in progeny, old Fritz, big professor, he was the whole damned cause.

Old Professor Fritz Strobel had been in Heidelberg *Krankenhaus,* the hospital. One month already; no sign of release. He had already suffered a trio of heart attacks, and now a stroke. Jutta had visited her mentor many times. Arthur had not visited, but at *Informationen* he was given the room number—a large private sanctorum on top floor for an honored man, *ein anerkannter Mann*. As belligerent as he could be, certainly Arthur questioned his own intentions. People speak of murder, or suicide, all the time: 'I'll kill you' is almost a commonplace. . . Upon entering Strobel's room—no, chamber—he saw the frail elderly maestro of Informatiks, whatever technical jibbityjabber that stuff was—the man was asleep, his long white hair a curtain over one of his gray eyes, his neck a spine's twig, his pale skin like straw. Pathetic (Ironically he resembled a concentration camp survivor). . . But the less pathetic as Becker stood and watched, and as his malleable mind began to transform the helpless man, this "brilliant" invalid into a monster, a Mengele—and himself into some version of Simon Wiesenthal, the Nazi hunter. Just as his son Mick-ah-yell was ambiguous over his religious heritage in this nation,

Becker careened this way and that over his intentions. He did have a plan, although it had been more in the nature of a minor league pitcher imagining his tossing of a no-hitter and then being forthwith swept-up into the major leagues. Yes, Arthur was his father, Moe, a man who could bring *schwartze* ballplayer buddies home to Eva's dinner—*eat those latkes, eat!*—and despise them, their "sloppy" talk, their jangly limbs, especially when they got called-up to The Bigs. So, when Moe's son saw Strobel huddled-up in his hospital bed, *as* he saw Strobel now no more than an uncooked shrimp curled purple in his bed, sleeping so snort-peacefully, he imagined Strobel's dream-nightmares, where Jews took all the Germans' monies, where Israel did the same, and Becker entered Strobel's hatred, he shared it, and too easily, too naturally—he *was* it!—and then he took one pillow from beneath the man's head, brought it round and over the man's face, and not-looking he pressed, he pressed, until there was no longer any breath to hear, and Becker listened hard, and he did listen long, as long as he could bear that silence, that no nothing. Strobel was dead. Becker had worn no gloves, he was too impulsive to consider fingerprints— he'd probably believed that he would not go through with the murder; and, after all, a man near in age to ninety, in hospital after three cardiacs and a stroke, his just plain ceasing to breathe, just peacefully conking-out, who'd question it? The Honorable Strobel had already been smelling, no difference there as yet. The cleaning people, foreigners (like Tibetans) they didn't care, they would just roll the bedding down to the hospital laundry room, sheets and pillowcases would be sanitized, and that would be the ballgame.

ALAN GOLDFEIN

Becker even went to Strobel's funeral with Jutta, observing his widow's tears and observing his own ambivalence at his own wife's deep mourning.

Which had him slow-spilling down to the alternate end of his bipolar being and unquestionably swallowing sorrow.

For Strobel or for himself?

Or were both possible?

But it cannot be denied that a reason at least equal to the six thousand mile flight towards the assessment of son Mick-ah-yell's Chinese intended woman was the escape from Germany and guilt and, who knows?, someone might have seen him—pursuit. But, damnit, there had been the Stern gang, there had been the Irgund—Jewish goyim-killer killers. There had been that Jewish plan after The War and the six million (seven?), to poison the Nuremberg water supply. And Strobel was no all-Nuremberg.

And anyway, those Jews had abandoned their Nuremberg poisoning.

Guilt. Humanity.

Becker had one; did Becker have the other?

IV

TIAN'AN MEN SQUARE

In almost every way imaginable (to Arthur Becker) it seemed that Arthur Becker was, saddeningly, the polaric opposite of his son. For instance, unlike Mick-ah-yell Becker, he was not *verstopft* in Beijing, but instead he was stricken by an insistent *durchfall*[3] that had him that first night, sphincter on auto-clamp, in rapid ricochet between bed and toilet—so his sleep was intermittent and surface poor, and to compensate he just had to sleep late, until eleven. At that hour the late morning light was already being attacked by a thick ascending smog, an indigo substance that seemed monstrously lifelike and devouring and inferred Get Your Ass Back to Bed; but by that overdue time Arthur Becker did manage to get his ass down to breakfast. (Closing his room door he noticed the Do Not Drink the Water sign, and on the hall floor rug beneath it a thermos, obviously filled with potable water, with a teabag hanging from it, and swinging. (And what

---

[3] diarrhea

37

strikes him?—"Strange Fruit", the heart-tug Billie Holiday song). It was still breakfast-time for Arthur, but lunchtime for the Chinese. Thus he had to entreat and implore to be served a touch of "English Brekkies" (tea-[Jasmine Green]-toast-jam, strawberry) in the small Hotel Prince Gong dining room (cellar: no windows, low ceiling, lamps spindly, lamps massive, table sticky-marred with some spilt something.). . . He then met the trio in the lobby, which seemed an incongruous paltry/posh amalgam of Chinese Greatness of the Past and Chinese Insecurity of the Present: lit-up emperors and dragons and lanterns and temple reproductions on the walls, surrounding a central circle of mosaic tiles, modular chairs and sofas and a "Free" Nespresso coffee machine, which was visited so frequently by staff and visitors that the coffee-getters did continuously bump into one another and dribble driblets onto the mosaic tiles from their smallish-dainty mugs. Becker's ass-crease itched (*a rash from last night's quick nigger-shower Nivea!? a consequence of the mega-rapidfire durchfall?*) while Hung showed no sign of her having been heartily slapped the night before. She wore faded jeans and faded T-shirt with stretched V-neck collar; Mick-ah-yell was similarly smart-scruffed; but their companion, Nyemo the Tibetan, stood out, a sore thumb: (His first words were, "They've cut the Gmail, not to just known Tibetans but to even you and yours. I cannot write now to my father, Norbu." [Hung hush-responded, "Don't say about it."]. It seemed everyone could speak English.). Chunky, robust, hunkered-down into itself, into laconic (seeming) *himself*, this Nyemo was an oblong ochre flatland of a face excavated by pinches of pockmarks, a blood moon or a map of

Central Asia, with eyes just about anthracite and too widely spread above a near to bridgeless nose—those eyes worn with a weariness, a too major resignation for any young man; yet there was something, something avid in those eyes—a pilot light begging. That was why, despite his innerness, his hiddenness, this Nyemo appeared ripe-ready to leap out of his Ultimate Fighter corner in The Hexagon for full-out bone breaks and gloveless knuckle bangings; he hardly resembled any wiry-devoted Tibetan scaler-guide of the Himalayas or "mindfulness" meditation boy. Nyemo the Tibetan wore a Yankees baseball cap (backwards, you bet) and he clung tautly with both hands to the folds of a wide-lapeled tan sportscoat that cried out Seventies-Oklahoma City—he held to those flaps as if his jacket might just sprout wings and soar off, leaving him naked in this enemy Han hotel lobby. Needless to say this Nyemo resembled not even minutely the only Tibetan man whom Arthur had ever seen (consciously albeit electronically)—the Dalai Lama. He exhibited a checkered shirt which had a tendency to pop open at the belly each time he gestured or shuffled or even deeply breathed, which seemed to be a product of his robust but touching nervousness; his shoes were camouflage army surplus or imitations thereof. Round his neck he wore what he later called Tibetan *dzi* beads—they had been his mother's. . . It also appeared to Arthur that this Nyemo had a strong attachment to Hung. He kept staring at her with concern, with protection, and yet it seemed for guidance—proper in-public behavior. And he looked at Mick with concern as well. But this gaze was different. Wary? Distrustful? Even down-his-nose.

There was this swaggering annihilation about

Nyemo—a sharp resonance in eye and jaw.

Perhaps from what he endured: The Tibetan was being shunned right there in the small two-bit lobby. The Han-folk, they'd walk by and they'd turn their heads away, and oh they made sure this Tibet-creep took note—or they looked down or they looked quite through him; broad berths, purposive bigtime egregious detours. As if Nyemo smelled (which he did). (Nyemo would later tell Arthur that the Beijing citizens referred to Tibetans as "green brain people", as "terrorist-potentials", "though they just *'love'* Tibet as *super-so* exotic".). Peoples with great respect for hierarchy obviously had great disrespect for the low.

Arthur *Der Jude von Deutschland* decided he understood.

Arthur the son of Moe the rare Jew-tough horsehide-hurler decided he understood.

Arthur the murderer of a (closet?) Nazi decided he understood.

Arthur the feeler wanted to hug, absorb the guy.

Arthur the deluded misled himself: *I'm You!*

And that full-fledged gaze of The Tibetan fell often, just too often, on Hung. Unembarrassed it lingered, heavy, challenging, entreating; and vaguely barbaric.

How does Mick interpret those looks?

The Tibetan Nyemo then insisted, "I am schooled few Tantra."

Out of nowhere, a declaration like a chest-pounding, his voice a harsh dry scrape. It sure rang no bit like bragging. Like a "liberated Reform Jew" declaring 'I've never read from Talmud *or* Torah. My kids will *not* be bar mitzvah.'

Had he avowed this non-Tantra for Arthur's benefit?

"He means," said Hung, "the doctrines of Mahayana. Everyone expects that because Nyemo is Tibetan he knows all such ways." Hung then said something to Nyemo in Mandarin.

Lobby people stared frowned gawked: Disgusting unabashed *Tibetan*.

This was *chiru*, which meant, son Mick whispered to Arthur, humiliation: "They call the Dali Lama a wolf wrapped in a monk's robes."

Does Mick have to keep showing-off he's so in-the-know!

Mick certainly never showed his ounce of Yiddish-savvy to his German-boy compatriots.

Hung herself looked toward the tile floor, then away, toward outside, as if people were waiting for her. She took Mick's hand. She never touched Nyemo, but somehow that non-touch seemed charged with electrified touching—it seemed more potent than her touch of Mick.

"Many Tibetans," she said, "they are not Tantric peace. There was a Tibetan, at The Great Monastery that we Han Chinese attacked. He was named Yunri. He killed a Chinese General, and more. We did not learn *that* in school."

"That is true," said Nyemo. "Tibetans can kill." He said that with a proud triple-nod. "I taught it you."

"Yes." Hung made a quarter-bow, and it was not sarcastic.

Nyemo now went to touch Hung's hand, but then he gave Arthur a quick bold once-over and held himself back.

As if having been fueled-up by Hung's praise of his people's bravery Nyemo went, "We had a Great Revolt against Mao and his PLA and their desecration."

He said it too loudly. He might or might not have meant to.

"It was a Holocaust," verified Arthur's Mick. "Mao had made a *Kristallnacht*."

Mick seemed more scandalized by the Tibetan disaster than the Jewish.

My own Mick!

Hung smart-shifted them from competitive Holocausts: "Nyemo, he has lived with us. My father offered. Nyemo would have had to live underneath a basement—or under the underneath. In the Beijing under-city."

"Rats!" Nyemo's hands had gone busy making resonant rat-killer fists. Unfortunately, Nyemo's fists looked eager.

Hung: "When Nyemo came to Peking University from Lhasa, it was a rare privilege: The Support Tibet Program was on dead legs but Nyemo had done so well on the *gaokao* they added him."

"The entrance test," translated grandstanding nouveau-Chinese Mick.

My kid's annoying me.

They began walking out of the lobby. Again, people gave them the broadest berths. That humiliation, that *chiru*. Like a demon-mask, The Tibetan plastered-on his murderous jaw-jut face. He thrust it into what he must have experienced as the abysmal unkind darkness of Han people's souls, and he looked happy for the opportunity.

They had a Chinese car, an old one—in view of the new Chinese prosperity and Hung's father's importance (if true) Arthur expected at least, say, an Audi. But this thing was an Xiali, painted blue-red, but in geometries, all quadratics: Blue fender, ripe red door; blue-red strips along the trunk. From its rattlings, scattered scuffings and arced windshield wiper trawlings its origins appeared maybe two decades back; it stank with an updraft of crankcase oil and it pressed tight with friction heat as the floor itself vibrated (tin?) and the multi-cracked rear seat scraped Becker's raw ass (that damned Nivea!, that diarrhea), it harried his hamstrings, even through his pants.[4] But the Xiali was also replete with overdone-overwhelming new-car-aroma (to cover the engine oil and tinnish reek?), most likely sprayed on days ago—perhaps for Arthur Becker's welcome (allergic, he couldn't contain his swollen sneezing). Hung drove, or rather "negotiated" The Great Perturbation: the engulfing Beijing traffic—cars bleating-growling-veering-swarming as if in spawn downstream towards stores and offices, no few blaring music so potently that the nimbi of their bass-beats reverberated off the many orange-red building cranes and shuddered the skeletal fabric of the small Xiali—even with its windows shut tight. One skyscraper collapsed, caved right-in on itself, a controlled im-plosion, a controlled observing crowd. "It was a new skyscratcher," said Hung, "and it happens all the time. Nobody rented. China has built too much, so now, while it builds, China goes tearing down." "China is dumb," commented Nyemo the Tibetan; Arthur let the absurdity go unsaid. Hung did not employ her seat belt. (Nor did Mick wear his—he certainly would have in

---

[4] Old Chinese joke, related by—you guessed it—nouveau savvy Mick: "How many Chinese does it take to drive a Xiali? Four: One to steer and three to push."

Germany). Hung turned on the car radio and hummed along with a popular singer (they said) who never changed key—Faye Wong (Nyemo claimed, "She is not so good as Yadong"—the top Tibetan singer). Hung hunched over the steering wheel—her hands in the unusually awkward (boxing?) locus of five past seven (except for the occasional casual switch to a two-handed six-thirty or, worse, a two-handed twelve-on-the-button [picture it!], or, worse still, she abandoning the wheel thoroughly to gesture—effusive—when she spoke); she jerked her head about so rapidly, as if breaking a bronco while on the lookout for cattle rustlers. In the West it was sallied about that because of their queer sense of space and distance the Chinese were such terrible drivers that you could be legitimately jailed for 'Driving while Chinese', but Hung drove so unflagging herky-jerk—but casual—one might have believed that young Beijing operators were warned by joke that 'You can be arrested for driving like a snail American.' Arthur was cramped into that narrow rear seat with the inscrutable Tibetan Nyemo—who was hardly inscrutable.

Hung had said, "Now we take you to Tian'An Men Square, I know a shortcut."

"Everyone in Beijing knows a shortcut."—ironic-mad Nyemo.

If her side-street "shortcut" route had been designed to avoid bigtime traffic and save time Becker wondered at what a continental trek the longcut route must have been. Their trip took them one hour.

"Tian'An Men is where all Westerners wish to first go, although most Chinese wonder why they wish it. Most Chinese, they don't know what had happened there—that is *true*."

"It's true," echoed Mick; damn he was so annoyingly on-the-in.

Hung said, "Tian'An Men, it is outblocked in History, called *liu si*, which means a rule with no rule; but my father taught me of Tian'An Men. He would not allow me to not know."

Arthur summonsed-up that infamous picture: the lanky, backpacked Beijing student—the stubborn righteous "tank man"—braving the Army *Panzer*. That radical faceoff had gone round the world: admiration and anonymity—was that paladin still alive? It was astounding to realize that most Chinese could conjure no such confrontation. No, Arthur had not summonsed-up that vital picture: it had arisen on its own.

He said nothing about that.

"I don't go," piped Nyemo. "I never go to Tian'An Men."

For a moment it seemed that he and Hung were a long-married couple, tied taut by their jagged ins-and-outs, their cantankerous seethings and sunken-in furies; their swirling love yet their settled love. They looked as if they could not escape from one single censer placed within them.

Leaning forward, Nyemo rapped Hung upside the right shoulder. He felt he had a right to do this? This was neither a love tap nor a punch—more a reminder of some double-binding. Did Mick see more punch than punch was?—he reached to grab the Tibetan's offending hand, and the Tibetan's turned look towards Mick was more wondering, more startled, more confused, than a counter or a confrontation. Mick stared at Nyemo with near threat.

Arthur had never seen such a daring expression escape from Mick-ah-yell before.

He liked it.

Hung said, "The Tibet temple is there in Tian'An Men. It is the most beautiful in all Beijing."

Nyemo said, "The Yonghegon, it is Han fakery, not real. It is plastic, and you know it. You Han, you destroyed the *real*."

Frozen offence now—*ain'nobody gonna turn me round*: "The Han," said Nyemo, "they have made our Lhasa temples into *Han* cinemas, do you know *that*?— and in other temples they hustle-scam your tourists by shaving their own *Han* heads, they wearing monk cassocks and asking *yuan* for the bestow of Tibetish Buddahood—it is *obscene*!"

(Of course Arthur saw those Nazi Buchenwald guards posing as skeletal Jew prisoners when the Russian Army moved in.)

"*Other* temples," said Nyemo, "they have made into the mini-golf courses. Our music, it is gone, it is *Han* music all round now. The word 'Tibet' is even banned from Chinese Internet—The Great *Fire*wall. So many *Tibetans* cannot now speak *Tibet*."

He sneered and repeated that one: "So many Tibetans cannot now speak *Tibet*."

Hung said: "You are *known*, Nyemo. You *know* you are known—what are you *doing*!? You should stop your *talk*."

"And *you* should stop *your* talk. Hung, I am not your *sanwu*."

"*Sanwu* is charity," explained Mick-ah-yell, endless happy to take part.

"I hate the *sanwu*. It is why I am a thief."

He's a thief?!
Neither Hung nor Mick said that he was not.

They approached Tian'An Men Square, by way of the Avenue of Eternal Peace, into which they *had* swerved from Hung's "shortcut". Hung found a small spot on a side alleyway called Qian Jie and bumper-bumper touch-parked as if she were handicapped or blind or maneuvering an amusement park crash car. A woman leaned out from her second-story window and hollered, and Hung hollered back. "She says it is her family's parking place, traditional. That is fullish rid-dick."

There were *thousands* of tourists in the enormous square.

"I could kill."—Nyemo. "And I do not go *into* Tian'An Men. I have *never*!"

Nyemo had already worked himself to a pitch—a salvo seemed natural from his rounded near bubbling head—pop pop pop; that broad desert-face had gone ripe as any painted balloon, it was fierce and it was comical—it might just topple-over onto you; Nyemo—or the Nyemo within Nyemo—was so quick-angry that when he opened the Xiali's cranky rear door to get out he just about tumbled and was near struck by a passing car—and he did not even notice. Nor likely did the tunnel-vision Beijing driver: just a matter of course.

At the entrance to the Gate of Heavenly Peace was suspended a bright red slogan, thickly imprinted: *Long Live the Great Unity of the Peoples of the World*. From an unlocatable speaker, Kenny G (for Chrissakes!) was syrupping away on "Going Home". Hung and Mick led Arthur about the many temples and The Hall of Mental

Cultivation.

Hung said: "Their motions are saying their silent wisdom words they believe to believe and think."

Huh?

Hung was describing now an arcing string of Tai Chiers in the Square, their arms moving slowly as in a very thick sea of dreams:

> The world is wide
> The universe is vast
> My path is narrow
> My path is small
> I must work hard
> My small and narrow path.

Hung added: "That is old China. We do not take that serious."

She seemed too sure of herself.

And Arthur was attracted to that.

She said: "I only made up what their Tai Chi has said. Not that it is secrets, but I do not know the Tai Chi."

Arthur remained attracted.

Appearing, the great towers, with their ornamented archways and concave-edged roofs, with exotic (to Arthur) inscriptions on their "flying eaves", maybe of uplift prayer.

Mick announced, "What a place to *live*!"

Arthur felt a vague competition forming with his son. This time not for Jutta.

He said: "Are the two of you sure you are not in-toxicated by the newness, your differences. That can be quite subtle and feel, you know, so authentic. Not that it—" He ventured, "Your marriage might be too soon."

"Father," went Mick, "that angers me."

Mick had never before spoken like that to Arthur.

Arthur addressed Hung: "Has your father approved?"

"Jin Jianxin," said Hung. "That is my father's name." Even the assertion of naming her father was done with an enveloping-attracting strength.

The towers now before them, Zhengyang Men and the Bell Tower. They resembled giant wedding cakes. The stark split of East from West, from Gothic or Classical. Different human beings. Different constructs in which to live. The Picking Flowers Temple had underwear hanging out front to dry.

Arthur remembered what he had read in *Die Zeit*: China ranked 112th in a poll of world human happiness. That was awfully low.

How might that happiness have been measured?

"Please do me a favor," he managed. "Just think hard. Think hard about what you two are doing." He rubbed the bone at the base of his neck as if that scrubbing motion belonged to some form of Tai Chi that remained within everyone. "I don't mean to—"

They simply stared at him and his, what?—Dismay? Distrust? Stupidity?

He was drawn by Hung's acute glare. There was a violence in it—he was surprised to see that now, but he did see it—it resembled the vehemence that resonated within the eyes of the Tibetan Nyemo. And there was a hidden mercy. . . But Nyemo's eyes contained this last as well.

Did Mick's, Mick's eyes? Arthur did not see his son as having much sophistication. Sorriful feeling there.

Live life, boy. Live LIFE.

"I've come here with an open mind," he lied.

Coward. Only a *Feigling* resorts to lies. Arthur Becker had heard *Feigling,* but the person who had laid out that wisdom, if wisdom it was, had been his mulehead bitter-end father Moe.

Mick hugged Hung, so tightly, as if she might fly off. To where? To The Tibetan? Mick kissed Hung, but that kiss was just too long, it seemed to have strands of son-stubborn-protest in its wake. . . And of begging too.

Damn, that pulsation Hung had had with the Tibetan—that was real, inescapable. It had taken place, what? a half an hour before. But it still pressed in on you.

Long Live the Great Unity of the Peoples of the World. That was what that banner near to them had read.

Hung went calling, calling "Nyemo, *zai na*!?"

Mick translated (quite unnecessarily in this case): " 'Where are you?'."

When they next caught sight of Nyemo The Tibetan he was indeed within the Square; he had just hollered out, "*Confucian!?—No one* here is *Confucian.* It is all the *lippest* serve to cover." Nyemo appeared scarlet-faced, as if he had just exploded out of not Tian'An Men but Pandemonium. It was clear that Tian'An Men had brought out his most passionate violences—and his threatening, defiant lack of fear in exhibiting these. His face was jerking about catercornerish, his eyes had rolled back, seeming in a permanent palsy, bearing the usually covert whites. What were his intentions— lecturing? imploring? menacing? or even, arms flailing, chasing people out of the Square? His breath was blasting outrage, so exhibitionistic with his pumping the victory V into the air—V! V! V! V! V!—and not in a deranged look, at least not fully. Which fact was quite amazing. As was the fact that his rage did turn his face also into a candied cherubic lucent. "Conqueror injustice," he hollered, "masked as glory grandeur!" By now, it was surely not just tourists gawking and snapping fotos of this "hilarious" Tibetan spleen-venting nut, odds-on there were tourist-got-up undercovers—as if Nyemo didn't know it: he seemed trying now, or risking, permanent escape *into* where else but a Han Chinese prison. Self-destructive pleasure fulfilling righteous fury. And Arthur Becker was put in mind of himself, a compact earnest distillation of revenge. The Tibetan looked then towards temples and gates, then away, as if their beauty, their indisputable ancient beauty (all Han fakery, he'd said) were also evidence of indecency and injustice preserved.

"Nyemo!" called out Hung.

Nyemo was approaching, still blathering.

"Do not come unbridled."

It was a bit late for such a caution, but Hung continued talking to the Tibetan—now in Mandarin. . . . Then to Arthur—

Hung said: "Nyemo is already known. He is being a self-immolator like a Tibet monk, without *burning* the self-immolation—except by his substitute. He is his own fire. They have let him off once before, because likely of my father. But Nyemo, he tempts and he tempts them—and in that way he also *denies* my father, his works for him."

"Who?" Arthur asked. "Who is Nyemo tempting?"

"The *chengguan*. Secret police. Who are not so

secret."

Mick said: "I wonder what's today got Nyemo's tantric juices so uproared."

Mick was beaming as he said that: slapping himself on the back for his having mastered what was apparently a hip street Chinese idiom.

Nyemo had not lost his look of haggard volatility. His smile went thin and maddening.

Hung went to the Tibetan, her eyes were now compassionate and urgent. She said mildly, "Nyemo."

She cradled the sides of his face; above her palms his eyes suggested bulging needles, so black they came off a pulsating silver. Hung had cradled his face to silence him of course—but it also appeared erotic. Intimate. Welded.

Didn't Mick see that?

"My Bodhisattva," Nyemo said to Hung, not ironic, not hostile—more as if resisting.

"It is his ego," said Mick. "His trying to be important."

"No!" Hung hadn't missed that ego-crack. Her right arm twitched, it jump-jolted, as if she'd been struck by a police taser. It looked as if she might have slapped Mick her fiancé. . . For insulting another man she loved?

Mick had even flinched.

Arthur waited for his son to do more. Hold Hung. Something.

"Nyemo, you do go crazy," Hung said. But there was admiration in her voice—as if she felt that, all things considered, he shouldn't not go crazy. To her Nyemo was not just all ego. He was so much more.

Nyemo said no more.

On the spot he was not arrested.

Later, when he was alone in his room at the Hotel Prince Gong, his thoughts were interrupted by the tingly-tiny ringing bright yellow telephone. Becker barely heard it—*maybe in a year I'll hear silence*—and once again he noted to himself to get his ear-drums checked on return to Heidelberg. And once again he was prompted to imagine that some nurse or attendant in the hospital might well have heard the stifled snortles of his strangled intellectual bigot Fritz Strobel—and then seen Arthur the Strangler. And the nurse or attendant, eager for a back-pat (most were grateful refugee Bosnians, Herzegovinians, Croatians) had notified the authorities. Were it not for his wife Jutta, Becker could have booked his return flight not to Frankfurt but to SFO. Go East to America, not West to Europe. He had so often prided himself on his sacrifice some twenty years before in giving-up his longtime community in Berkeley to become a Deutsche *Aufenthaltstitel* guy, a holder of the German green card (which was not green). . . Why had he done that? Jutta the Visiting Scholar at Cal had just not been like Berserkeley girls. Paradoxically her honesty, and her formality, were relaxing. Even her shyness, or what seemed like shyness, these shone as a politeness, a quiet intelligence, a patience to learn the other's opinion, to wait for it, to absorb it—a built-in empathy. And, she was good-looking: penetrating eyes, that direct-thin Germanic nose. Although Jutta could not have looked in the least like his son Mick-ah-yell's Hung Huang, the Chinese girl's way-of-being reminded him of his wife's: that strength bolstering the politeness and the concern softening the strong face. There had already been those moments when Becker had wanted to embrace Hung, to bring her into him. It felt as if he had already done this. . . *Tell the truth: you'd like to make love to her*.

Nyemo was on the phone. "It is just only me myself, in the lobby, of your hotel. Only me, alone. People are staring as they do at me. I could kill them."

"Don't do that."

He'd meant it as wit, but Becker did believe Nyemo could kill.

Of course he knew Nyemo would not pick up on the humor.

Humor? Was that really humor?

"May I come up to you?"

After a worried pause, Becker said "Of course."

Christ what was this about?

Recollecting that cuneiform of harangue to which The Tibetan had subjected the rubbernecking tourists at Tian'An Men, Becker sped through this strategy of avoidance, that scenario of placation, a hamming-up of "understanding"—he drew himself a blank.

Best not to work too hard on what you haven't the vaguest conceivable—

Nyemo's door knock was not what Arthur Becker expected. It was so light, so tentative and apologetic, it seemed unlike the voluble Tibetan's roundhouse flailing ways. Perhaps this was because, yet wrapped in his "dress-up" tan Thirties Oklahoma cowpoke sports-coat he was squatting, reaching-out longitudinally to the door, while being perched spreadeagle on top of the pinned-down shoulders of a skinny young perplexed uniformed hotel attendant. The slight-built lobby-boy (whose livery was so bedecked with gold buttons and epaulets that he resembled a Gilbert and Sullivan potentate) had obviously been told to stop the "green brain" barbarian Tibetan from his hairbrained Tibetan intention of ascending to Herr Mister Becker's room, and had been summarily table-turned in what was unquestionably too arduous a task for him alone. "It's okay," Arthur told this orderly manque, as if it were the "orderly" who owned the authoritarial hand here; and instantly Nyemo's mouth fell from the grim-set to the innocent-ajar; he raised himself from the hotel boy, saying something in Mandarin perhaps on the order of "I'm sorry but I had no choice since you were about to clobber me had I not proactively clobbered you. Next time your Hotel Prince Gong should send *two* men." . . . The swarthy broad young man from Lhasa was now allowed into his room by Arthur, who had not yet undressed for sleep. Nyemo sat, for some reason, likely elder-respect, on the wide green low plateau of an ottoman situated at the room's center. For balance he leaned forward, elbows on quadriceps—which put Arthur in mind of a man on a toilet seat, or The Thinker, or one who might blast himself off at any moment and run the 100 meters full out—with his checkered shirt's buttons now force-popped-out by his belly, and the shirt now looking not unlike a dolphin's mouth—this quite evident from his having unbuttoned his Okie sportscoat (which now put Arthur in mind of The Surrey With the Fringe on Top). Nyemo's face had now gone so still it seemed vacant of every emotion but the effort to not weep—or to not explode. Arthur fluff-propped his pillows and lay back on his bed. In a tense effort to be casual—or therapeutically important?—he locked his fingers behind his head, which act felt so artificial and superior (and theatrical) (and uncomfortable) he immediately abandoned that posturing and, inadvertently, he double-hand-covered his groin— a finger-arrangement as languid as it was false: The Disconcerted But Casually Protected Man.

Nyemo said: "Herr Becker, there is something I very must of inform you."

"Okay, inform away."

Again unsettled Arthur had tried a disarming humor slant.

Again, not picked up.

"It is to do with my Hung—I mean not 'my', but Hung. Hung Huang, your son Mick's to be. His."

"Ah."

Arthur's first thought: *My son's fiancé is not a virgin.*

Well, quite the natural conjecture: who today would expect otherwise? Even in China. That flippant Brit in the arriving limo had quick-clued Becker pretty thoroughly.

"But now I am before you I do not know if I can inform."

Inform?

Arthur leaned forward from his bed and took the man's jacketed arm, he lightly stroked it. This gentling surprised even him: it was his hand's own will more than his own—his gesture did not feel inappropriate but it did feel so sorryass New Age, an indulgent chutzpah, more a, well, female thing.

A bigot hostile to his bigotry—that's me.

He experienced the Tibetan's arm strength and then ditched that rubbing of the Tibetan's muscles.

"You are a Chew," declared Nyemo.

Becker got it. After first digesting that "Chew" for a pair of milliseconds.

"Yes. A Jew. I'm a Jew."

I'm now going to be garnering some anti-Semitism from a Tibetan?

"I understand your Jewness from your Mick-ah-yell. And I wish to know more of Jews-ishness—I just do not understand what Jew means. Mostly Mick is mum."

"Yes."

I thought he was about to unveil some Hung hiddenness. Already he's changing the subject?

Be polite. Tolerant. Indulge. . . As best you can, you being neither tolerant nor indulgent:

"It's hard to explain, Jewishness. Even in the West it is. But in an Eastern context, it's . . . "

"Complexity, I do understand. Tibet is too— complex. We are a relaxed people and we are a nervous people."

Jew-wise, couldn't have said it better myself, but Can We Get To HUNG?

Nyemo swung out one arm—Becker flinched, his groin-covering hands tightening involuntarily on his balls. The Tibetan was only waving away a giant flittering butterfly that resembled a helicopter or a decorated flapping drone. Becker must have left his wide window open in the morning when he'd joined the trio.

"Do you know that at one time your CIA, they helped us, Tibet, with the training. Against Mao and his PLA?"

"I did not know that."

"Under-blanket advisement, they did. But they, uh,

curtailed?"

I bet they did.

"They needed their China more."

"I'm sorry, Nyemo."

Can we get to HUNG?!

For the first time Nyemo gazed about the hotel room, his lips retarding an obvious curl-up of vague distaste on the order of: 'So this is the kind of craphouse chamber they give to Jews. Well, they'd give the same to us Tibetans—likely worse, if any room at all.' Of course this had been Arthur's cynical deconstructing of the Tibetan's cast. But Nyemo now did try a smile, a pained sort of downhill grin; it looked like a satisfaction that had got deformed in the process of its own relishing. No, that was a Western thing, all labyrinth, all jockeying. Nyemo studied Arthur squintingly: trying to comprehend The Jew American? Didn't he see that his squint was impolite? Well, Western squint-smiles were definitely sadist, ironic, heavy on the shattenfreude. Was The Tibetan then perceiving a shared but hazy pain?—his and Arthur Becker's peoples. He stood from the ottoman and walked to the room's window, looking out on the small hotel room's view-poor courtyard: a blockage?—an impasse reserved for Tibetans and for Jews? One might think such were one of two related minds. But come on, these two men were not that, not remotely. . . Nyemo turned back to Arthur: "Always, they should fight. Down to the last and final Chew."

Huh? . . . He's talking Israel?

Please, can we get back to Hung!

This time it was Arthur who swung at the gigantic headstrong butterfly, and whiffed.

Why did I try to kill a butterfly?

Nyemo said: "There are rich Tibetans, did you know? It is true. They rub-bones with VIP Chinese, and I hate them. They try so to rub Han bones. Those Tibetans, they go to clubs together with the highest Han who will take them—because those Han, they want things from such Tibetans, land and our resource; and together they all get girls. *Together* they do. Tibetan girls. Those rich Tibetans, they like doing that. It prides them, and I so hate them. The Chinese, they grit their teeth (*Like a pit bull Nyemo showed vast eager teeth*) and they suffer the associate with 'the green brain people'—even the rich ones trying so hard to be VIP. Hypocrites. You never read of *that* shame-sin in the *Internationals*."

Arthur decided to look indignant. That felt phony and he changed it to a nod of knowing: *Human beings, what the hell can you expect!*

Burl Ives appeared: Big Daddy in *Cat on a Hot Tin Roof*. Big Daddy hated "mendacity". Burl Ives hung in there while Nyemo went on now about Norbu, a *non*-shame-sinner, his own father. Norbu, who taught children—he loved geography. He taught children by his sculpting in wood the shapes of nations in Africa. Wood maps. Nyemo had helped him, with the color-painting. Nyemo said Norbu a score of times. He hummed Norbu like a bass, he honked Norbu like a clarinet, more deep instruments. The filial reverence was so familiar to Arthur the Moe-child—so annoying. Truth be told it was very annoying to this father of Mick-ah-yell, Mick-ah-yell who likely never extolled his father. Nyemo told Arthur that Mandarins had come, businessman, and taken-over map production, "mass and cheap, for sale out in the wide world." They had payed Norbu nothing, as Norbu had no "ownership of production"; all he'd had was a teacher's idea of Africa and wood and a teacher's crafting love. Despite sympathy, Arthur's thought:

Can we already get to Hung!?

"In Beijing," Nyemo said, "I believe now—no things."

"I understand."

Arthur understood nothing, almost nothing; he wished he could show more fellow feeling to Nyemo than merely his stupid empty nod.

Nyemo then reached-out and shook Arthur's hand, and with that very powerful rock grip. "Thank you," he said. "I must go."

He comes to give me the lowdown on Hung and he chickens-out on Hung!?

Arthur following, Nyemo hunched sluggish towards the room's entrance door—then he stopped and turned: "Sir," he said, "I do see-into why Mick-ah-yell counts himself not conjugated in the midst of you, your Jews. I see-into that that hurts you—it must, it would be terrible if it did not hurt. My father Norbu would die if I denied Tibetan, even as being it becomes so small." Then startlingly he rushed back to Arthur, who was holding the door ajar, polite invitation for the Tibetan to go already? With an apologetic shrug Nyemo took the lever-like doorknob from Arthur's holding hand, closed the door, and he embraced the older man, the Jew, now stupefied. . . Then, suddenly, The Tibetan swung round, trudged straight past Arthur as if the American were a wax statue or a block of wood, and returned to sitting on the hotel room hassock, leaning forward in his sunken-readied style, again as if on the toilet. He chafed his hands as if warming up or demolishing a broad itch—Arthur saw the considerable dirt under the Tibetan's fingernails. Nyemo's turn-about said determination rebuilt? A conscience twitching about him like that butterfly.

"Hung," he said.

Gentlemen, start your engines!

"I have created for my own, a monster. And for, I think, your Mick. It is my only way for honor, if I tell you."

"Hung you're saying is a monster?"

"No!"

A more rigid-alarmed look could not have stiffened Nyemo's face. As if a ten-ton trailer with its brights on and its warnings blinking red were bearing down on him.

"But you just said that she is—"

"A monster, Hung, but she is good."

Clueless, Becker did not wish to appear in the dark. He showed his palms and shrugged, wise man style. It couldn't hurt.

"Please, you see: In China it is held that taking the virginal from a virgin can make a man a man. In Tibet as well. This wisdom may be true, but I am sorry."

So we were crawling about, knuckle-walking in The West, a zillion years ago.

Becker said nothing.

Nyemo held to his button-popped bulge-bellied shirt as if comforting a stomach ache. He looked down as if truth were that swelling ache.

Silence.

Arthur remained standing. He started towards the

hassock, then he stopped short. He realized that he was afraid of the Tibetan, who might smother him with love and tears—or kill him, with love and tears.

"You had sex with Hung?"

"Truth is truth. Hung is no longer *chu*."

"*Chu*?"

"In China the word for virgin is *chu*. It is praise and it is insult."

That *chu* did chug-out undissimilar from a sudden sneeze.

"*Chu,*" explained Nyemo, now so earnest, "it is the main of the word *chuzhang*."

Etymology: I could give a shit just now.

"And *Chuzhang,* it means section chief."

Despite himself, Becker hacked-out a laugh: *Section chief?* So, to break a girl's cherry in the world of Han was to show you had the best boss stuff: Section Chief yet. A wonder China hadn't shot up years earlier on capitalism's grueling charts.

Nyemo said: "I so want to be moral of it by telling, of myself and Hung, and honest. I have as to yet not told to any one soul. But you are the father of the wronged."

Wronged?

Seated on the ottoman Nyemo the wronger folded his arms. He now put Arthur in mind of Yul Brynner as the king of Siam, except that the Wronger here was arm-folding not out of total domination but for supreme protection and forgiveness, a warding-off. His face had suddenly, like that, cascaded from its own bewronged muscularity (as a "repulsive green-brain" Tibetan) to a near wreckage. "And the father of the *other* wronged, Jin Jianxin, *he* is the cause."

"Jin Jianxin? Hung's father? *He's* the *cause*?"

"*The-fuck-up-the-ass,* yes. It is called that? I will come to this."

"The—you . . . ?"

"It is not a nice thing to say, that what I did. It hurts, to do it, to receive it. I know, I did it but I don't know how I did—that hurt, that scream, even to the Hung. Even *by* the Hung."

You fucked her up the ass!? You say you will Come to this?! Come Now!

Becker backed-up to his spot on the bed. He sat but he did not lie down. He folded his hands and he stared at them. Prayerful could be a habit of even out-striking hands. His hands were small. Flimsy things—he despised his measly piddling fingers, Lilliputian jobs. He had often blamed his hands for why he, the son of a pro pitcher with cigar fingers, had been able to play only high-school ball. He hadn't even made inter-fuckingcollegiate. He pictured—couldn't help it—the Hung ass-fucking. That sweet strong girl with the intense dark sympathetic absorbing eyes. Not the worst match for his more watery son. . . Or, the worst match.

"It commenced by accidental," vouched Nyemo.

Nyemo'd said that the great ombudsman Jin Jianxin was the cause?

Becker unfolded his hands. He rubbed them along his thighs, which was an habitual hurler motion of his dad Moe—also in prep for temper-Moe's whomping him, which Moe did do a lot—at least such seemed so in memory. Becker said not one thing.

"Hung and I, we went onto the roof of the Xiushui Building at the university. It was night dark, as we had been studying so late long, practicing our English, and in the idiom, and laughing. It was a clear night. We climbed up the stairs to see the stars and the constellates—they are so seldom visible in Beijing, you just have to believe that they are there, and so they help to keep your *chi* up, and even more when you see them."

'Keep your chin up' was Becker's initial grasp.

"But," said The Tibetan, "as we, Hung and I, we—"

"But where was my son? Where was Mick?"

"This night was before your Mick came to here from Germany. Oh months before. Mick was not then known to us as a man."

Which phrasing sounded so strange, comical but accurate. And unpleasant. And pathetic. And, especially to Arthur, clobbering. A reflection on Mick's un-involvement in Hung's de-*chu*-ing and on the boy's own virility.

Is Mick yet known to Me as-a-man?

"We walked, Hung and I, to a bench on the roof, where many students sit, at usual in the day, at the lunchtime. But in night's sharp we did not sight the bench, and Hung tripped her foot over it, she bumped, and then she fell, and then she laughed at this, and as so did I. And because we were laughing, and so having fun, when Hung stood herself back I had more fun, and I pushed her, in play I did it, I swear to you to that—I pushed her back to the bench again, and again Hung started to fall. But she didn't—not fall. Not this time, not total. She was bent on knees. And rather then she pushed *me* back, and she laughed, and I did not fall either—as we both then knew just exact where the bench was in its being."

"Nyemo," said Becker, "I don't need the details. It's

uncomfortable, for you. For me too (he added, although it wouldn't be: prurience with this garnish of the personal—are you kidding?). You don't have to tell me all this."

Tell me already, tell me!

"Hung's father. Jin Jianxin. He was in-mixed in this."

"So you said before: The 'great' Jin Jianxin? The brave reformer. The moral Confucian." The irony. "Nyemo, please, what are you talking about?"

"I will say of Jin. I will tell to you. At the point that it comes to right."

Patience, old boy, patience.

Becker stood once more. His arches ached. All that slow stop-go treading round Tian'An Men, and the tension now. (Like Moe he was afflicted with fallen arches; but ache or no, Moe had made it to the mound—of Roanoak, of Hagerstown, and to the top farm club of the Senators, Triple A). Becker wanted to take his shoes off and deep-tissue dig-in with his thumbs. How would the Tibetan see this? Weakness, likely, a mockery of an Achilles; and too much informality. In China, perhaps, contempt—especially to a hearty Tibetan. Becker refrained from deep-tissuing. False dignity prevailed.

"But as Hung was down low," said Nyemo, "I could see her smile (Nyemo smiled now), and it was different, different from her usual. Which made my look down at her also too not the usual."

Damnit, tell me about "the great" Jin Jianxin, the defender of the undefended—His role. How could he have a role?

"Hung joked then: She teased that she had heard that

65

Tibetans enjoy to be in the naked a great deal—and I said No, that was Han myth, the slander or its praise. But I was lying, and Hung, she could tell; and she said she would push me off the roof, which was mere some meters over, so she was taunting—and she pushed, and I pushed her back, again. And this time, Hung fell once again, although she did not have to fall, I don't think so—she helped her fall. And this time she stared up at me from being down, and it was like as if she were asking, waiting, questing?—she looked mixed, like I was going to shoot her for a crime, or whip." The Tibetan shook his head, conveying to Arthur that he had been confused, puzzled by Hung's victimized expression, trying to figure it, as if it were false, not her at all. Especially as, said Nyemo, "Hung did not arise herself. She just kept staring up at me, Nyemo. She stayed down. It was as like she was mixed-up herself, like Hung was captured into this mysterious *asking* and its fearing. Hung you can see is not usual a victim of a girl."

"Yes, I agree. I have seen that."

And I've also seen her slapped good by that woman with the hair-lipped child.

And taken it stoicly. Sympathetically.

And also I have seen how I, on the plane to here, made Strobel's smothering Strobel's fault, his own, not mine. We humans do do that.

And also I have seen how I, already, admire Hung . . . Already?

She can handle abuse, not that this episode, sex or not, fits that ravage category. This apparent episode.

I'm beginning to not trust Nyemo.

Tibetans—easy to understand their motives.

"Then" said The Tibetan, "Hung, she held out her hands, to which I felt she wanted me to pull her up, as in a sporting game. So I did that, I took her hands, and I felt Hung pulling me down, or trying to. So, it was part of the game, and I came down, easy, on the top of Hung—which made her from my pressure bump her head on the roof floor—which you could hear, the bump-bump, but I don't believe it hurt so much or at all, but it made her look at me in that strange way again, as if I were a Han conqueror and she, *she* was the Tibetan being hurt and being conquered, and glad: 'what will you *do* with me?!' "

Nyemo's broad face had gone broader with this improbable boasting—and its apparent torment? Pathos duking it out with erotic male big talk. And Arthur, no stranger to such a sadness of masculine inner warfare, split Arthur, he identified: a Jew living in Germany (even in now-times) he might step into the psyche, even the body, of a Tibetan living in Beijing. But for the ass-fucking of his son's fiancé, that steady girl of what seemed a serene humility, a girl who Becker already saw at moments as sublime, as "his" (he needed to see this?), he wished to inflict harm on this young man, the intruder, the refugee, the Tibetan hillbilly-shitkicker outsider who had acted-out The Protocols of the Elders of Tibet; the, well, Asian Jew; even if such bungholing act at this point was merely implied.

A teaser?

Standing before his bed, but not dropping onto it, not even onto its edge—which might present a diminish-ment, and also might allow Nyemo's staying for who knew how long—Becker said, "Nyemo, you mentioned Hung's father, Jin Jianxin. His responsibility for the—.

It's about time you told me."

Becker sure did covet that Jin detail—that strange, baleful father-implication. Especially as The Great Ombudsman, who did not fear jailing—*really!? Chinese jailing!*—had already, just by his existence, made Arthur feel so damned diminished. As, in his way, old Fritz Strobel had. And dad Moe, of course.

Nyemo: "I will say how—but soon—how Jin Jianxin enrolled?"

Enrolled?

"But, I have to say: I was feeling like that Hung had planned it—our us. I mean, I was feeling that queerest, but I did not believe that feeling, as I was so knowing Hung." The Tibetan shut his eyes for a moment, as if to picture the two Hungs he knew and then merge them. He then shook his head: Hung was Hung and Hung was no Hung at all.

He opened his eyes.

"Now, please, Nyemo, you've said that her *father* was involved. *Please.*"

"I will say how that soon. Very soon."

"Look, Nyemo." Becker said it very softly. And now he did sit on his bed. "Your feeling that Hung had planned it all, or her father"—which really went a universe beyond belief—"this allows you to feel less, what? guilty? bad?"

"Hung is not Hung," said Nyemo. "To that concluding I have come."

" 'Hung is not Hung'?"

"Not Hung who you see. She is that changing color little, what?—chameleon. I mean, she hates her father Jin Jianxin."

"It sure doesn't seem so. She's in awe of him."

"She is in the awe. Yes. She speaks of the awe. She is full of the awe."

Becker held his tongue: no time for pun-instruction.

After all, he was 'full of the awe' for mixed-chameleon-not-so-awe-worthy Moe.

"But she is also in the hate—no, not the hate, but—" Nyemo's brow rose and wrinkled in its word-search, his brow-ridge jutted, suggesting a lower primate; it looked as if his eyeballs were chasing his eyelids—"Hung is just the quick patch-quilt."

"She resents her father?"

"Resent. Yes. Times resent. Jin Jianxin's too-good-being-and-helps-for-all. His super *chi*. For the good of everyone. This is imprison for Hung—in some times—can you understand? It is all on Hung's head, it loads. She tells to me she feels, she can feel, the trapped, she wishes to break away. She is not who you think she is. She is not who your Mick thinks she is. One time Hung Huang, she goes on train to Hong Kong, in risk of a psych-condition."

"A psychiatric condition, from a *train*?"

"Yes. This is known well in China: travel-claustro, travel close, the skin-on-skin too much." The Tibetan covered his mouth, as if people might be watching. People ear-scrunched against the next hotel room walls: "Even the train-fucking, it proceeds. By stand-up, with the clothing, in the aisles. On the crowded days, the Chinese homegoings."

Sounds like eager-edge Germans saturating each other, choke and elbow, at the exits of their supertrain ICE: The GERMAN travel-claustro. Sans the fucking. German traingoers don't fuck, except maybe in First Class.

"Hung," said the boy, "she is in thought that from Hong Kong she can go to America by meeting people from America and being nice."

"Does my Mick know any of this, about Hung's leaving—wanting to?"

"Mick—I'm sorry. He does not know anything. I'm sorry."

She is using Mick?

"But," said Nyemo, "Hung turns back, first train stop of Harmony Express: Tianjin. She could not leave. That would pain her father. Hung, simple loves her father. There are just two Hungs."

Nyemo's hands, for some reason, went to his own testicles.

"I too," he nodded forcefully. "I left my family so far back. I still see the road from Lhasa, the Gobi Desert. Bears and gooseberries." He did not smile. "I left my family with all their hopes."

Although there was scant comparison, Arthur had felt the same when he had left America to live in Germany. His son Mick just hadn't seemed to show his own rupture. Maybe to Jutta Mick had given-out the awkward pain; certainly not to Arthur.

A wind might have swept through the wide window now, pulling the two men now together.

Nyemo bleated, "I *love* Hung!" Then—

"Hung's father Jin, here he comes in at now."

My pulse, it's fucking beating in my eyes? I can see my pulse popping its shadow on the ceiling. Stroke? I've never seen that shadow-flap before.

"We could not stop," said Nyemo, "Hung and I. We needed no help from the maca."

"Maca?"

"African-dee-see-yack, from Peru."

"African, from Peru?"

Ah, aphrodisiac.

"Looks like turnip. It is used in China, very muchso. I can retrieve for you some portions. The gratuity would be low."

The nice Tibetan kid does deal dope?

Becker waved the offer off.

"Hung and I," said Nyemo, "we were taken hold and we carried. We couldn't halt. This had us do these deeds Jin said."

'Jin said'?

What could Arthur say but "Yes?"—while picturing.

Hung sweetness, Hung soft temperament. Hung's wild nature lure.

"Hung, her nails, her whimpsters, her bumping her head as if *I* were bumping her, and I was *not*. Her way of spreading-out, *and from the rear!—and spreading with her hands!*—this frightened. Herr Becker, I live in the Jianxin house, I am in their debted, I am a 'green brain' Tibet boy, I hate but I am grateful. So I told Jin Jianxin the happenings—I had to. I was frightened to tell, but I had to. And Jin, he then told to me what in next times, in future, how to do. To advance. Hung, the rolling over. Jin, he did not appear upshotted at Hung's behavior."

"Rolling, onto her stomach."

"And her knees, the rise-up back."

"Jin told you this how-to?"

This Tibetan kid's a liar, pathological. Didn't the Nazis believe this shit about the Jews, sex-power; didn't all goyim believe it, deep down. . . Now they probably hate us, deep down, for the disappointment. It's the

Tibetans' turn.

"But I did not roll Hung—I did not have to. *She* rolled her, as *like* I had rolled her. And she *waited*, for my fullest nerve."

"Your . . . entry, up her . . . rear end."

" 'It will hurt', I said, I knew it would, and she said no words, did she clutch her teeth?—and I could not achieve, what you say, the wood. . . At first."

With that I will not sympathize.

"Since, I have tried myself, with my finger. It does hurt."

Arthur nodded.

Shocked Arthur trying to talk flat-unflappable as old-time TV cop Joe Friday: *Just the facts ma'am.* Shocked Arthur who'd never entered Jutta this way—never. *(And why haven't I tried?).* Shocked Arthur imagining the "event", eyes prurient and eyes wishing to shut-off their demanding hardcore vision, like some creep hung-up on the dirty cable channels—and, tell the truth, eyes wishing to imagine further further prurience: This girl Hung, this daughter-in-law potential, this tolerant consoling girl whose benevolent eyes had embraced Nyemo at Tian'An Men when he was off the deepest edge, this child whom Arthur has already seen as generous, as radiant in calm, the radiant love of his son Mick, she has now a radiance alright, a sharpest filament of the rogue. . . *But since when am I so naïve? Since when am I not human?*

"The Jin, *he* gave me fullest nerve."

He fucking gave you permission.

My daughter-in-law?

Hung with her proportions perfect, her custard coloring, her Asian pubic hair (was it really straight, not a lick of kink?), her face to the floor as in Allah prayer, her fingers curling with some fervent wish— self-abnegation? what? Jin obedience, or dis- obedience? like her aborted train ride. And what does Arthur, tough Moe's son, see while wishing to see and not see?—Eva's ass, his mother Eva's ass for godssakes!—then again Hung's ass, her begging ass risen as she's on her begging belly, her coccyx bone protruding into high triangle, a so-wanted good-felt- painful yielding. Constance Chatterly and lowly Oliver—the woman, a decent upright Han, she subdued, bent, humbled, by a TIBETAN, a "worthless" "green brain" alley dog from the Shtetl Lhasa—a Chew. . .

Well, no Chew maybe: this here, it's a hangover, modern, of the Chinese female feet binding?

A hangover as an emphasis?

The world is so parallel in lies. And how could it be other!

My daughter-in-law!

Jin Jianxin is as human as I am.

Okeydokes, if I wish to kaibash this Hung-Mick marriage, I now have got my ammo.

"And Jin Jianxin, he told you to do this?—to his daughter?"

Arthur could not picture his Mick-ah-yell in Nyemo's role. He tried. Mick on Hung's ass? Gimme- a-break: It came off miscast, undone Romeo 'neath the balcony that holds high his sweet "mansion of a love". The balcony kaplunks.

"I am sorry," said Nyemo. "I am very sorry." He started towards the door; one leg asleep from the awkward hassock, he limped, a one-oared gondolier. "But I had to tell you, Herr-Mister Becker. I wish to be moral."

Arthur stood from the bedside. A titillated priest forgiving the titillator. Did his son Mick-ah-yell live by some naïve idea of Chinese primness? That was also prejudice.

"And Jin Jianxin directed this?"

"You continue to inquiring. I said Yes. 'The rear the once,' he said. 'That is all'." Nyemo went to touch Arthur, but he seemed unable to find a correct respectful placing, not now. As if at attention, he dropped his arm.

"But once began," he said, "we defied Jin Jianxin and we did more."

My daughter-in-law.

Becker had surprised himself upon Nyemo's leaving: An urge had taken hold. He had wanted to embrace Nyemo, but that urge was tangled, he was not sure why. A peculiarity of Arthur Becker, but a good decent one, he had often felt, was that he experienced a brotherliness to certain men—an inner cohesion; he'd wish it if the man was right, appropriate, had the fitting slump and ease yet strength and honesty; and then he'd feel this feeling spread within himself a kind of whooping-tingling. And then he would fear it. *Gay!?* And then he would lose it, that brotherhood, he'd watch it subside with something akin to regret and something akin to relief. The cause was Moe? *Is everything the cause of Moe!?* Take credit and take responsibility, as the psycho-socials say. And they're right. *But, damnit, no!—this male bloodship Was because of Moe.* Moe who beat, Moe who clipped his kid behind the ears and "upside da haid", Moe who hurt and Moe who'd failed and Moe who thus hurt more. But Arthur Becker had never experienced such tying-tight emotions with his own son Mick-ah-yell—and he had never hit his son, no matter what. Great disappointment—how weird to think that—*disappointment!?*—of great accomplishment, in view of his own upbringing (or downbringing). In any case Arthur had *not* held this departing young man Nyemo, this demi-dopplegänger, this familiar, whom he had wished to hold. . . Especially after Nyemo had reached into the small watch pocket of his jeans, extracting a slim charcoal-blood-red-mustardy piece of wood no larger than a two-piece euro—it looked like rising smoke—and handed it to the Jewish American.

"I made it," he said.

He said it was the nation of Malawi.

Malawi?

"I employed a knife and chisel, and then I smoothed and polished—with sap from mountain ash trees and laurel, and with leaves. I used beer to paint it, and also Coca Cola."

Nyemo here told Arthur the story of his father Norbu's creations for his father's young students in Lhasa, bringing alive the shape of Africa, and of his own, Nyemo's, determined helping. . . Sure he had already told the story. His face was a sudden-softened chord. He loved repeating that story.

"So, you are The Tibetan Picasso."

"I and my father, Norbu."

"You should hang on to this. Keep it."

"I wish for you to have it."

"You have others?"

"Yes."

Arthur suspected that Nyemo did not have more. Of

Malawis anyway. But he could not reject the gift that Nyemo in some time might regret having given. He placed it within the circumference of the strap-circle of his wristwatch band on his nite-table. Again he thought to embrace Nyemo; but he envisioned two wooden planks collapsed on each other and swaying in no wind. And stuck. What a strange thing to envision.

The two men did not embrace.

Once again alone that night in his room: Would he tell his son about Nyemo and Hung? Did he have to? A spreading lassitude was the consequence of his indecision. . . And Nyemo might be lying—a Tibetan spite. . . But if truth, wellthen, this roof-begun Adventure of The Tibetan and The Han might just well be ongoing, a sexual rondo, what of *that*? It might continue during Mick and Hung's marriage, no? Hey, Mick with Arthur's murder genes: a suspicious Mick might then go the Aeschylus-Becker route and put to death any issue, not knowing whose was whose? Well, he wouldn't serve the infant up to Nyemo at a banquet, par for the course in Homer's Greece—and triggering the abduction of Helen of Beijing? Thus jokes the joker, overliterate while alone, because the joker is at a goddamn fucking intense loss: He feels love for the Tibetan. He feels that love as genuine, never mind its misplacements, glaring things. He tables the dilemma of his obligation to his beloved son.

Now Becker did, first time, take a second look at *The Heaven in Beijing*: that hooker-service card slipped under his door two evenings before; he stared, he considered, he rubbed his right index finger over the card as if the oldtime tactile might be a blind substitute Facebook; and, yes, he touched his cock; and no, he vowed to not go pneumatic. Be he broke the vow and he buckled-down for a few fast plumb-liners, a trifle of the full course—*hey already, before you come make the hooker-service call*. But then exhaustedly, even while hardening, he fell asleep amidst the backdrop of the loud crashing shouting newfound omnibus of down-town post-modern Beijing (even the giant cranes still clanged at their building work—and so resonant they were, did they go at it 24/7?). And, despite the clamor and racket he dreamed, not of suffocating Professor Fritz Strobel, and not of anything so violent-painful as fucking anyone up the ass, but—what dunderhead couldn't guess it?—he dreamed of his father Moe, who had committed suicide by Magnum 357—because he hadn't made the Majors? No way: thousands of young hopefuls had had their dreams dashed by not stacking-up to the Bigs. Arthur Becker's dream was an affection-ate sublimation of a repression of a sublimation—that's what insipid habit-torment *that* dream was—he even knew it as he dreamt it. . . And Arthur Becker did remember that that episode of Moe-dream was indeed followed up by a slight *cinéma vérité* trailer of Nyemo and Hung. No dissolves, no fade-ins—just the quickest truthful slash-cut: The Tibetan had slowly, respectfully, taken-up the bentover Hung's skirt, what Oscar-winner dreaming couturier Becker (invoking his internal Edith Head) had designed: a pleated white silk crinoline so like an extended veil (such as all girls wear to study in the Xiushui Building library at Peking U); and there was nothing so obscene, so pornographic, so erotically sad (and enviable) as Nyemo's ugly hurried unbuckling and pants-dropping to his boots set slumped behind that sweet white number of a girl.

V

BEZOBORO

His freedom day, on his own. Hung and Mick had classes at Peking U, and Arthur was glad of it. He'd walk Beijing, he'd investigate. Truth was he was a guy who liked to be alone, even to talk out loud to himself—and sometimes to answer. He'd been an only child, he disliked parties, meetings, cabals, even teaching—which he had suffered through for one year as a T/A at Cal. He just wished to discover Beijing for himself, in more intimate prospect, i.e. to fart when he wished to, to just sit and think about the whole enterprise: Believe it or not, there were the more noble, or intellectual, considerations: How had the Chinese architecture evolved as it had?—what did such arched, looping and vivid shapings of home and holy place say of the Eastern personality? Such brainwork might take, what? fifteen minutes. Then the real deal: the marriage, the Tibetan sex, especially the Jin-prescribed nature it had found itself taking; and the unlooping (cheated?) innocence, apparent, of his son. . .

His cell rang. He had been planning to call Jutta, but
. . . but what?—too much strange world to digest? No
greedy reports seemed to be fermenting—a form here
of single child selfishness trailing on into the Arthur
Becker adulthood. After all, wouldn't such Beijing
uniquenesses as he had already seen tweak his appetite
to call his wife?—hold out of course on the Hung-Tibet
rear-entry business. But otherwise, on that oriental
mindset shouldn't he have wanted to get The Jutta
feedback. Jutta had been to Beijing and Shanghai—and
more than once: Economic theory exchanges, trade
conferences, junket whatevers concocted semi-
conscientiously by academics—obviously Jutta had
encountered plenty. So why didn't Arthur just call his
wife? Was he simply that glad to get away?—to let
Arthur be Arthur, even if that meant a less-informed
Arthur. And why did he not yet wish to bring Hung into
his little private debate? Be honest with yourself: Hung
Attraction.

Well, all that didn't matter because his cell had rung:

"Hi, Poopyhead." His affectionate name for her for
twenty-three years. He hadn't the vaguest recollection
how he'd come up with that typical ripe-lame
insipidity—and he cared not to work on remembering.

"Pardon me?"

If this nonplussed questioner was a Poopyhead it
was a brusque officious male one with a German
accent.

"Arthur Becker? Your name is Arthur Becker?—
no?"

"Yes. Sorry about the 'Poopyhead'." Was he about
to apologize for his sophomoric Americanishism? No:
the kraut's stout voice was so Reichish it foreclosed-on

any Becker-abjectivity.

"Here is Doctor Schiffer. Ludwig Schiffer, *Oberarzt*[5] from Heidelberg *Krankenhaus*—the hospital."

Where I smothered Strobel.

Becker's silence. Except for an ongoing sputter-jitter beginning bubblework in his colon—which he not only felt but heard.

"Your wife, Professor Koenig, she was kind enough to allow for me your cell number."

"Ah." *My kind-obliging wife.*

"Mister Becker, I will take straight to the issue: there is a film of you entering the doorway of one of our patients—we have posted cameras high above, at the transoms, within the wards of our most serious cases, such as that of the late Professor Fritz Strobel."

"Ah. . . ." *Say something*: "Good idea."

No, be more sympathetic, you ninny: "What a terrible thing, the professor's death. We were all so shocked. Of course, he was an old man, but, well, his mind was clear, and you never do expect that final . . ."

Like a wisened judge, Becker's colon interrupted his concocted sympathy; his intestines were fast becoming a sliding board for hectic passengers on a just-landed jet with flames afire: He experienced an impending need for an irrevocable and swelling shit.

"Sir, I am sorry to disturb you in Beijing, but as the patient involved was an important man and he is now deceased, likely due as you say to his advanced years; yet there are circumstances in which are troubling and they ought to contain clarity. Might you, sir, help provide?—as to why you entered the private room of

---

[5] Second in command, under the *Chefarzt*.

Professor Doctor Fritz Strobel? You may well be the final person to have seen him living."

Silence. Becker again heard that compulsory colon rumble—by now passing the fail-safe sigmoid. He said—

"Well, I . . . I knew Professor Strobel, as my wife was his protégé—we had had him to dinner on numerous—"

"But you did not know him *so* well? You yourself."

"No, but . . . "

" . . . as to enter his *Krankenhaus* room without accompaniment by your wife, who did of course know her superior in extremely."

In Extremely?

Hell, this was no inquiry; this was a goddamn uncamouflaged interrogation, a five thousand mile cellphone grilling. This fever-prone Son-of-Fever-Prone-Moe Becker, never having lain eyes on this *Oberarzt* Schiffer, imagined him—he could not help it—as looking precisely as his dead victim Professor Fritz Strobel, and of course he wished to smash him.

"No, I didn't know the professor on even a first name basis (*a GERMAN first-name basis, which comes pretty close to having sucked the guy's cock, or at least seen it—you formal fuckers*), but . . . still I . . . as he was an old man and you never know when—"

"You do admit then that it was you, sir, entering the room."

"Yes. Certainly."

How can I deny?

"Wellsir, I will then remain in touch. I do not wish to disturb you further in China, as I said, and please excuse me. But perhaps you might provide some information—when you return to Heidelberg of course—as to the state of Herr Strobel, the final state, as it does seem, to repeat—you were, from our camera prints, the last person to see the Professor, it does seem so. Would you please, sir, contact me when you return?"

"Certainly." *Oh shit.*

Well this development sure as hell threatened to put a chink (no pun intended) in Arthur Becker's anticipated freedom day. With invariable ease, stubborn ease, it torpedoed his thinking focus: Trial. Defense? Guilt verdict. Judges judged in Germany, not juries who might be soppy—but he had no soppable "peers" there anyway. *I'm finished.* But then again—judges might be better for him than a jury—judges, "wise men" ("and women": even within his worrying now he was frightened to egalitarianism, didn't want to jinx himself by male chauvinism—*now this is real true worry!*): A judge in Deutschland would consider the international, his nation's reputation—a judge freights himself with greater considerations than does some kraut bricklayer or housewife (house-husband): A judge might ponder: "*Ach*, A Jew in today's Germany imprisoned for murder, and murder of a suspected fossil Nazi, the papers, the Internet, the TV—*Nein*, this cannot be! Germany cannot sustain such publicity?" Well, especially not now that the fatherland is led by such an admired Chancellor, a Chancellorette (Germany has become thus a *Mutterland*), a woman who had even welcomed refugees from the Middle East. . . Cool out— take that Beijing walk you'd planned.

The Hutong district, one of many. Old narrow

alleyway Beijing enclosed, placid in a seeming tealike hush, it attracted—this antithesis of a European old town or ghetto. Antithesis as the small, connected, shuttered Hutong houses, often dilapidated, were on the outside, rather than being protected by a medieval wall, as in, say, Frankfurt, or Nuremberg, or even Jerusalem. They were the opposite of Thanatos, a dense denial of denial, in that these feeble houses *were* the wall, as if, say, a man's hard bones were on his outside, protecting his skin within; and the Hutong courtyard, if one could call it that, was within, the skin, protected by the linked-up houses. Then, Becker's Brilliancy: you protect what's most valuable. In the West, privacy, the family—the wall shelters your own; in the East, public, the community: the courtyard, the place of gathering, that's what's guarded safe—at least back in China's past. (Figuratively Becker slapped himself on the back for that "grand insight", which he knew might not have been in the least true). In any case, the courtyard was a kind of mews, shaded by wisteria and crab-apple trees . . . Now, alone and walking about for the first times in a strange environment, an oppositional one, or even residing there, and for years, this can have one feeling not even human. It can have you see people gawking at you, even when they are busy with leaf-blowers or scooping their doggies' poop. But: It can have one feeling wonder, as much as it can have one caught-up in that hostility-for-the-other, caught and manufacturing mockeries one keeps to oneself, criticisms, urges to correct these people's "failures". Such had been Arthur's life in Germany, even familiarish Heidelberg—and he'd never got over it. But drifting about in Beijing, especially in the old Eastern world of the

Hutong district, Becker couldn't but find himself worlds beyond Western Heidelberg. And now he'd begun seeing himself as not merely an Other but a Negative Other, a creature strolling within a glass cage, such as the one in which the Israelis had held Eichmann during his famous Holocaust trial; Becker was now a man thinking only to himself, transported by a sorcery that might not even allow his words, the sounds of them, to exit from his voice-box—if there had even been anyone to speak with. The Hutong world did not exist, or Becker did not exist. Still, within all this abnormalcy—*which was a kind of normalcy*—here was the weirdest part: he began to see that, even within this Hutong world, once you've seen one you've pretty much seen them all—you *expect*. . . Except for when he came upon this one particular oblong warren, which had hollers and cheers within. A party? A religious thing? A political protest assemblage? Maybe just a delusional Becker by now hearing things?—a flimsy Hutong was nowhere near hideaway enough for rebel-plans in this close-watched "despot-benevolent" megalopolis, even of fifteen-twenty million.

And so, in the absence of anything corollary what did strike Arthur Becker was not really a Chinese concealment at all but a Jewish: Chizuk Amuno. Murderer, he had edged his way down the Heidelberg hills to this synagogue rebuilt years after *Kristallnacht* (prayers?—he had never before visited the place), he'd gone to the House of Worship no more than one week after that worst crime (short of mass extermination) that man can commit that he'd committed. Confession? Expiation? Forgiveness? Just purest acknowledgement and understanding-sorrow and regret? (*and regret for not having more regret?*)—the telling to a rabbi, with wise rabbi words eased to him in return? Take a chance that the rabbi will not report you. *Go to synagogue!* Absorb it. *Be* in it—and he, no sobber, had choked back a sob—here before a dilipated Hutong he remembered that sorry sob. . . And the "new" replacement synagogue from the past sure was no Daniel Libeskind prizewinner, as in Berlin. It did sit round the corner from a row of beautiful *Jugendstil* residences, but this new, camouflaged, unadorned, unguarded Chizuk Amuno was a small quadrangular building that might have been mistaken for a moderate-sized real estate office, it looked out on Heidelberg with the dull defiance of a man blocking his head from blows with his forearm—such the protective point. And after standing outside for at least one minute, Becker had opened one of the relatively heavy doors of the House of Worship, he'd had to bend and lean and enlist his hamstrings and quads and his full right shoulder's strength (which he hadn't called-upon since using all-of-himself to suffocate Professor Strobel.). As he would now, in a moment, at the Beijing Hutong he'd peeked into the synagogue with two-thirds of his body still lagging out (for escape), and there were folks in discussion, not in wooden pews but seated on thin mocha-backed folding chairs arranged in a semi-circle: Germany, Europe, anti-Semitism (now by Islam), this was the talk, the usual, plus some local events such as marriages and interfaith gatherings—when one woman came out with this horror: Israeli soldiers were now "taking their own lives 'in disproportionate numbers' ", guilt-suicide for their "murder of Palestinians"—as the world turns. And then there had been silence, and then there had been denials. And then, arguments, even excuses. And Becker had brought back his peeked-in head, brought it outside this Jewish Hutong and let that heavy synagogue door close silent-slow of its own leaden will—or urgency. He had not even caught sight of rows of seats, or pulpit, or tabernacle, or Torah with its silver-armored trim, or Ark of Covenant—he had forgotten to look for these. (Had he ever wanted to?). Had he then known Nymeo the Tibetan he would have known that for those moments *he* was Nyemo, who could not bring himself to enter the "faux" Tibetan temples at Tian'An Men.

But that Beijing Hutong. That hiddenness. As with Chizuk Amuno after the murder Becker pressed-open the unlatched dilapidated and low-arched gate doors. Boldly, surprising himself, he walked through:

A baseball game.

A baseball game!?

Are you kidding me?

Chinese men in uniform, gray one team, white the other, an actual diamond of pitcher's mound and basepaths, rough-hewn, jagged and pebble-strewn, and considerably smaller than a by-the-book ballfield. More softball size—except this was *baseball*—with the bats however kaplunkey metal, not goodwood Louisville Sluggers. The men were young, in their twenties, Becker would have said—a few though his own age, mid-forties. Christ, you seldom see this type activity in the U.S., the home of The American Pastime (which of course it isn't anymore: that's football. But still, speaking historically…). But okay, aside from some Mandarin "chatter round the infield" (which sounded to the American out-of-whack, goofy-funny, a Three Stooges caricature) these guys were no great shakes: the pitcher wound-up bigtime but pitched anemic, the batters practice-swung masterly but whiffed at the ball anemic, occasionally fathering a dribbling grounder, which had Becker recollecting that most *unter*-apropos of monickers for a baseball, "spheroid", and which was at least well-fielded, as why shouldn't a dribbler be. Hey though, you'd expect more, no? Chinese kids won sometimes the Little League World Series, whipped the asses of America's best pre-adolescents—what happened to them?, they gave up? For ping-pong? Gymnastics, with those monkey bars? After all, the Japs kept at the game, the Japanese Pastime?—some burly Japs made it to the U.S. majors (unlike Moe), pitchers and homerun hitter Japs. (*Hirohito up on the mound today, ho ho ho!*). But no chinks made that leap, not as far as Arthur—a maven—could recall. Really?—what's the story?—baseball discouraged by the government for being the sport of their total world competitor in GDP? . . . And Becker, he was noticed, how could he not be. He was watched watching. Mister Guts—and also because they all stunk, and also because he had played (high school), and also for that desperate reason of induction, belonging (more than in *Germany*, actually) he asked to play (*by making motions [that might have looked like some mime of I'm you, you're me—hands across the sea]*), *he fucking asked to play!?* The current pitcher was a sin, way off the plate, struck batters, bounced balls off the ground before they got to the plate (*which actually was a plate!*) (made the game look more like cricket), so by charades-throwing Becker asked 'pitcher?'—and, Hutong hospitality, he got brought a *uniform,* and he donned it quick within a Hutong hut offered as a sort of locker room (so excited he barely surveyed the front room of the residence: it didn't look so bad, as its walls were lined with thickly calligraphed scrowls; but the shower and sink were in the living room and there were some few stained strip-hangs of old-rained paint on the ceiling and the floor was of a commonplace floral linoleum [bizarrely, the long old sofa was covered tight in transparent plastic, as if it had just been purchased at some Beijing Ikea and had to be preserved for years to come—even in the new burgeoning Beijing]). Becker being no American giant, the gray (visitors?) uniform loaned to him was not the worst fit, just a tad waist tight and pinched in the underarm—true, not the best for a pitcher.

He stunk: way off the plate, threw behind one batter, struck another (no, not imagined as his murder victim Fritz Strobel—until he realized that he was not imagining that, and then he imagined it).

"You *suck,* you eat fuc*keeng sheet! You should take a frying FUCK!*"

He hadn't noticed the character acting-out as the opposing third-base coach, in white uniform, slapping one knee like crotchety Walter Brennan might have, or crotchety Walter Huston (the only man on the "field" wearing spikes) and laughing laughing laughing laughing.

Such gleeful cackles, artificial-forced.

"*Peecha's up da reeva!* Too bad dere ain'no *barn* heeya, cause you cannot heet da side of *eet!* You call you'self an *American*?!"

The razzing catcalling jerk giving Arthur Becker the raspberries was not Chinese. Needless to say. From his perch on the mound Becker observed a man roughly Arthur's age, a leathery man who resembled Shakespeare in that famous old portrait—the moustache-beard (but this moustache a pencil-job), the long-haired demi-baldness, the big-eyed wary look; but this guy was a Shakespeare with serious swarth, who now walked to home-plate, took up a metal bat, ordered "*Peech* me!"—which Arthur did—he tried a (supposed) fastball, and watched it get clobbered out of the park, or in this case it cleared the cramped Hutong: "We Cubans *play* baseball! *Fidel* could play, his wish before he revolted us was to join the *Yankees*."

"I knew that."

Arthur prided himself he knew.

Moe'd talked about that piece of baseball-revolution-lore all the time.

Arthur couldn't come up with what to ask this Cuban, but asked: "How come you come here to coach?"

"Baseball love—I love it. Good customer relations. Advertisement for my lot. Word gets round. Long *story*, my man."

"Your lot? Your . . ."—Becker pancaked with the ball—"Your *what*?"

"You'll see. You're just the kind of guy I want to take see and hero-adore. I dream of guys like you."

His *lot*?

The Cuban had a face one could only describe as guileful-innocent, as stupid-cagey-smart, depending upon how you yourself felt about you yourself when you looked at that Cuban face. If there was such a thing as a salesman's face, this was a salesman's face. When the two men shook hands this "Ricky" seemed to be doing his level best to crumple Arthur's finger bones.

Later, quick-buddied-up, Ricardo "Ricky" Rubalcava changed to a flannel plaid shirt, pleated brown
pants, shiney black tasseled shoes. He made the change
in a Hutong house out in what might have been called
center-left field. The Hutong house looked at first the
same as the others about, except perhaps for its cleaner-
scrubbed walls and artfully chiseled door (looked like
teak, or teak stain), and well-tended garden with little
accumulated Beijing dust—perhaps only that very
morning's; then Arthur caught sight of the carved and
painted roof which was singular here and had obviously
required some pretty expert sculpting; and when he
rejoined Arthur, Ricky admitted it was his own
residence, and that of his father, a Ricardo as well
("He'd changed it from the *Jésus*."). The elder Ricardo
had met a Chinese girl years before—Communist
Chinese tourists had of course been begged-for in
'Nineties Havana after the USSR imploded—and then
Ricky Senior, "a Latino charmer, my dear padré", left
his Cuban wife—Ricky Junior's mother, "a balcony
warmer" (Ricky actually *said* this of his mother)—and
"the ex-Jésus hotfeeted it" to the socialist-salvation
future, China. "But China's capitalist these days," said
Arthur, and Ricky plastered a shush-finger to his
mouth, hushing-out a weirdly-sinister-sibilant-rasping,
"Hey, I'm in *business* here." . . . The Rubalcava
Hutong, Ricky explained, was "ritzier" than the others
here, although from the outside it looked fairly much
the same—there was even, off to its left, a practitioner
administering acupuncture, while glimpsing up and
about to catch the non-progress of the baseball game

(With but one needle he was treating only one ear lobe, no other bodily part. "Exquisite", Ricky called this method, explaining [lying?] to Arthur that this "superior one-ear style of aku" existed only in China, it was so "precise" in its repair of "all the total body.").

"You wish to try it?" he asked Arthur.

"Sure."

Now why did I have to say Sure?

No, when in Rome.

Becker lay on the acupuncture table out in center left field and waited for the worst. He was, he'd admit to anyone, a man major-bigoted. He prided himself on that. "You believe in a placebo," he'd often said, "then it works. Even when you know it's a placebo."

Arthur Becker just did not believe in this goddamn shit—he even had contempt for Westerners who did believe. But let the Chinese believe in their own shit if they wanted. . . Be respectful.

The acupuncture needle was twirled pretty good into his left ear lobe.

From that "treatment" his left ear lobe hurt. Stabbing-bad it hurt.

The remainder of him felt no better than it had since he'd murdered Professor Fritz Strobel.

Perverse schmuck, his own thought of himself: you actually do feel better now that the "alien" Eastern treatment has *not* worked. You're validated.

Calling his home a "villa"—and sounding as spirited as a real estate dealer—Ricky Rubalcava explained to Arthur that underground they had more "spacious" rooms to his "*palazzo*" whereas the usual Hutong house had no underground; and Ricky's had a "workout gym" and sauna, and that their Hutong neighbors did not mind their "wealth" as it was not a "show-to-the world", as an outside mansion might be. He said that there were other poor people Hutongs in Beijing that contained similar "wealthful" setups, as rich mixing-in with poor was a "good-tradition Chinese together taint". (Athur let-slide the inapt English). Ricky's father Ricardo had founded "the lot"—the Cuban had still not revealed what it was—on a "pica" level with only two "chintzy" cars. "I'll show you what we have made of it—you will hero-adore." Ricky now drove Arthur way out to the suburbs through amazingly infinite lanes of superhiway traffic and excavations, past marshy fields and then expensive modern enclaves—"they are combination-locked"—all stainless steel and black granite, with names like Full Gold Garden and The Ultimate (and what seemed a billion overpasses, which gave you an underground sensation, as if you were driving a subway car; or as if there were belts and straps squeezing taut across the gray-imprisoned sky); this trip was in Ricky's '54 Buick Special (which had been near too wide for the narrow Hutong alleyways and which rocked you left-right-left, as it cornered like a tank), thus to Havana Heaven, "my Cubana used car lot—hey hey *hey!*".

"Your what?"

"I'm in *business* here, as I say. As with China, Cuba is now on the road to capitalism, you know that, it is slimpering that way (Arthur let the onomatopoeia go), and I am on that road. I keep the Cuba connect, I must, it is nowadays quite easy. And it is a necessary, considering my stocks-in-trade."

Stocks-in-trade?

Ricky's lot was situated along Gold Panning Road. It broadcast Latin jazz from cobra-coiled speakers mounted on both sides of the tar roof of the office shack: Celia Cruz was singing, her flute backup thick and raw with a kind of brilliant shriekiness. Between and above the speakers and a spanking metallic archway was a Havana Heaven sign. Lit bright rainbow bulbs of course.

Dodging prospective Chinese customers Arthur and Ricky walked the lot maze. The possible buyers roamed and slipped into this car, that, slamming doors for that more than half-century ago respected heaviness, they marveled at the thickness of balloon-type tires with white walls (some of them anyway), the pearl-shininess of hubcaps (which Cuban Ricky said were copies, welded by Cubans from original designs); with chancy admiration the Chinese lightly patted the hinge-sloping-movable metallic sun-visors external to the windshield, maybe a half-foot wide, their lengths stretching full across and so adding to the intimation of bullet-bounce-off war machines with which years ago their fathers might have rumbled south into South Korea; and those front windows were often half-split by pewter bars—unexplainable but surely of some smart strong aggressive once-great American function. It was all as if these were the most brilliant inventions made by automotive man—and why were they abandoned for the dull dead-designs of today? The Chinese lay down on the expansive no-longer-made bench seats in the cars' fronts (Ricky neck-swiveling in caution against buyer-abuse). These were 'Fifties U.S. cars, exclusively it seemed, all buffed to a reflective shine: the Chevvy Malibu, the Buick four-holer, a yellow Pontiac Trans-

Am with the amber Indian hood ornament, a two-toned red-white Mercury convertible with white-walls (Nudging Arthur playful: "We call them Mer-crappies."), an ancient Thunderbird four-seater angled upward from its rear so as to suggest a rocket ship at takeoff?, a Packard yet, a Desoto yet, a shitpile lineup of Plymouths (hood ornaments the set sails of the Puritans' three-masters) and plain Ford Fairlanes. Through all that well-honed polish one made out few scratches.

Arthur asked, "How'd you get these cars? How'd you get them here?"

Ricky's right hand launched a stiff hold-your-horses, which he then swept about his inventory of those classic cars. "This is how the new Chinese feel about their newfound wealth; they want the old-found goodies. They will like nothing better than to snub the nose at the American and his past greatness by driving his past sharp color-cars with wings. Americans will see this on the TV Newses and chew their eyes to green."

"So how'd you *get* these cars?"

Ricky gave his solipsistic happy-con-man grin. His thin moustache went elastic.

Well, it was like walking into a dream of your adolescence—although the adolescence dreamed-of wasn't Arthur's, he was too young. He was sidetimeing his way through his dad Moe Becker's youth. Moe had told Arthur that before he'd got cut from Triple A ball, he'd owned a "battleship gray Corvette with plush-bucket red leather seats, she was all fuck-a-duck *fiberglass,* whatever *that* means"—which he'd had to sell "when *you* were born, kid."

Thanks a lot, dad.

Moe had then had to buy a used Plymouth Valiant. Such a pathetic shabmobile it seemed that Ricky had even declined to carry here.

"My team-boys," Moe had revealed too often, "they called my chariot a *Jew*-vette." Moe had actually disclosed that slime-slur putdown with nostalgic-braggy eyes.

"You know," added Ricky, "when America cut us off we all got 'stuck' with these babies in Havana. They decayed and we improvised. Cuban geniuses, we kept them running, we got T-bird carbs, points, plugs, reworked them for Dodges'n'shit. We Cubans are *great*. You don't think our Teofilo Stevenson couldn't have whupped your Ali's ass?—*sheey*-it. But we kept it *amateur*, we being *commies*." His happy-derision smirk, again the skimp-moustache gone elastic. "But our main attract all these years was our *cars*, man, fix and preserve, fix and preserve, a moving auto-*museum*, that drew us the *world.*"

Arthur asked, "But how'd you get these cars *here*?"

He couldn't imagine how. And being a writer, albeit blocked, particularly by being a murderer, he considered an article, an exposé: "The China-Cuba Carriage Trade." The sidewise style of humorous revelation. He liked Ricky but he certainly had no allegiances.

"Ever heard of a ship?" said Ricky. "How the cars got here. Same as with the parts. My inventive Cubans, we've been concocting parts for these antiques to sixty *years*. Chinese trust Cubans to make the parts. Chinese wouldn't know a 'Fifties carburetor from a pressure cooker. And *Americans* couldn't now make them either."

Arthur laughed. But his question had meant money, arrangements. Secret deals. As a writer he'd have loved to uncover "secret deals."

Ricky did not elaborate. He did say that they were negotiating with "Six" for a weekly TV ad, "on some *telenovela*. "Six" must have been a local Beijing channel.

Thinking of himself in Germany, Arthur asked, "Ricky do you like it here? I mean really."

"Really?—you ask. Well, really, with all I say to you, the honest is *no*—the Chinese are too hidden, too polite while too calculaters, because they are too scared shit. They have been too scared for too long a time, though now they are trying to be natural, once they figure out what that nature is. It is very hard to *calculate* for yourself a natural and then *manufacture* your natural. So, I put on the good face and I think of Cuba, especially now that our Cuba is becoming our *Cuba* again—the *real* Cuba. Very natural."

"But you can't move back because you're in good business here."

"Waiting list, long as your *layygs*, an' I ain't *sheetin* you."

A serious smile stuck to the Cuban's face. This time the smile appeared depressed.

"But Ricky, what about pollution? These giants are gas guzzlers, you know that, and Beijing's the most smog-ridden city in the world."

Ricky still maintained as Mister Grin, his thin moustache that stick of licorice.

Arthur had wondered of course how this nowhere Ricky from Havana had gotten the bucks to import.

How much baksheesh to the Chinese government?—their own baksheesh allowing Ricky's shipping-in?

"Arturo"—Ricky suddenly went friendly, although that friendliness might easily have been interpreted as diminishing, as hostile—"Arturo, why are *you* here?"

Arthur told him. He tried hard at not showing his disappointment that Mick had chosen the East. He did not mention Hung.

"I have a son," said Ricky. "Geraldo. He was twenty when he came here with me and my father."

"Is he, Geraldo, your partner here?"

Ricky's eyes took to the ground, as if he had just lost a few coins and with them no few hopes.

"So much," he said in an undertone, "so much money to be made."

"I can imagine, with the Chinese and their conspicuous consumption."

Ricky squinted, as if trying to crunch that phrase into some discernible meaning.

I had to mention Veblen mishigas. Pretentious idiot bastard.

"Geraldo," said Ricky. "He soured. My son. He went home to Cuba. After only one year. I tried to explain to him that we would prevail, that it was not all so alien here and primitive and awkward. That we would have more money here than ever we did in Cuba. But this strange China was all he saw: the music, dong-bong-dong, even the way Chinese people *walked*. He was *none* of that."

Facing Ricky's so quickly devastated face, Arthur worked-up a look of sympathy, as if he shared the Cuban's emotions—and perhaps, he feared, he did.

"I can understand so full why Geraldo did that,

leaving." Ricky had turned miserable with this understanding, as if knowledge of the universe, of God, of the inevitable future of life and of oneself could only bring deepest sorrow. Even his Shakespeare beard had gone to droop. Not to understand was to understand. He wanted his son back.

He said: "I am doing so well in this country here."

It seemed as if Ricky wanted Arthur to go tell Geraldo.

"Does Geraldo return? For visits?"

"Geraldo says that I should not be draining-away my nation's treasures, the American autos—that is a sin. That Havana will not be Havana without the old Cadillacs and the Lincolns and the others. I said but that I am only taking away a few compared to all that ride in our land, but Geraldo said that 'a few' is 'an all'—these cars are not even *American* cars anymore but Cuban cars—*America* cannot make them—and we *deserve* them for all our struggling sweat in keeping them, keeping them alive. If Chinese people drive these wondercars in Beijing that detracts from Havana and our future, now that we *do* have our future. Geraldo, he hates China, the most for *that*. It is like taking-away our heart—and that is not true. Geraldo called me, his father, a *traitor*—he could not be a part, a partner to *that*." Ricky simply shut his eyes, while it resonated in the mind of "Arturo" that he, Ricky, like his son Geraldo, still called his Cuba "we". . . He did not say if Geraldo ever returned to Beijing.

Arthur doubted it.

The Cuban let Arthur sit behind the wheels of a few beauties. Arthur had never realized how huge had been this steering gadgetry with its wraparound horn-honk chrome—it made you, the driver, feel so puppet-small—*and* so large, a ship's captain. So, here it is, this Great America of Moe's—and this Great Cuba of Geraldo. And there *he* was, Arthur, strong enough to have opened the heavy-leady car door (with serious tugging effort) and perched behind the wheel of one of these gilded whoppers driven thirty years before his own time; there he was, face it, wanting to be what he had always wanted to be with his delusions and his illusions, with his toughy Jewboyish moving to Germany, his becoming a writer (of sorts) as if he might morph his way to a burly blustery Norman Mailer, who, being a plain old Jewboy himself, brainy-but-jockless, had mimed his way to Irish toughass-poet; or maybe he was now a delicate refined clotheshorse-but-lyrical(ish) Saul Bellow—and this was why, even, stretching things a bit to implicate his failure-hurler-hackie dad Moe, why he had "taken-care-of" Fritz Strobel the Nazi. Somewhere in there, in here, this was true, but don't think of it too much—who needs Truth!? Not when you are here behind the wheels of these motor yachts, when you are here with the shivers you ascribe to America's great past. So Arthur asked if he could drive one of these chariots.

"Not all over Beijing, Ricky. Just, you know, around the block."

"Can you drive a stick?"

"Yes."

"You have driven before in the traffic of Beijing?"

"No."

"You've got an International Driver License?"

"No."

"You have got International Driver Insurance?"

"Uh-uh. No."

"Then no, triple."

Ricky wagged a punitive finger at his absurd companion.

After a few more stationary behind the wheels, a marveling at the chromium station buttons of old car radios and a tour of the perhaps two dozen other spanky-shined vintage American cars, and the endless sad annoyance of Ricky's Spanglish (and Arthur's lack of Spanish) they ran out of things to say or do. So Arthur, despite his want of the requisite certifications, asked again:

"Please Ricky, let me drive."

"Shit, I like you. I'm a softie."

Arthur was allowed to take the wheel of the machine he pointed to: a dinky Plymouth. Reasons: Relatively, this was a small car, easier to handle; if he smashed it this would be less of a Ricky-loss; and Moe had bought Plymouths for his smalltime hackie business (three cars). This chosen job handled terribly, but it sat high, almost at the level of a today's SUV—of which today's Beijing had an astounding shitload (there was even a Chinese brand)—and its tires roared, and its floor vibrated, the feeling was as if he might have Parkinson's; and it was no picnic to periscope all the local swervings from his spot behind the outsize steering wheel and the endless hood with its Puritan sailing ships hood ornament, so he sat stiff-up as he could—and hit his head on the inside roof (Ricky laughed). But just now Arthur was The Captain of the Past, and he even half-expected that if he turned on the radio—if it worked—he might hear Sinatra or Chuck

Berry and not Beijing agitprop—there was so much of that: Harmony Shmarmony, etc etc etc.

He did come down with this idea:

"Ricky, do you need help here?"

As son Geraldo had stayed in the Caribbean—but Arthur wouldn't mention that sad thing.

"I do need help, *you* need a *job*?"

Ricky's incredulous eyebrows shoved-up into forehead furrow-waves.

"No. Not me."

"You got someone? Hey, I don't trust the Chinese for hire: Too greedy, too needy. Big on the cheating. I tried one out. He did kickbacks for cheap sales. I couldn't leave the place with him in charge. All I use Chinese for is the polish-up, and the scratch rub-outs."

"How do you feel about Tibetans?"

A distant smile, closed-eyes.

"I like Tibetans, Arturo, but I don't know none. Being Cuban, verses America, I understand them, their problems. Arturo, I feel for them, that's instinct. But talk of *primitive*. What?—they're gonna go meditate on The Buddha while behind the *wheel*. A few Tibetans have tried to *steal* some of these beauts, resell'em. But the fuckers can't fuckin' *drive*—they crash-up. For Tibetans there ain't nothing I can do."

Hung had said that Nyemo was leaving university. He was failing, as he did so little study work, out of spite for the domineering Han-contempt. Despite Nyemo's blowups (because of them?) Arthur Becker sensed that the guy was trustworthy—he'd revealed his betrayal of son Mick even though that had happened way before Mick's arrival on the scene. It had hurt Nyemo to tell. A righteous Nyemo wouldn't cheat his boss. . . Becker hoped that that were true.

He said, "I know a smart Tibetan who isn't into the Buddha shit and might need a job. Anything, scrubbing-up, I don't know—until he learns to drive well. You could try him out."

Ricky just stared at Arthur as if the American were a world-vacuum idiot.

Ricky drove Arthur back to the Hotel Prince Gong, this time in his lavender Thunderbird—he referred to it as a 'motor car'—an earlier 'Fifties job four-seater, it rumbled like a small prop-plane (Ricky said "My guys are scrabbling-up a big muffler, but it ain't so easy").

New brainstorm: Arthur formulated it, rejected it, and then asked it: "Ricky, may I drive one of these cars of yours to my son, where he's staying? To show him America's grandeur of sixty years ago."

Ricky got a gander at Arthur's shabby-lame hotel.

He didn't even bother to answer Arthur No.

VI

GUILT'S GOOD FAMILIES

This evening he would be meeting Hung's father, Jin Jianxin. Which got him on his (well-travelled) road of reflection:

Arthur Becker was nine or ten years old he and his dad Moe had been walking along their favorite Chesapeake Bay beach just south of Annapolis. Moe by then had come to be characterized by a too-often wounded and confused—and *distant*—expression that was embedded in the lines and cavernous in-wedgings of his face. Like somebody had thrown a rock and got him right sideburn full-on to eye. To little Arthur his dad even resembled, though vaguely, Boris Karloff—and once an event, or rather a seeing, took place, that had "Artie" squirming terrified, if but for a few seconds: he saw Moe as Karloff's weak-demonic Frankenstein. But that Moe look changed, it transformed, it smoothened, it leaped, when a beer-bellied full-bald man went hollering-out "Hey *Moe!—Moco!*" This chunky character was about Moe's age, and after their embrace (the guy had kissed Moe's right ear) he had hurried off-off-and-away down the sands of the Chesapeake. A getaway while the getting was good—before Moe might burden him with memories, requests, complaints, whatnots. "That, m'boy, was Otts *Lehrer*," Moe had proudly announced, and little Artie knew the name. Otts was now—then—the manager and coach of the major league Orioles, and it turned out that he had played Double A ball with Moe in Hagerstown (Maryland) years before—and then he'd made it as a "hotsitot" catcher in the Bigs. This chance meeting with a man of super-substance and elevated presence had for young Arthur been bittersweet, the tingling recognition of his father's grandeur to have been on hug-and-kiss terms with a "great" known all over Baltimore and really the American League, but this sadly churned-up into the ambiguous confrontation with Moe's ungrandeur, his own failure to be known anywhere outside the Baltimore taxi business (the minor-league "Independents" yet)—a schlump to be, finally, run-away from by a thrilling super non-schlump. So, firstoff at the beach, youngster Arthur had been overbrimming with worship for his father, gladness for his father (except that recollection now, in *China?* yet, had him wondering if his son Mick had ever brimmed for him, much less *over*brimmed. Well, not that Arthur Becker, straining to recall, could recall: 1. Maybe for his first book?—a fable-novel about Jean Jacques Rousseau [*The Grunge Idealist*], whereby he had won the Johns Hopkins Young Writers Fiction Award. But nah: Mick was too young at that time to understand and thus do a daddy-brim. And 2. Germans didn't much brim, at anything—and *Mick was a German*.). And now, this very evening in Beijing, Arthur Becker would be meeting another great, one of an important adult nature and thus greater than baseball's Otts Lehrer or Moe Becker. Well, true such greatness was putative: Arthur was to be breaking bread with a Mender of the Social Fabric (or at least one of that good-body of menders), a saint of altruism, a brave leader of men, a purported bulwark of nobility-honor-service-bravery-modesty—*caveat the ordered diminishment of his own daughter by way of a galvanized Tibetan penis up her rear* (if the Nyemo tale were unvarnished—and *how could it be!? And how could it Not be!?*)—*and* this man he would meet, this father of Hung, was a man (if the Hung tales were unvarnished) who had helped reduce the Chinese death penalty *"by half"*. Intimidated Arthur Becker. Suspicious Arthur Becker. Hung had said that her humanitarian father Jin had been in jail for his good works with the New Citizens Movement for people's freedom from arbitrary everything; he had been under house arrest, he had worn one of those GPS ankle-bracelets "like that great Burma woman from Myanmar"; Hung had said that everyone was sure that Jin was followed, perpetually tracked, "like a prey better than the preyers." Great Badge of Courage, a trail of fascist spooks behind you like huffing black bears in pursuit of campers well-stocked with Yoohoos and Hersheys. . . *Or:* Hung's sanctified father Jin was a megalomaniac—of the modesty persuasion. Oriental Enigma Braggadoccio. Could be, no? Moreso than even that of Cubano Ricky Rubalcava of the vintage U.S. cars (You just *knew* some kind of monkey-business had been going on there—which must have been why Ricky's kid Geraldo had begged-off). Face life: small gaggles of exalteds were always bounding round, as the

unexalted (everyone, just about) always needed to see
the exalteds' exaltings—and needed to bow down
(Becker always saw cakewalking Mussolini as the
prance-model). *Or:* Jin might be kind-of like a
cantankerous-softie-hardnose-others-blaming Jewish
loser Arthur Becker had once known in whose house
(small downtown apartment: no money) he had "once"
for eighteen years lived, a man who'd never made the
Majors. . .

But of course such would be the buzzing bees-in-
the-bonnet of him with his own deep unbounding, that
hospital-pillow-smother-blot on his own morality.

So, thus, dinner, Arthur having been invited for that
evening to the Jianxin household, that Lair of the
Selfless Ombudsman. In Arthur's honor, they had
decided to hold the repast for Hung's "German" fiancé-
father not in their daily residence, which was a
condominium in a gated community of the upper
middle-class and wealthy Beijingoisie, the *suzhi*
(people of good quality) ("robbers," confided Hung,
"*do* climb our gates"), but in the family lineage
ancestral hall,[6] which was located on the outskirts of the
large expanding city and shielded by a high hedge over
six meters, and where on the way, under a pallid gray
sky (that normalcy), one saw super-malls, one with a
Walmart, then a huge two-level Apple store, a
Starbuck's, a Pizza Hut and a Kentucky Fried Chicken

---

[6] The other reason was that this day also happened to be a national
holiday—Tomb Sweeping Festival, where folks trecked to visit
their ancestors' tomb site, which was nearby their family lineage
ancestral hall.

(no KFC here[7]); the malls also contained auto dealerships unlike Ricky Rubalcava's sui generis one, with their lots chock-full of stark black shark-shaped BMWs and stark black shark-shaped Mercedes and (for some inexplicable reason) Buicks—many many Buicks, modern ones, unlike Ricky's four-hole oldsters (*and what's the queer deal here?—if you're gonna go GM, questionable in itself, why not Cadillac?—were the millennial-success Chinese anti-over-ostentation in their middling-ostentation?*); and strange large Quonset huts with bicycles lashed to them ("These are for artists, legal and illegal," explained Hung. "Sometimes our government is generous trying hard and does provide." "Better than does America," contributed German Mickah-yell, who knew zip about America—but was right.) . . . Arthur had not been aware that such homesteads existed as family lineage ancestral halls, and he was properly impressed (it was a great idea, if you had a family lineage: he did have, somewhere, Moe's *talis*— amazing that Moe'd even owned one of those fringed prayer shawls; but *talis* was all there was remaining of the baseball-worship Beckers and their American family lineage); but regarding the Jianxin family hall Becker buttoned his lip, he did not express his awe: He feared not so much ignorance itself—sure he had plenty of that—but its detection and dissemination: the father-of-the-(foreign)-groom did not need any more moron-limelight than nature and international relations would make evident.

---

[7] Becker wondered if perhaps the absence of the acronym had to do with the absence in Beijing of *"schwartzes"*, American ones, who had taken offense at the bonhomie-bullshit face of the whitebeard Southern Colonel.

Hung and Mick had picked up Arthur at his hotel, The Prince Gong—this time without in tow Nyemo the Tibetan, the unwanted outwrestler of the hotel's poor uniformed bellhop and the (apparently ached-for; and Jin-ordered?) ass-"abuser" of Hung Huang Jianxin— and outrageously brave (and suicidal?) haranguer at Tian'An Men Square. As Hung drove her crappy-exhaust engine-clang Chinese Xiali (well, at least she wasn't spoiled with a BMW—*but what about the environment!*), as they were heading westerly, the sun performed that magnificent tangerine-blackberry trompe l'oeil setting through the Beijing coal fumes— which Hung pointed out embarrassed-proud (as if God had mix-blessed Beijing with such a "natural-beauty" cover) while Becker couldn't help but see her bent-over and rectally infringed by The Tibetan. And it was continuously that Becker saw this. He also saw his son now next to Hung in the front seat. Did he feel solicitude for his son?—sorrow?—hard to say. No way Mick would penetrate his beloved's back door. At least, no way for Arthur to picture it. Mick would have to have another face, one where the angles and crevices and juttings and cramping-snearing eyes said Don't You Fuck With Me.

"Where is Nyemo?" Arthur asked.

"Nyemo was invited, to be sure," said Hung. "But he informed us that he had his 'prior business'."

Mick said, "He said that very strong. He said that he has *got* something."

"Did you believe him?" It was difficult to imagine that Nyemo had any "business" whatsoever—prior or prospective.

"No, no belief, " admitted Hung. "We have no

belief. Belief is in Nyemo's mind. Life as Nyemo sees it is in his mind. He is very creative, but in his mind. He has a Tibetan mind."

Ah, so even Hung had her prejudices stuck and clinging, likely from childhood myths. Hung could be a Tupaloo, Mississippi racist pig if the kindred chords were struck.

She said: "But we accept Nyemo in his desires and ways. Although it seems to anger him if we accept *or* if we doubt his words. He has a bipole enscattering psychology." From her attentive driving on the crowded street Hung had now speed-turned back to face Arthur, a bit bipolar herself.

Don't do that!

Arthur reached forward and gently guided her vision back to facing traffic.

She hardly noticed—if at all. . . But Mick noticed. His gripped expression said that he did not appreciate anyone manhandling Hung, not excluding his father.

Arthur's taking-in of that annoyed Mick-look had him imagining his son's learning of Nyemo's penetration of her rump.

"But Nyemo," Hung said, "he is so rather brilliant and sometimes not so wrong."

"Really?"

Arthur doubted that with Hung's 'not so wrong' she was picturing the anal-intrusive graphics Arthur was.

"Especially this in the sciences," Hung said. "And in literature. Nyemo knows now more of Chinese classics than do I. Although he swears, if he does not leave university, he will go into the 'Business' degree"—her face went to a sniff-sneer sourness, she stuck out her tongue, acting-out a gag. " 'Business', as wants Mick-ah-yell. To be the big."

"Correct!" Mick squeezed Hung's shoulder with male top-dog affection.

Which clutching seemed, despite Arthur's not wishing it to seem, artificial: For his father's benefit.

"I wish," said Hung to Mick, "that *you* would not do . . . 'Business'."

Ricky Rubalcava's "motor car" ventures. Gross 'business'. Cash-in on the newfound land. Carpetbagger creativity. Even Ricky's son Geraldo had found it too distasteful. Crumbled Cuba for that faithful kid was better.

"No foreigners," now insisted Mick, "come to Peking U for anything but 'Business'. We come 'to-*do*-China', as the saying goes."

My son the know-it-all. He really is not the Heidelberg Mick.

"That is *false*," said Hung. "Foreigners, they come here for art and culture and humanity. Mick, you told me you came here for that—for some of it."

Mick nodded sketchily—whatever that meant.

A fight? Did they have many of these? Where did Mick pick-up this new combat-readiness?

Arthur was not sorry that his kid was showing he had some balls and wasn't just a striving suck-up to the privileged daughter of a high-admired Han.

"I do so dislike," said Hung—but now staring straight ahead—"when people think of China as only *Business*. As crass. Even *you*, Mick-ah-yell Beck-er."

Mick leaned over and kissed her.

As they drove Hung and Mick agreed that Nyemo was likely at The Tibetan Bar, a "bistro" frequented by, well, Tibetans—"and Chinese Han who think that they are beatnik hipster Hans and learn the Tibetan folk music and dance, and this makes them groovy-wild—they wear Buddhist beads on one wrist and a Swiss watch on the other." Hung then laughed, a hollow ironic cackle that Arthur had already heard many times in China. "Except," she added, "The Tibet Bar group, Vajara, it is all American punkish rock-a-roll and 'billy-rap."

"And like Nyemo," supplied Mick, "they all are smoking up that K-2 Space Trip shit."

"Don't curse," said Hung.

Arthur had never heard Mick utter "shit" before.

K-2 Space Trip? Arthur asked what that was.

Hung told him it was fake dope, "chemicalled marijuana" that was illegal and could kill you or make you crazy, and was probably what was inside Nyemo when he "went crazy" at the *June Four*.

"The *June Four*?"

"What they, the unders, call the Tian'An Men, for the date of the Massacre—which few know about today. It is said that at The Tibetan Bar they publish under their ground a 'truth' underground samizdater called *The June Four*. It reveals for those who dare to take and read it how China is all controlled." She spoke through a shoosh-shoosh finger. "Nyemo works on *The June Four*. While he is on the K-2. He has not said, but I am sure."

Could be that K-2 "Space Trip" was inside Nyemo when he bungholed Hung.

Could be Hung was on it too?

"The Tibetan Bar," Hung said, "it is the only locale in Beijing where Nyemo does not get himself stared at like as by a shooting bullet-eye, and he can speak quick-street Tibetan like he likes—and they do do this Tibetan rap and they wear their pants below their unders like do your American blacks like Doggie Dog—see, *we* know Doggie Dog!—and they throw darts at a board with a big Mao's *Little Red Book* on it center, that red star is the bullseye—hah."

Mick happily echoed his fiancé's "Hah".

Mick, you're slipping back now to Mister Leash-Led! Watch it!

I'd never have believed a Chinese husband could be henpecked.

What are you, Mick!?

"Except," said Hung, "they should be alert, the Tibets, as there are watchouts in that Bar." Hung shook her head at all such craziness and spy-injustice; her straight black hair flew and her hands leaped-off the Xiali's little steering wheel—as if she would strangle the traffic and all unfair China—her hands then dropped back on. "At that bar Nyemo is even envied. He is a star at The Tibetan Bar as he was a star in Lhasa, far off, for his scholarship. And he is a star at The Tibetan Bar because he is a man of university, *Peking* Uni, the top, where no one else is, of Tibetans—or very few anyway."

She added, "We do love Nyemo."

It seemed—the way she slowly turned her head and tilted it upwards—that a ceaseless watching deity had prescribed her sentiment.

"Yes," insisted Mick, back-to-his-goddamn-striving. "We do."

Hung said that once she and Mick were married they would gain an "Official Certificate" which would allow them to rent a flat—and Nyemo could live with them instead of within her entire family condo, where they all lived now.

Arthur presumed that agglomeration already included Mick-ah-yell—he wouldn't be living by now in his assigned grim dorm. He asked—

"How large are the rental flats allowed?"

"One bedroom." Hung must have perceived Arthur's disapproval, his Aeschylus nightmare tragedy: "Nyemo would sleep in the living.

"With Nyemo," added Hung, "it is just so impossible to not to worry. About a living place. He could find himself in the most horror-rific."

Arthur responded with the Americanish "I hear you."

Hung said, "I am sure you hear me."

She's literal as a German:

Arthur smirked.

Mick said: "With Nyemo, as he is a thief, with others from the Tibet Bar, we fear the arrest and the *shuanggui*."

"Nyemo"—Hung—"he is *no* thief."

Nyemo is a thief?

"*Shuanggui?*" asked Arthur. "What's that?'

Hung gave Mick a narrowing repressive look for his creep divulgence, which might not even have been true; and she held those large dark eyes on Arthur's son as she drove—that damned herky-jerk Beijing drivership. *Shuanggui* was obviously bad stuff. Torture certainly came to mind. Habeas corpus not a chance. But, again, this was Arthur's thought.

Hung again insisted, "We just do *love* Nyemo."

Again Chinesing-up Mick insisted the similar.

Nyemo-love simply filled-up that Xiali, sucked the

crapcar air right out.

Gimme a break, Mick: Don't protest your bullshit love so frightful fucking much!

I wonder if Mick even likes Nyemo.

Brave Arthur: "Can we detour to The Tibetan Bar? Quick sidetrip?"

Ulterior motive for the writer: A piece in *The New Yorker* or *The Atlantic*. He would not deny his incentives. Not to himself anyway.

"What—*no*!?" Annoyed Mick. Frightened Mick? "A sidetrip? We are going to the family *lineage* hall. There's *dinner*! In your *honor*, father. There's no *time*."

The kid was decidedly apprehensive.

To see the time, Hung turned her wrist on the steering wheel; like so many Chinese (even those partial-paltried in the Hutong) she had one of those modern Dick Tracy omnibus watches and she seemed to hone-in on the data for quite some time.

Anarchic other-disciplined chink driver.

Arthur refrained from cautioning (for the fourth time?), 'Watch the *road!*'

"There is time," Hung said. "A little time."

"I wouldn't like to go," said Mick. "Not now."

Mick did seem scared.

"I would like," said Hung. "I was there but only the but once."

"With Nyemo?" Jealous Mick.

"With Nyemo, yes. And I ask why not?"

"But," said Mick, "we are overdressed. They won't want us there."

True: Hung wore a dark cocktail outfit with white pearls. Mick wore a dark suit. Arthur hadn't known the boy owned one. Perhaps great Jin Jianxin, Hung's father, had purchased it for his soon son-in-law.

"Don't be scared," said Hung to Mick.

By just a touch she sounded too solicitous, her voice a chord higher than her usual; it was not a coo, but it could be interpreted as on the sketchy frontier between care and mockery. The tender petting of a pet.

"I am *not* scared!"

Hung's voice-cradling had obviously got Mick offended.

They turned down Bei Lu, one mile or so, alongside broad government buildings, including a pale pillared megalith that looked as if it belonged in 'thirties Berlin or smackdab on Wall Street. Hung said it was once The City Bank of New York and was now Beijing Police Museum. (*Police Museum?*). A bit farther on, just past a treeless square park (as super-well-mown as any German park) and then Peking University with its skyscraper pagoda, its halls with the inevitable concave roofs and its intricate archways, and they were there: The Tibetan Bar. Parking in an alleyway behind the narrow dark-windowed club (as if it were a VIP limo), opening a door of intricately frosted dark gray glass (spook proof?), entering a tight large room where most everybody chain-smoked and wore commie-denim (or prison-denim) workshirts (with major underarm sweat blotches [perhaps from the endless playing of the video games lined along one concrete wall]—those grungey ideological shirts were so predictably profuse they might have been purchased equipped with that "added labor-sweat attraction"), and beneath your feet came the crackling of sunflower seed shells like cockroach colonies, infinite and slippery. The room was low-lit, blackout-like black curtains, body-shadows through the

117

cigarette smoke and a musty odor that had Arthur the film fanatic picturing Fred Astaire slink-smooth in "Limehouse Blues"[8]—except there was one bright wall sign that read: BAN CAPITAL PUNISHMENT FOR JAYWALKING, and another: I HATE THE CHINESE DREAM. ("Is there actually a death sentence for jaywalking?" Arthur asked Hung, feeling inordinately stupid. "Almost," she said, "but that is a mockerize-joke: We do have the capital death for the sell of fake sports tickets." [Was she bragging? At a loss, Arthur nodded].). Mick had lagged back a step as they entered, and consequently he bumped into a sunken-eyed, orange-and-spiky-haired fellow holding an iPhone like a weapon—it was playing (inscrutable of course) Talk: "Free Tibet Radio," said Hung. "Only bar outside Tibet and part Szechuan to play it. That man," she said, "he is a fake artificial Lama." "That's terrible," said Arthur, "it's obscene." "No no," said Hung, "He dresses in his berry robes and he blesses rich Han, and they give him much money for the bless. Tibet Buddhism is quite the pop now in Beijing amongst the money-people, as it was in the West, no?" "Yes," said Arthur. "Our fooler Buddha here," Hung said, "he gives his swindle money to the underground, *The June Four*. He is brave and a good Lama actor." She looked quite proud of him. They three stood beneath a broad-bladed slow overhead fan as they looked about for Nyemo (Hung said, "No bar in Beijing has these neatly fans anymore." She said that proudly too, as if she had been in on the big-fan-purchase.). They couldn't locate Nyemo, and egregiously consulting his watch (a plain old watch it

---

[8] The first ever music-"video"—extracted from a film of The Ziegfeld Follies.

was) Mick said, "Let's go, we ought to go." Hung allowed that they could wait some moments, her family at the lineage house was "precision-slow" in their preparation ("And they try to be a smiter late, like they are the smartest French.").

The three waited—for what? They did not order drinks, as they did not wish to appear at the family lineage hall in various off-kilter states and with "drinky breath". Arthur saw nothing that one might label Tibetan here, not as far as he could tell—a few young men wore their hair down their backs like ancient hippies, or they sported ponytails like Willie Nelson. Cui Jian (said Hung) was being played: "The Chinese Bob Dylan" (Hung said she was surprised they played someone so "old vogue"—he'd effected a Chinese Woody Guthrie twang, which sounded insane, like a guitar with broken strings.). The bar was a bar, that's it, more Shitkicker Austin Texas than anything else Leftist, message T-shirts (in Mandarin and in English: one read GRASS MUD HORSE [a homonym in Mandarin, explained Hung, for FUCK YOUR MOTHER]), such when not the prevalent denim workshirts and jeans (that read not Levis but Dickies and obscure Westernesque names like Hobo Boys—the usual one pool table (old style scuffed mahogany, with pocket nets), a few booths with high backs. "Here they publish an underground?" Arthur asked Hung, in an undertone, she who was nodding to a few boys roundabout. "Maybe underground *is* underground," she hushed-out, "under is just under the bar floor." She shrugged-dumb while speaking (Arthur suspected she well knew) just as Nyemo entered. And not a moment too soon: Hung was about to be hit upon, a slim good-looking guy, opaque silver specs yet. Mick-ah-yell did show a protection-face for Hung, but it was also compromised by a frightened face (and his undertaker suit). He did stand his ground, Mick did, while Nyemo intervened (his T-shirt read THANKS 4 NOTTING)— Nyemo placed an arm about Hung, possessive, he eerie-smiled, and that was that. "You should go," Nyemo said to Hung. But it wouldn't be offbase to take-in what Arthur did: Despite Nyemo's upset at Hung's presence, her intrusion into *his* Bar World, he was glad for this chance to be, in a way, her boss, her protector—her superior. You saw that in his unbent buccaneer Bluto chest-blurt, his "manly" smile—which Arthur hadn't seen before (certainly not in his hotel room, where Nyemo had been close to apologetic tears): Now he was The Tibetan Emperor with the Mandarin-girl servant— who still appeared to want to stay. (While Mick's irked expression said, 'Please, do we have to drag her out?'). Nyemo maintained his Emperor smile with Hung, but it was also, underneath, a tightened smile, wrong but hereabouts prolongable; and then—just like that—he walked away from her, to this group. It was now up to Hung to push it, to walk to Nyemo—which she did, with Arthur and Mick following, they had little choice, leash-dragged doggies in this environment—you didn't know where to look, don't offend anyone; don't *not*-look, don't offend anyone. Hung asked Nyemo to come with them to the family lineage hall, where *Mister* Becker was to be honored. "You asked before," he said, not covering his annoyance. However Nyemo did turn to Arthur with apology, a sadness that leaked its embarrassment and seemed reserved for only *Mister* Arthur Becker. He said he could not come. "Why? Why no?" asked Hung. "I am not your family," he said. "You *are*," she said, and you saw in the harsh dilation of his nostrils, in his strained containment, how he despised Hung's condescension, how he knew that she, even *she*, did not know that her condescension was just that, you saw how he had here his rebellious Tibetan Bar options, his elevation, his localized importance, his *worth*. . . And so Nyemo would not abate his stone stare at Hung. And he liked doing that, aiming, eye-darts— you couldn't miss that. "I am sorry, sir," Nyemo did say to Arthur Becker, to whom he now acted not deferentially, not superior, just simply flat—man-to-man. He had ignored, completely, impolitely, (cipher?) Mick-ah-yell. . . Arthur made note of that.

Hung drove away nervously. Something had struck home, but not possible the clarity that had just spread itself out and honed-in like a stage-play before Mister Arthur Becker: Nyemo had come to Beijing—or China—so as to reject Beijing—or China, to tackle his life's subordination; and Mick-ah-yell had come to Beijing—or China—to reject, not Germany but America (a famous university, *any* famous university)—which was his Jewishness, which was in effect his own life-subordination. Two Beijing tacklers, Arthur saw the pained parallel for some moments: Two young men trying to crash through the swinging double-doors of their own divided souls, and those doors, swinging, swung back, crashing into the fronts of their own souls. Here were two ever-dividing spirit-calculi that might have led them years ago to join up with the French Foreign Legion and challenge the Arabs and their Atlas mountains. And then, as with most epiphanies (of men who are not much on epiphany), this Becker-seen drama dissolved with just the buzzing, vaporized feeling that it was there—that he, Becker, *knew it*, that he could call it up. . . But with Hung a drama had played-out as well, a parallel—and perhaps she had known it earlier, probably she had; but now it had projected itself with speed's immediate force and closed-in loudness in The Tibetan Bar, with an audience about; and while driving away from the bar she kept clutch-releasing too soon, too often, and stalling the Xiali; she peeled wheels (the tires were likely bald anyway, but the rubber-squeal said a lot); she ran traffic lights on the tail end of the warning orange; this jumpiness had been from Nyemo's strong hold on her and his equally strong let-go, pull-push-pull-and-push—and the awareness of her potent hold on Mick, which could be an annoyance she—who knows?—might jettison. Hung had likely expected that Nyemo would have been more glad to see her and then he'd drop his shady Tibetan Bar doings and come to the family lineage dinner—which in a way he'd just about spit at, which was hardly necessary. Hung's spirited disappointment, however, her called-forth recklessness, brought forth in Arthur just the opposite of what one might expect—what even *he* would have expected at that moment. He was drawn more to the girl, he awaited more impulsive reflex display, he actually wanted to witness it, to be a part of it. Hung was calm—Becker had seen that cool head confront the slapping girl in the restaurant, and the same with crazed Nyemo at Tian 'An Men—and she was inflammable. Becker's own wife Jutta was calm, there might not have been an explosive bone in her body—which "lack" had surprised him at first, and impressed him, and had him honor her even in his broodings—and in truth it also disappointed him. In truth it always had. Jutta would never have joined the French Foreign Legion—although maybe Doctors Without Borders, had she chosen to be a physician.

In order to reach that family lineage hall, they had now to travel far past what was called the Fifth Ring Road, and amazingly it looked familiar to Arthur: they actually passed Ricky Rubalcava's Havana Heaven lot of vintage American cars, Hung declaring that Ricky's place was indeed famous in Beijing and that these "monstrosers" were "degenerate hoggers" and "smoke burpers, which smoke is come to be a perverse pride *if* it is from one of these old American chariots", but still that she would not mind owning one, "a least for one day", and "cruising our Beijing biways like a Queen and *waving*". Quelle girl! (Mick said he could not believe that "even America" would have manufactured such "crude dragons as at an amusement park. What silly people.") (Arthur wanted to clobber his kid, like Moe did.). Arthur refrained from mentioning that he knew Ricky, had driven and been driven in a T-bird and a Trans-Am and that son Mick was by birth one-half that silly-American-person. . . They went through what Hung called "ant tribes"—poorer residential areas of the solar system of this megalopolis, where there were bunk-bed boarding houses for college graduates who could not get jobs; and just outside of these were bedraggled day laborers bunched-up at corners and holding signs, which Hung translated: CAN BUILD; CAN DRYWALL; CAN BRICK; CAN PAINT AND WATERPROOF; DRAIN UNCLOG; MAKE FINE

BRAS (yes, that's what she said); and it seemed these grim warrens would never end—quite the contrast to the flaunted Cuban-American motor-carriages housed nearby. Hung was driving in that black dinner dress, she had pinned-on a turquoise brooch which she said that Mick had given her (Mick smiled, but for some reason when he looked at Arthur he curtailed that smile). Mick's black suit was the nearest imitation to a tuxedo Arthur had ever seen, too near. Dressed like red-carpet Academy Award nominees they passed gray dilapidated remnants of what must have been public housing and what appeared now to be factory dormitories—as clothing drooped and jutted out the narrow windows: some, all shirts over slacks, appeared like suspended ghostly humans, large puppets flapping-flopping devivified. Then two churches, a brownstone Catholic, a gray-slab Protestant with sharp spires. No synagogues.

"Many here are migrants." Hung still driving her puny Xiali in that frightening anarchic mode. "Many here were in The Tibetan Bar, I think—it's cheaper, and sometimes they forget to take money. Some out here are thieves and some not thieves. Some work and are cheats, as they do receive the *dibao*."

"Welfare," contributed Mick-ah-yell, again in his impress dad mode: 'I already know Chinese ins-and-outs.'

"It is very low," said Hung.

"The *dibao*," explicated Mick-ah-yell. "Far lower than in Europe or even stingey America."

"Even stingey America, eh." Arthur's annoyance at his son.

"That is why, in China," said Hung, "we must take

advantage, to our fullest, of our educations."

"And that is why," said Mick, "I am to be majoring at Peking Uni for my degree in Business. Peking U is now in the top ten worldwide—it overtops most Ivies and the OxCam, and all Germans as well."

What two-bit chink poll said that?!

"I wish," said Hung, as she play-struggled with the stubborn Xiali wheel, "that Mick you had more social care. More feel for the spirit life."

Like Nyemo?

"But I do," said Mick, "the spirit. Do you wish for me to take a polly-polly?"

It was explained to Arthur that it was not uncommon in China for prospective couples to take a polygraph, to determine whether or not they were lying about their interests and accomplishments and potential futures. (Arthur snort-laughed when he heard of this bizarre emblem of this Eastern face culture).

Hung said: "With a faith, Mick, then you might not be having your problem what you have."

"I do not *have* a problem."

"Call it what you will have to call."

Problem? What problem? Mick has got a problem?

"I *have* no problem," Mick swore again.

Problem? What problem?

"I meant . . . "—Hung's voice now in apology, regret.

"I *don't*."

"I am sorry. No. You don't."

What problem!?

Arthur remained silent. He discovered that he was holding-firm onto the central armrest in the Xiali's scruff-torn rear. There were chrome loops for seatbelts, but there were no seatbelts.

Mick turned back to his dad, to emphasize his problemlessness. That was how it seemed. But an odd white grime was holding to the corners of Mick's mouth. Arthur had never seen such form on his son's lips before—and it looked especially weird with Mick got up in his semi-tuxedo. Arthur held the narrow armrest even more tightly. For a moment he was not facing his son Mick but Tibetan Nyemo, and he liked that—and he caught that he'd liked it, and he did not know what to do with that ambiguity. He certainly wasn't comfortable with it. Mick then leaned to Hung and kissed her cheek, his love-show forgiving her for her having mentioned his "problem".

Except: The kiss did look to contain, what? a hate-touch in it?

That Arthur-Moe problem?
What's the kid's damn problem!

They arrived at their destination—and everyone about started-in with their super-thrust huggings, which seemed unforced, quite genuine. They told Arthur that they would speak only in English, as everyone there could (to a degree)—and then they occasionally spoke in Mandarin. Hung had a sister, Heibin (so Jin Jianxin had once had clout, sidestepping the onetime Chinese one-child policy); Heibin was the mother of an eight-year-old boy, Kuan, who rambled about, un-controllably, chasing cats from worm-pecking birds, and then chasing the birds as well—and of course not speaking in English. Heibin was either divorced or estranged—nothing was said about that, only that it was monetarily difficult for a "single" woman to manage the tuition of the "exceptional progressive" *Fortune School* for the boy, which happened to be a Waldorf School which (Heibin made a point of saying) followed "the deep-wise principles of the Swissman Rudolf Steiner, who understood Confucious and could do the blend." "We *do* contribute handsome," Madame Jianxin did want Arthur to understand the family's assistance at *Fortune School*. There were no grandparents present— very surprising to Arthur (in familial *China!?*) as he was awkwardly drawn into the hug-whirlpool: Hung hugged her father Jin Jianxin, who hugged Mick-ah-yell (who thereupon dropped his eyesight, a fawning reverence which sickened Arthur Becker who had never to his recollection received such fawnings from his son); Mick then hugged Madame Jianxin, who graciously hugged Arthur Becker (with considerable rigidity and drawing-away her pelvis, and a tightness tugging at her chin), who, not knowing if he was supposed to, nonetheless hugged Hung (he felt no resistance here, thank god—he'd wanted badly to hug that girl, and keep-on holding her too: it was that twinge of erection coming-on that had him keeping its pert off her by assing-out, as good rebounders do under the backboard in basketball—god it had to have looked comical), and then Arthur hugged his son (and again here he did feel Mick's [unfawned] resistance). So: A hug Bacchanal in Beijing, its permutations might have allowed it to be mistaken for a dosey-do hoe-down honor-your-partner American country dance—minus however an Arthur-Jin Jianxin enwrapment, which must have stood out. Indeed, a hold-back shadow, a descent, had fallen over Jin Jianxin's face—a sorrow?—as if he were contemplating the full gestalt of this Mick-father, Arthur: 'Can this "German" comprehend my ambiguities in my land, my sacrifice—is he capable?'. Well, as Arthur later learned by boning-up, bigtime Chinese nuzzles were a new thing: in earlier years, before much contact with the West, the Chinese had hardly touched each other. Respect? Fear? Hygiene?—but now the "superfluous scuff and graze of adipose tissue" seemed de rigeur, these folk were hug-maniac obsessives (except for Jin). The zeal of the convert.

The Jianxin family lineage hall did not disappoint—it ought to have been approached with a trumpet flourish, or the annunciamento of fulsome Chinese woodwinds. Thus, Arthur Becker had to personify purpose, confidence, certainty. He had to justify himself. He was an equal here, no?—a prospective in-law. A (purported) intellectual, and an experienced internationalist as well. Same as he had done on entering The Tibetan Bar (and as the Berkeley Police advised people to do when they came face-to-face with a mountain lion), he held his head up and stood tall (at the Tibetan Bar this sturdy stance had lasted about three seconds). . . The pungence of thick incense burning in a large gray-black cauldron surrounded first the black wrought ironwork of the open gate, then came the white timber columns—which surrounded the edifice (fifteen hundred square feet was Arthur's guess; maybe four times the size of those *Schrebergarten* huts privileged Germans kept just outside their cities, for gardening [residing *verboten*]); and the columns were in turn bordered at their bases, in onyx, by phantasmal animals, these beings representing something on the order of tigers with humanoid heads and lion manes and humpy camel backs (How in the world had the early Han even known about faraway *camels*?—Marco Polo?). The stone walkway leading to the broad entranceway was as white as the surrounding columns, and it was bordered by black-white banners with Chinese characters; the banner above the entrance was yellow, also containing Chinese lettering in black, which Hung said read (what else?) JIANXIN LINEAGE ANCESTRAL HALL. Within, a scent; not of food quite yet, but of some taste wayworn: figurines with Bodhisattva faces—beside, weird, a *piano*: a stand-up studio version, branded ETERNA. (Made in China in Pearl River, in smaller print, just glued on). In America a comparable house with comparable adornment would be considered a House of Ego—but China was China.

"Families devoid of private lineage halls," said Hung, who'd observed Arthur's gawking inspection, "they go to rent the public ones where they *imagine* family lineage or furnish the family make-believe for the one family day."

She'd offered that with not the least contempt. Perhaps even with respect and sympathy.

Mick was definitely marrying up. If the marriage happened.

Jin revealed that he had spent time "in the West". (Later he would inform Arthur that he had learned, "as we do in the better China schools, the *Harvard* English." Arthur had clamped-down-tight on any smirkishness, as he couldn't but recollect so many Germans claiming proudly that they had learned "the *Oxford* English."). Still-and-all, the Jianxin clan was obviously special: Yes, Mick would be marrying above his station. Above the station Arthur's invisible station had conferred. Jin Jianxin and his wife Madame Jianxin had had two months of hearing-out Hung on "ultra-desirable" Mick—that was obvious. Hung had triumphed in discourse with them over skin-tones, hair, eyes and subtler physiognomies. All this pleasantness (and forbearance?) represented by the family's ministrations toward Arthur Becker this evening at the Jianxin family lineage hall reminded Arthur of the ongoing ping-pong attitudes by which Uwe and Lisa Koenig, *Die Steuer Berater* (tax advisor) and *Hausfrau*, parents of his wife Jutta, had welcomed into their family Becker The Jew. *So, was ist das Problem?* Nothing askance with a Yid. Jew?-Schmew. *Alles ist vorbei. . .* Nodding judiciously, his voice coursing steadily through the elaborate room, (and boorishly wearing-out the word "utmost") Jin Jianxin the paterfamilias occupied the lengthy table's head and talked and talked and talked as if he feared that Arthur's return-words, if they came, would be on even keel with a vacuum ("Ah, we are so living in utmost intensest times."); (Arthur fancied he'd detected Hung wrapped in a surreptitious yawn, which she camouflaged by whispering to Mick with a comical-urgent look); Jin's eyes were ever-augering, nailheads, his presence seemed even to refract the light: "our utmost China growth but oh so too material"; "*renminbis* inflates, so interest rate suppress for invests to help Jinping (who's that?) deal with the 'Siberian High' " (what's that?—weather?) and blah and low wages and blah and *no* wages, and blah and "health care utmost *paltry*—to *my* mind"; "our growth great, yes, but: no free press; suicides at factory concentration camps like Foxconn for your Apple Valley silicons—they have installed anti-self-kill *nets* around the roofs"; and *"fuqiang"*— which sounded in English like a gang orgy but meant too much concentrated wealth and power. "There is a hole in Chinese life," said Jin, "the *jingshen kongxu*— the void spiritual."

Jin was this and that: In a Western context it was hard to politically place the guy. Well, he did have to protect himself. For all he knew this Arthur Becker— *and* this Mick-ah-yell Becker, were agents of his government. Weirder things had happened.

"You know, we have a great deal of that injustice in the West," said Arthur, trying to accommodate.

He'd soft-squinted at Jin, as if to show respect. But squints can be misconstrued.

"Indeed," countered Jin. "You have injustice in the West, but injustice not like *here* in the *East*."

What's this?—a contest for top socio-econ shithole of the world?

"You would be surprised," said Arthur. "We in America, we come up short on—"

He saw Jin's steaming bulged-out labial lines and jaw:

"I *know*," said Jin, "what the West *has* and what are its *lacks*. I am not a naïve provincial *idiot*."

"I'm sure," said Arthur, shaking his head in a No-No-I-Didn't-Mean: "I'm sure you know more than I do about. . . ." His head swiveled within his shrug. "Far more."

Placate Placate Placate—Jin's weighty sought sage strain: those sharp opinion scars and creases. Becker remembered how harshly Moe wore his own sour grapes.[9]

---

[9]So, Becker's Brain: Why why why would a man as reputed kind and unprejudiced and reform-minded as Jin the Confucian, *the* believer in a struggled-for fairness and a national harmony (and a fierce regret for their lack), have instructed Nyemo to "manhandle" Hung? This made no sense, did it? (1) Jin wasn't so kind and unprejudiced and reform minded? He was as cynical-corrupt as that Brit huckster on the arrival bus had said the Chinese were?— even the reformers. Confucianism wasn't easy-harmony-fairness; it required disharmony to succeed, calculation and unfairness—as had China's Red Guards' "Great Leap Forward" mass killings for "good Communism", which resulted in more Mao backwardness. (2) Jin had really wanted Hung to marry *Nyemo*?—an egalitarian gesture for both of them, and for China: people would talk about it, and it would be a confidence-builder for a confidence-needing Tibetan? Ah, this sounds good—and it sounds absurd. (3) Jin had wanted Hung to *not* experience herself as privileged, to experience what POWER could do to her? (4) He'd wanted, despite his "liberal" self, to retain a part of that Chinese tradition of diminishing the woman?—really all along he'd wanted, not a daughter, but a son? He was just a normal Eastern guy. (5) He wanted to turn-in Nyemo, and thus rid himself of his burdensome obligations to an *abnormal* Eastern guy: He had too many commitments already, and his house was too crowded. Even the best of men must make compromising choices. And Nyemo might well have been compromising *Hung's* Chineseness, bending her down towards low-class scum activities like wearing dark glasses and showing underpants above the waistband, as nice-shy-respectful German Mick would not do—so Western Mick would re-fix Jin's good daughter. (6) Some fallacious idea of the "sophistication" of Western women in sexual activity, which Jin felt Hung should be equal to for New Women's capabilities in today's China, as sex was/is a shameful topic, wrapped in layers of patriarchal Confucian and Communist prudery—thus had come the neurosis of repression, and more of an ever-stultified homeland. Jin wished a new impure-purity, based on losing the old pure-impurity; so that, perhaps, Hung would not be "awkward" with a Westerner (*like awkward Mick-ah-yell?!*) or even a "modern" on-the-up Chinese—who might make her the best husband, better than

"And what then," asked Jin of Arthur, "do you think of our *Mister* Xi?"

Mister Z?

It sounded like the ad-name of a roofer or carpet cleaner who might, for some misguided reason, have wanted his business to be listed last in the Yellow Pages. Thinking *Z? Z? Z?* Becker paused and stared down towards his knee, as if he'd lost a contact.

And Hung, seeing the American's puzzlement, glowered boldly at her father, as if offended at his taunting, his undermining of her soon father-in-law.

Suspended in the Z void, stalled and mindshifting, Becker felt he loved Hung's daughter-bravery. Becker loved, not just her stalwart stance, but *her*, Hung. Had he been in his twenties, or thirties, he would have fought it out for her with his son Mick. He fancied he might have carried the girl off, right now, no bullshit, from the family lineage lair to his own hovel at the Hotel Prince Gong. Within, he laughed at his immaturity, his passion, which his son seemed not to have much of—and which, truth be told, was not considered by him as so immature.

And: Becker knew he knew "Z", damnit, but his nervousness had smothered his knowledge. Ought he then fake it?—in the midst of Jin's now pitying cast— already "the great man" was soured on him? But how the hell could Becker fake it? He'd earn further ridicule.

"The name, 'Z'," he said, "it's on the tip of my tongue. I mean that. But I'm afraid I can't come up with

---

this German Mick. Mick *and* Nyemo thus tune-ups, both to be jettisoned at the ripest time. (7) A toying-with Nyemo?—as Fritz Strobel had waged his cocky anti-Semitism weapons upon Arthur?—he probably hadn't even meant it. (8). I think too much.

it." He returned Jin's dumbfounded stare with hard-crafted innocence. "So, who, I have to ask, I'm sorry, is Mister Z?—I'm sorry."

They're Chinese: they'll be polite. Forgiving and polite. Hung was—he saw that.

"Xi?," went Jin. "Xi is *Xi!* Who could Xi be but *Xi!*"

Even Mick was looking stunned. Poor Mick. Mortified by his flesh-and-blood.

Rummage, your cortex, damn you, rummage: **Z-Z-Z-Z-Z**.

Self-dismay.

Self-hatred.

Then . . . Then, somehow, Something!

Ah: "Z is *Xi*? China's *President!*"

Shit, I didn't have to ANNOUNCE it like a bumptious dork-schmuck on Jeopardy: *'What is MISTER **Z**!?'*

Jin now tamped himself to a whisper: "Xi is Big Dad-dee, you can see it even in how he pumped-out *stands*. He writes *New Sayings*. China's best-seller. Perhaps world's, ha. Tells artists how to art. Tells everyone. 'The China Dream'. He is baby Mao now, *Mister* Communist. His mind is still nomenclatura while his hands collect the capital." Everyone was smiling at Jin's harsh irony—of which Arthur, before this Jin-performance, had not had a clue.

Am I supposed to grin collusive?

I doubt there are secret government WebCams in place here in the Jianxin Family Lineage Hall, as were in my murder-room in the hospital. What that Doctor Schiffer said there were.

Jin's face—call a sneer a sneer. A nose-riddling, an eyes clamping. A narrow face pinched and narrowed more; Christ, he looked near two-dimensional.

"Xi," hissed Jin, "Xi is *gang* and *er*."

No one ventured explaining the whispered *gang* and *er*.

Not even the Chinese-striving Mick-ah-yell—who did tell Arthur later: "macho kingly cruel and dumb. . . But great. Definitely great!"

And no one mentioned Xi again that night.

No one except for the quite unmanageable "progressively educated" eight-year-old Kuan, who had broken into a loud chant of "Xi! Xi! Xi! Xi! Xi! Xi!— an *idiot!*"—as if he had heard such declaration around the house all the time; and Kuan went banging his teacup like a prisoner, while his mother, Heibin, did nothing: she acted as if the boy were behaving properly, not out-of-order at all. Looked like the Chinese had mistaken notions of the "permissive" emotional freedom and "unmanacled thought" promulgated by the Swiss Rudolf Steiner and his Waldorf School.

That kid could get them into serious trouble.

I bet Jin knows it.

Nowthen, deeper Jin: He was tall, relatively tall—for a Chinese: Just about Arthur's height, and he looked to be Arthur's age (ballpark). He was slender, his face was quite smooth, almost as if buffed, and it really could seem two-dimensional, a wedge, if one stared at it straight-on; it might appear that he never required shaving. His cheekbones were not especially prominent, compared to the average (or what Arthur Becker imagined was the Han-average); his nose was merely a spot (well, not much more than that), as if it had been sawed-off or squished by a potent punch; but his lips were full, pulped-up (but not pouted) with authority. His bright brown eyes were large, like his daughter Hung's—or small when he used them to hone-in and investigate your own eyes. And bizarrely, freakish really, he wore a tweed jacket, checkered, cinched-in and belted at the waist, as might a Scottish lord—or Prince Philip of Edinborough. Or a pretentious phony who bought knockoffs at Barney's. To complement this amalgam he ought have been sporting a white Kaywoodie pipe—which he wasn't.

"My father was in jail," bragged Hung, suddenly— why now? She had once before exulted in Jin's imprisonment—jail seemed as if it could top the Nobel Prize, the only Chinese winner of which was in Chinese prison.

But there was something in her boast this time that said obligation, as if she had been prompted earlier to mention The Great Incarceration. Arthur saw Hung's contempt for her father—he was pretty sure what he saw was that: her head and her hands were even shaking as if it were cold in that family lineage room, which it was not.

Jin said: "I was in jail longer than was the blind lawyer, Chen Guangchen. The one who has escaped to America's New York Uni, and achieves himself famous for his blindness more than for his good helps."

Envious bitter dude, this noble Jin?

"Smartest people in the West," Jin then followed-up. "You Jews."

Out of nowhere? Why?

Again, Hung's shaking head and hands.

But she was not looking at her father.

What Arthur Becker thought was that she was

looking at him, with apology. And with something more. An intimacy, of origins unknown. Mick appeared to see it too. He couldn't take Hung's hand here in this Chinese family setting, but his glance toward Hung was not dissimilar from her father's—a brittle paternal scowl he must have picked up from her father—because he liked it?

"Perhaps," said Jin, "you did not know, Mister Becker, but those from the West who had come to help China in earlier days, they were in-the-main, in high proportion compared to Christians, Jews."

"No, I didn't know that."

What the hell's going on here?

"Do you, Mister Becker, as a good Jew, do you do anything yourself to help the less fortunate—Jew or non?"

"I do," Arthur lied, "lots of things."

And found himself the recipient from his son of the exact same sturdy stare that Mick had lain on Hung.

Arthur had noticed that the noble "selfless" (ruthless?) Jin Jianxin, "champion of the poor and the ill-treated", had watched with jaw tight and eyes narrowed when the dinner dishes had not been perfect-proper-placed by their two servant Uighur women, who did wear their hijabs with their robes and had seemed to float along the dinner table like white spirits. Jin had glowered at "his" Uighurs—a benevolent suppressive man. *Gang* and *er*. Things were mixed-up here. You looked into the depths of the human other and what you saw was—The Human Other.

When the evening ended, candle stubs burned darkly among the teacups as if dramatizing confusion's endurance and pantomime.

VII

REFRACTURED
REVELATIONS

When Arthur Becker finally found himself free of
The Jianxin Family Lineage Hall he was not sorry. Not
one bit. Free was the last thing he was. He'd been
troubled by what he perceived as Hung's attention to
him, and by his wanting more of it—and his trying to
not show it, especially as Jin Jianxin, due to what must
have been his own political balancing act, had to be an
excellent observer. (Good Jutta's face had appeared; not
only from Arthur's guilt [after all he did have guiltier
matters to obsess about] but because it was as if *Hung*
was the diligent scrupulous [approachable and
susceptible] Visiting Scholar from Germany who he
had, well, picked-up, in Berkeley [Andronico's Super-
market], by the broccoli and what Jutta musically called
the *"Spargel"* [white asparagus] some twenty-four
years ago.). Driving back to the Hotel Prince Gong in
the Xiali Arthur too often fixated on his driver, Hung—
her straight dark hair, that strong softness of her round

face when she turned back to him, which she found reasons to do too often (God, those mesmerizing eyes!—in Beijing industrial dusklight what?—obsidian?—those eyes *not on the goddamn road!*) (Didn't Mick notice this attention?—he was by her side: sure he'd noticed it. And why hadn't Arthur felt the way he felt now about Mick's earlier girlfriends? Because Mick had had no earlier girlfriends.). As insipidly sentimental as it sounds Hung's turning back to Arthur quickened his pulse, he felt that rapidity, he could see it bouncing just beneath his wrist, but it meant what? and it prompted also a hopeful why? Arthur Becker, forty six, was drawn to his son's fiancé, twenty-two—he *wanted* her!: her idealism, her youth, her knowledge, her talent (she had played piano at the family dinner—Jin had just about ordered this one song performance—of "Western" Tschaikovsky yet—First Piano Concerto: aka the once-pop "Till the End of Time": she'd flubbed chords badly—a bit like Victor Borge screwing around—but only Arthur had seemed to recognize that, as if it mattered), her bravery, her calmness and patience (when she was in possession of these), even (or especially?) her sexual gameness—and her rebelliousness towards her father (when she was in possession of *that:* She'd first demurred on the piano-playing: sullen grimace at her father); and of course that (what Becker the Bigot saw as) Oriental-perfect hourglassness of her body. Fantasizer, he had already imagined their embrace, it would be lust-blooded, headlong, as if they had been thrown together by defiant earthquake engines rock-running inside them (and no he did *not* see himself fucking her up the ass!). The old mid-life crisis, in the flesh—but Becker being

Becker decided there was more to it than such a prosaic stamp of socio-psych. No simple life-convention for the Son-of-Moe who had once upped and Jewed-away in Germany. He had certainly had enough already of father Jin's grisly enumerations of China's socio-politics, its dicto-economy, and of Jin's aggressive-weird (pointless?) naïveté about Jews. Things he, Becker, probably (certainly) agreed with but couldn't stand to hear patronized-out to him as if he were a no-nothing from Nowhereland. Arthur Becker was the *anti*-Jin Jianxin. Maybe his romantic lust for Hung wasn't so much different from his having murdered old brilliant professor racist Strobel.

No! Are you nuts!?

Anyway: Arthur Becker was destined to experience a busy room that last Beijing night of his four day visit: Mick; then Hung; then a taste of brutal Chinese beefcake in the hunch-rounded (but well-dressed) forms of two men who could have been offensive linemen in the NFL; then a Chinese hooker. In early morning Arthur was scheduled to fly back to Frankfurt, then train down the fifty miles to Mannheim, then cut across to Heidelberg on the pokey Regional. Ironic home sweet ironic home. . . First now however Mick-ah-yell came to him. Arthur was already stripped down to his Hanes, white cottons (Made in China tag—which rather annoyed him just now, although he smiled down at his cheap [worker-suicide-causing?] underpants.), blotted by, since his pre-dinner shower, a pea-stain, circumference in the area of three jagged inches. "I need a new washer"—he'd cracked to himself that old plumber-joke while staring at the repulsive unpatriarchal yellow blotch. . . Although he had been driven back to his hotel by Hung and Mick, the two had apparently not returned to the Jianxin home. They had waited down in the Prince Gong lobby, likely debating whether or not to go upstairs to venture their serious face-to-faces with Mick's father. They had decided that both of them needed such talks—and on the confidential levels of one-to-one. But Hung had remained down in the lobby, allowing Mick to have first crack.

Mick's take was a pinched one as he stood before his father while gazing about the meager overkill-certified 3-Star hotel room which should have been a 2-Star. . . Or starless.

"You don't have a *Fernseher*."

"I told you that before."

"You did not."

Arthur had. When he had first met Hung at this hotel, down in the lobby. But he let it go.

Mick actually now appeared spiteful, accused wrongly, as he had been in Heidelberg, when Arthur had attacked him for being a Pirate, one of those young Israel-haters of the Left. The sides of Mick's lips were drawn in, creating impatient jowls.

For Chrissakes, my accommodation's lack of a television, and my lack of emphasizing it, is what is bitterly pissing-off my kid?

Nah, more's offing: Brace.

"You actually didn't *ask* for a room with a *TV*?"

"Mick, I didn't think it was necessary. Hey, can we move on?"

"Well, father. Let me tell you. You were missing out. CCTV has English language shows. Lots of talk. It's instructive on this land, you'd have benefitted. Not much propaganda, if any. *I* watch."

Oh, He watches! Confirmation from the Highest Source.

"Come on kid," said Arthur. "This is not why you came up here. Gimme the real."

" 'Gimme'. 'The *real*'. You talk so *American*."

My son has turned into T.S. Eliot.

"Stop-it. Mick, I hate when you put down America."

"And *I* hate when you do what *you* do—all that Jewish Jewish Jewish."

So there they were standing face-to-face, real and posing hatreds. With his desultory Germanic, that polite distance, Mick was perfect in his formal attire, with Arthur merely in those stained Hanes jockeys. The Bloomsbury Group meets The Beverly Hillbillies.

"And, father, I hate how you stare at Hung, as if she is a freak show, from some alternating galaxy."

Kid, if you only knew what was in my stare.

"I stare?—actually I didn't know I was staring—I stare at a prospective daughter-in-law."

You deceitful-lying shrugger.

Mick had given his grudging nod. "And I do have other things to say." His voice had now dropped towards delicate, confidential; his eyes seemed suddenly fraught, even melancholy.

"Alright," said Arthur. "So say. Say say."

Arthur had crooned those 'says', a daddy-urge lullaby. He hadn't the vaguest idea why he'd resorted to that mode of sweet and mock—he hadn't wanted to.

Had Arthur-the-father behaved badly with Jin Jianxin The Great?—he thought not. Arthur fortified himself for Mick's coming comments, he shored-up. The dinner had been *in his honor,* and damned if he hadn't comported himself with dignity—he just *had*. The Honorable Arthur Becker. In that Han ancient lineage familial hall he had been good. Respectful. He'd shown interest. Deference. He'd looked at all the ancestral whachamajigs, and close up as a seasoned near-sighted antiquarian, as if discerning meanings and masteries, admiring, approving. Tom Hanks could not have acted-out a better job. Hell Arthur Becker had been the best Arthur Becker possible for Arthur Becker. He quite had.

"I am very glad," said Mick-ah-yell, "that you came here, father. I know it was not easy."

And Mick now bowed—he fucking *bowed*. A Chinese pickup, no doubt; but it did come-off devoid of irony—even with him shipshape in his tux.

"Mick said, "I am being honest when I admit that I was worried. That I would be uncomfortable here. Wouldn't fit—just couldn't." He shook his head in small quick arcs. "It's not easy here. I try too hard—I see that in your eyes too—I know it."

"I guess," said Arthur, "I'm kind of used to living in a land I wasn't brought up in."

Christ don't play that baneful Jew gambit. Not now, not here in China. It sounds so damned unsympathetic.

"Well I do think of all that," said Mick. "Father, your being alien, for all my life. I do forget about it, yes—and then I think of it, it rushes in. I am not sorry for you in Germany—I don't know if I even should be. I don't believe I should. But I have never full understood—I mean your place."

Oh tell me about it, kiddo.

"In life, like, I mean, your place."

"If there is such a thing."

"What?—" Mick's lostness squint: forecast inklings of old-guy dewlaps.

Arthur was pleased his son hadn't tapped-into the skepticism of "maturity".

Mick said: "But now I am very close to that, understanding. In China, by that way. I mean, dad—"

He called me dad!

"I mean you might have stayed in Berkeley California all those years ago."

True true true true true. But I didn't stay, did I!

"Mick, you wouldn't say I might have stayed in Berkeley if you'd seen your mom and me in action."

Mick's grin was walloping and it was embarrassed—he was so much more his father than he knew, than Arthur had really known, except perhaps at short disappearing moments. Those pursuing German eyes gone doubting Jewish, that sturdy German chin remaining German even as it slight-softened so it appeared to have a questioning brain and soul all on its own. What transpired between those two features, eyes and chin, had to accomplish a lot, make a lasting treaty, to resolve into a face believable—livable (forget comfortable)—for a young man who was an opposing two. Mick said—

"I understand now that living that surrounds home, one's home, and I want it. Around me, father, I want it. But I want to break it, too, because it can make you hate."

Arthur just said, "I know."

"The strength, of you and mother—now you know I know." Yes those honest pursuing eyes. "Father, I am so not Chinese."

Big revelation there.

145

"Just as you are not so German. And I see that as my union with Hung more approaches. Father, I love Hung, but my loneliness has made the love more, not the less. I am tied to Hung now, and that is frightening, and, no mistake, I still want it to be that way—tied tight. But . . . marriage?"

Arthur wanted to embrace his son, simply wrap him up.

It had been a long time for them since an unrestrained enfolding had happened, just plain happened: one forged and welded from within.

So, there stood Mick in this getup, his best top-evening dress—and Arthur smiled with a curious bemusement, considering his current pea-stained getup in his (once) white Hanes underpants. . . The comicality of the two men together, quite discovering each other, that resonated, it made waves of elements; and it really was so endearing that Arthur couldn't but, finally, embrace his son; and Mick held Arthur tight as well. God Arthur loved that tightness, that crush-feel of his son's arms, so much stronger than expected: such emotional honesty hadn't even broken-out when Mick had first taken off for China. At Frankfurt Airport, after Mick and Jutta had held each other, a brisk handshake had been the father-son currency du jour—what a failure! Arthur now went and, standing on this leg that, pulled on nearby pants and T-shirt.

"There are problems," Mick said now, unexpectedly, and on the verge of mourning. The oblique distancing of Mick's voice—he couldn't mean father-son complexities this time. Arthur made a quick ransack:

Nyemo!?

Maybe, good girl that she was, Hung had told Mick

about her "depravities" with The Tibetan. And how had his son handled *that* Breaking News?

Careful, neatly pressing with thumbs-and-index, Mick preserved the crease of his slacks as he crouched himself down onto the ottoman, just where The Tibetan had sat the evening before. Arthur employed his bed for his customary laydown, fingers interlocked between the back of his neck and the plumped pillows and cushions.

"Father, Mister Jianxin said that he liked you well enough, despite what was your ignorance."

My ignorance? And that's the problem?

Arthur grinned and held his tongue—until his tongue won out:

"He's a good man, Jin. A-very-good-man. Still, I . . ." A cock of the neck, a shoulder shift, indicating All Men Must Have Their Doubts. He thought of businessman Ricky Rubalcava's balancing act with the wise fashion-chasing Chinese.

Mick wobbled on the ottoman, as if it had lost some stuffings. He leaned back and began crossing and uncrossing his legs. He said—

"It is hard these days to be a good China patriot and not be considered a traitor, so to speak. To the Left line of things. It is a fine tight-line."

"Yes. Why Hung was slapped the other evening at the restaurant."

"Yes, and it was not the first time. Sometimes it is just bad words Hung must receive, in substitute for her father—and then to not speak words back. Holding-in herself. She is so marvelous."

Mick went nodding, his eyes shut—as if he were envisioning that sudden slap and others, and Hung's temperate saint-absorbing powers. Then, boom—

"I am impotent with Hung."

So that's the problem, not Jin's judgment of my ignorance.

The kid had revealed his sorry sex news with his eyes closed, as if covering-up failed visions; then he opened his eyes. His gaze was bleak and empty and expectant: *Help!*

To make light, Arthur smiled sagacity. The smile stayed in place to show that the impotence would not.

"Did you hear me, my admission?"

"Mick, what I heard were my own feelings, in my teens. *My* fears."

"Really?'

"Really."

Well played: Except I wouldn't have told tough Moe of any limp dick experiences: man of impulse, the rough guy would have gone weak with that telling and decided I was a queer-homo-fag non-son son and both our lives were thus kaput: No purpose in having had a kid. Moe'd have given up the ghost. . . As of course, come to think, he did.

And: Arthur saw Nyemo the Tibetan's thorough lack of impotence. He saw Nyemo standing over Mick's Hung with his schlong out, conqueror-trumpet, then fucking her up the ass—as noble Jin Jianxin had advised? *Advised!? Stipulated? Demanded? Jin Jianxin!? "You are hereby evicted from my house if you do not give my Hung what-for!"* Crazy thinking, Becker—cut it out, what's *with* you!?—obviously Nyemo lied. . . But: this love-act of non-love—to *Hung—with* Hung—can't get it out of your mind, Hung Huang's overrun of pleasure. What would Abelard have said? he'd probably have thrown-up. But, then again, there was Ovid with his rape-swamped *Metamorphosis*. *El amor brujo*. . . And, come on, it's compounded by, how not?, Arthur's own personal quirks, had *he* been the *auteur*. Moe's son, *he* had never fucked anyone up the ass—and he regretted it—so of course he obsessed about it. . . But Arthur tried to reassure his own son:

"A let-down, kid. Impotence, it's not unnatural, at first bite. Happens all the time—more than you think, *mein kint*."

" 'Mein *Kind*'. Deutsch, dad. Not your Yiddish."

'*YOUR Yiddish*'.

Even now he corrects me!

An instant then when Arthur wanted to clobber his "*Kind*"—impotent or not—slam his ass, clobber it, not fuck it. His own slip to Yiddish was his own rush to his born soul—he couldn't help that surge, he'd wanted it. *And Mick puts it down!?* He tries to help Mick for Mick's failure and for that *Mick puts him down!?* Mick the non-circumsized (big battle with Jutta over *that* one). Mick the kid who'd chosen to be called the Germanic Mick-ah-yell. Mick the non bar mitzvahed. Mick the belittler of written Hebrew as pathetic, bassackwards, its characters so much stiffer than those of its brother Arabic.

Come on: Christ, Art, the kid is Suffering.

Becker said, "Mick, you're young, that's all. You'll be alright. Don't worry. Chrissakes, don't worry. It's nothing. Hibernation is hibernation, I swear to you. I'm serious."

Oops, hibernation is not hibernation in German. It's *Winterschlaf*. 'Hibernation' lends itself to fun-metaphors and puns. *Winterschlaf*, forget it. Arthur was about to synonym-hunt when Mick went—

"Father. . . "

The kid was holding onto the ottoman at both edges, as if he might tumble from a precariously great height, or was about to perform a dodgy gymnastic number. Nyemo's hassock-perch had not required any such edgy doings. Mick insisted, "It's not the 'young', that I am *young*—I am sure. The 'young' is *not* the impotence—I truly am sure of it. And it is not a problem we can discuss with Hung's family. Or should."

"Not a one I'd've been able to discuss with Jutta's people either."

"You had the problem then? I was preparing to inquire."

Arthur lied: "It's been so long. I honestly can't remember."

He could remember. He had *not* had The Problem. He couldn't decide whether Yes or No was the better answer with which to soothe his son.

Mick now placed his hands in his lap, overlapped as if to cover up his middle: A Declaration of Impotence? Mick saw that his father remained in search of bolstering consolations. He went staring momentarily at his father's groin—weird, unintentional, as if his eyes had been pulled down there, were trapped there, locked there by a mischievous golem, like he might go questioning Becker's own fathering genitals; then the kid jerked such odd sighting away away.

"You did have such problems with my mother?"

'*My* mother'? As if Arthur were an alien, at best a second husband happening along tra-la *after* this boy's birth.

Smartly, to cover-up his first lie, Arthur lied:

"Yes, Jutta and I: We had problems, in the

beginning. But they worked out—and in short order too. Yours will too. . . I'm promising, '*Mein Kind*'— with a '*d*', okay?—not with a Yiddish '*t*', I am guaranteeing."

Mick allowed himself a smile, albeit tightened-thwarted, lips in-tucked at their edges. He said—

"I am not impotent. I know."

"I've no doubt. Like I said."

Again Arthur saw Nyemo travel like a NASCAR heaviweight straight up Mick's Hung's rear end.

"But I think it is that."

"You think that is what? Impotence? How can you think it is that when, as you just said, it *isn't* that?"

"It is hard to explain."

"I'll bet."

"Don't *mock* me, father. Please."

"I wasn't. But, explain?"

"It's not the easiest."

Sex-talk had definitely altered the room air—it seemed hot and it seemed cold. Mick again allowed himself an uncharacteristic self-mocking grin. The sort of expression more at home on his father's face, and in fact a look that his wife Jutta said she 'adored', as you never saw it "skookle" (Jutta's invented word) on the faces of German men, just as you never saw in Germany a gait as slumped yet as "prettyful languid" as the "patented" walk of Arthur Becker's (it had been dad Moe's way of moving, as if captivated by the cipher of the sidewalk's random cracks)—which rolling amble was *not* to be found motoring the longish legs of young, Germanicated, *Mick-ah-yell* Becker.

"The impotence," said Mick, "how can I say?—it is there and it is not—even when it's there."

"Okayyy?"

"And when it's *not* there, and *there is potence*, 'it' doesn't rock-up like a, . . . a rock, it's more a, a . . . a *pulse*, I guess, so it doesn't allow time-for-taking, you know, any . . . 'liberties'? inventions?—time wastes. It's a, I don't know"—he looked into reclining Arthur as if his father had the best word possible—"a *stalk*, that is what it is, a bean? Strong but it's, well, it's"— Mick's eyebrows lifted as if a hawk might be about to land on his head—"it's, in-the-wind, it's—. . . weak."

What to say? "Mick, I'm telling you: with practice —"

"I think it is that I see Hung as"—another shrug— "vulnerable?—too muchso, in this day and age. As I could be hurting her."

Ohboy kid are You on the wrong Autobahn.

"Mick, don't worry about hurting her."

Mick went shock-eyed: his sensitive father could seriously advise such a callous thing? Mick looked as if he had just witnessed a man leap and plummet from a building.

"Hung," he said. "She has ever been a demonstrator for rights of those without. A *demonstrator*—the most dangerous thing in China, unless you are demonstrating against any *anti*-Chinese, like Tibet. I love Hung's way to be a woman, her kindnesses but that she does not suffer the fools like that slapping lady. I love Hung's way to be a woman, so not like German girls—she's stepping back but it is forward."

Arthur nodded total comprehension—which he felt that he might possibly possess.

"But yet," went Mick, "I don't know why, I feel I must stand before Hung and cover her like a weapon-proof vest, protecting. It is not her lookways, I am sure of that, the Asian facialness."

"Mick, I never even considered that," said Arthur. He wanted very much for his son to know that there was not the slightest chance of his considering the boy a bigot—at least regarding Asians.

Then, a brainstorm: "Mick, have you considered what, well, what they used to call the female-superior position?"

"Hung on top?"

"That might make the . . . the 'rock' easier to—"

"I have considered, father."

"But . . . ?"

"It's the Chinese."

"Huh?"

"I am not so experienced, but—"

I figured that.

"But, it's the Chinese, the Chinese woman. I don't know if, by now, although they are so advanced in these days, that the Chinese woman is ready, or knows how quite natural, the—what you call the Chinese woman superior position. It leaves them so full exposed."

Full-doubting Becker let that slide.

"And then, my feelings for the embarrassed Hung would—I'm afraid—well . . . soften me."

Mick pressed and rubbed his cheek, a probing psycho-sociologist (youth jowls were forced outward by the rubbing—not a pretty thing to see):

"Maybe it is the presence of Hung's parents, so close, so much *in* everything. I've said this to her, and she has sworn it is not necessary, China changes—and I believe her, when you consider who her father is and how he risks his life and limb for rightness. He is like an angel."

Some angel, the ass-fuck prescriber. Guess Mick doesn't know about Hung's hopping a getaway train for Hong Kong. . . Well, she did turn back.

"It is like, in deeply, the Chinese are so different," said Mick, "Still they are. They simply are. I just have to say that."

Then it hit: *Die Juden in diesem Deutschland.* Arthur said: "Mick-ah-yell, you are a Jew here, more than you were in Germany."

"Father, I wasn't a Jew in Germany. Not at all."

But Nyemo the Tibetan: HE was a Jew in Germany. He is.

"Those Chinese *ways*," said Mick. "The difference, the problem: Our home, Hung and mine, it could be occupied at times, at many times, by Chinese relations—and many."

"You'll handle it."

"The privacy: we Germans, we love our privacy."

We Germans!

"But they, the Chinese, they will walk right into the toilet when you are in there doing. What you Americans call, 'doing your duty'. Can you imagine?—they will walk right in and talk like nothing. They put, perhaps you have noticed, they put covers, plastic covers, over all things. Over the remote of the TV. Over sofas, chairs, bookcases."

Arthur recollected his original entry into this room at the Hotel Prince Gong: his puzzling bizarro confrontation with the plasti-coverings over chair and hassock—which were already so well-used, rumpled, on tear's borderline; even, with the transparent plastic, they had dust-drifts. It was annoying, crinkling-noisy, as if the butcher were wrapping up your steak or grinding it.

Mick was still talking: " . . . and they push their children so too hard: the piano, the maths. They are like stones rolling upwards. I don't know if I want to do that. . . . I *don't* want to do that."

Yup: Hung and her poor Tschaikovsky. That resistant painful wrestling.

Arthur stood up from the bed, just before his worrisome complaining son. He expected his son to stand from the ottoman, to face him. But the boy did not. As if he were about to drink water from a spring, Mick cupped-up his palms before his mouth and nose—it looked religious. It also looked like Mick just wanted to be small, an acolyte, a son.

"Kiddo" (Arthur, just wanting to be a father—but a father-light), "you're looking for roadblocks. And so you're making them. Once you get a handle on your blockages, you won't have any trouble with the sex. I'm sure of it. Once you get relaxed here and get going you won't be a Jew-in-Germany-in-China."

Damn did I have to say that last: Shit, it flew out, me the insistent crow. Jew-crow.

"Father, *blöd*," went Mick.

"I'm sorry. I shouldn't have said the Jew stuff."

Mick finally stood from the unpleasant lumpy ottoman—he even wobbled in his rise. "Father, I have to say: I did not *choose* to be Jewish and I did not *choose* to be *not*-Jewish. As I said, I was *not* a Jew in Germany—as you keep *thinking* it. Your thinking, it is like an, well, it is an impotence."

Of course he's right.

But, damnit, I can't change on that: I'm sorry and

I'm not so fucking sorry.

"Mick, I'm sorry."

Mick was still part-awobble, he looked dizzy, his blood hadn't risen with him when he stood?

"I too," Mick said. "For you, father, sorry. You have so seemed to have *needed* it, the Jewish-me, and I have always needed to *deny* it." Mick had borrowed Hung's protuberant ocean stare—or it was his standing dizziness? "No, for me too I am sorry."

Hesitantly, amazingly, Mick-ah-yell now touched Arthur's arms and he maintained that electronic-appearing linkage."Father, oh, you know, I turn the truth a little bit—I have had to: Maybe I did feel somewhat your Jewish, its being inside of me."

"Thanks, kid."

"No, I do say it not for you, but for me. I must now: In China now, being not what everyone is, yes now I can feel to see it, I can feel your need for me for it. Father, when I was little—you will laugh now—I tried to look myself all over and locate the Jewish parts or possibles, and sometimes I felt that they might, well, quiet, secret, crawl up in me."

Crawl!?

Oh well.

It was as if there were a deeply honest second self within Mick that had been bottled-up, by let's say that *Deutsche comportment*; and China, or Jin Jianxin, or Hung, or even Nyemo and his alien place here, they had all gone and popped that Mick-tight bottle-cap. Mick might gain now some hardwon self-possession, far more than that lame core he had lugged here in his psychic luggage. . . Hoping it might foster a real honest embrace, Arthur followed-up on his son's holding of his arms. Hold the holder. Had such enfolding *ever* happened before? It felt as if they were clutched-up underground in an air-raid, bombs falling.

Me struggling to be Moe's boy.

"You want my blessings, then."

"For the Jewish?"

"For the marriage."

Mick went actually grinning. A wan grin that exploded.

"I thought at first that you thought I was asking for your blessings for the impotence. For the marriage with the impotence."

My kid Does have a sense of humor then. Hoorah.

"For the marriage. I do give my blessings."

Did I just honestly say that?

Mick wished the blessings of a man who knew that the young woman of the blessings was not exactly the young woman beloved of the blessed son. Truth, the ruiner.

And what if "truth" were not the ruination?—and Mick married Hung anyway, knowing all.

Mick would. It was possible. It was likely. It was almost certain.

"Mick," said Arthur, "I love you."

"*Gott*, when have you said *that* before?"

Arthur could not remember. If he ever had, exactly.

He repeated it: "I love you."

Their embrace, honest, but an honesty relying on a dishonesty? on a withholding—a blessing of omission.

How tender I feel now; it's almost unbearable.

Had I ever felt such melting way with Moe?

Arthur Becker forgot that he was a murderer. A rare thing, that forgetting. An inhuman thing, such fatality of memory. Of memory of fatality. Of sin striving to be blessing.

This lasted seconds.

"Like me," said Mick, "our children will be split halfs and halves."

"Mick, I'm sorry, for splitting you."

"No."

Just before opening the hotel room door to leave, Mick said, "Hung, if it is okay—she would like to speak with you. Alone. All alone. Without me in presence."

"That's . . . nice." *That's . . . interesting.* "She's a fine girl. Woman."

Despite her dicey activities with The Tibetan, but because of everything else about her, *everything*, Arthur did believe that Hung was "nice". Hung was very "nice". Nice as you can get—he could even admit to himself that he envied Mick, that if he were younger he would love this girl. Hell, he *did* love this girl. He felt strangely flushed about that "love"—he thought it might be somewhat on the order of discovering religion; but he also felt creepy about that "love"—this was not religion.

"What about?" he asked. "Hung's speaking with me?"

"I don't know. She will not say."

"You have suspicions?"

"No. No, really. But she feels she must."

Hell, boy would I not prefer this. Courtesy-deference-respect for The "German" Father might in this case include premarital guilt admissions and guilt pleadings. Tears and consolations and regrets and promises and explanations and, from me, wise-man holding-hugs and understanding and—more promises . . . And urges, my own I can't stop. Those definite decided urges. In a trice of seconds Arthur entertained a sex fantasy—and then he entertained the guilt.

"Father." Mick with one hand on the door and one on his father's hand. "In China I have learned to not probe private intentions with another."

Ayah, Mick, come-on: you learned that close-to-the-vest business in Germany too. The Beijing-Berlin Emotion Axis. I'm not sure it's even politeness—maybe fear.

"China history," said Mick "says the within is a sacred space. Like as deeper. Like as touching." He looked at his hand on his father's hand, and he let go.

It was a feather-light liftoff.

When Mick left he did it backing-up, treading backwards. So as to continue facing his father? Theatrical, such dissolve, such reduction, Hollywood, were it not Mick's inborn polite *Mittleurope* way.

When Hung appeared Arthur couldn't help but up the sex-confession odds. In her dinner dress, Hung small-to-teensy-stepped into Arthur's room. ("As if her feet are still bound," that image inescapable [and perhaps intentional]). And she entered frowning, nicks forming beneath her narrowed cheekbones; and she was damp-eyed ("As if she is leaving Mick?—on 'The Midnight Train to Hong Kong'?"). Or, this is a contrition face?—and an excellent one. Or, rather, once she had entered and confronted an attending Arthur, who was doing his best to wear a sympathetic look—which likely came out as a confused look (as he *was* confused)—she brushed back that falling filament of her straight black hair and touched a tear at the corner of one eye, not to point it out of course (although this possibility also occurred [or appealed?]) but to suppress it; then she moved her finger to stifle the tear in the other eye (which nose-crossing might well have seemed a cryptic religious sign?). Then she circled the room, more of a circumscription it (as it was kidney-shaped), nervous, a skulking stalker who was being stalked. It was clear that Hung was taken aback that her fiance's *father*, Mick's estimable Amero-German writer dad, a man of international experience (well, she *might* have thought that, damnit), should get himself holed-up in such pitiable quarters as this grungey economization provided at the Hotel Prince Gong—a lodgings of which she'd likely never heard tell. . . Ought Arthur touch her? Ought he hold her? He did wish to, badly, perhaps as much as his son wanted to marry her. Such cravings—and we must call them cravings—are not perverse, especially (he told himself) when the girl in question, or young woman, is so foreign in a manner one has never quite witnessed as normal in the West (not considering even one's own good wife): the politeness intrinsic with its idealism, the brave-vulnerability, the absence (seeming) of anything ulterior, all like, what might you call them, Arthur, you idealizer (part-time idealizer)?—leafs of colors tame, even dry, yet flashing too, and an intelligence that has learned its own right temper—no, a cognizance, that's it, a knowing when-and-where, that's how she fits herself. Alright, the *humanity*: one wishes to enclose her humanity, to embrace it. And the beauty, don't forget Hung's beauty in that gamin heart (again, seeming, seeming); one would not even trust such a heart in the West, one might even laugh at it. Except (or especially) on a theatre's stage—of a play set before, say, 1900. So, not yet, Arthur Becker, no clasping and holding Hung to oneself—your estimations are likely so wrong anyway—so driven by your own problems—you know that. Anyway, Hung would have first to slow down on her room-rangings for a hug, just bring to a halt these edgy circumnavigations and inspections. And still Arthur's touches would be too rash—even if bolstered by his newfound bear hugs with his son. He simply tried now to set his face into a mature innocence, Mister SuperNice Tabula Rasa. At one time he'd been good at this, quite good (his dread of a dad Moe welt-boosting belt-whomping had inaugurated it—and perfected it); but now he could not dredge up innocence.

"I am so a whore."

Holy Jesus, I would have preferred a bit of beating-round-the-bush.

I would have preferred no bush, no beating, no admission.

Hung made her whore declaration not with the meek sorrowful or repentant voice that might have been expected to accompany tears, but with the sort of sharp-swollen black-eye vehemence that one might have employed to announce, 'I am a patriot!' Or 'I will fight for the inalienable rights of all the world's dis-possessed—*damn* you!'

An obsidian declaration.

Then, she repeated the whore-phrase faintly, thinly, all lament.

A tattered whisper meant to solidify.

161

At a loss Arthur found himself a kind of flagless semaphore—whipping-up, flagging gesticulations of Gargantuan disbelief.

As cockeyed as it looked, this seemed so natural, a staunch denial by dumbass kinaesthetics.

It also seemed un-natural, quite phony.

Considering, from Nyemo, he did know the total score.

For protection? for bracing?, Hung held tensely to her collared pearls, pulling her neck downward slightly, as if in small prayer. She then collapsed into the room's one large easy chair which for some reason had been rejected by both Mick and Nyemo, and which crinkled and rustled due to its plastic wrappings. So bizarre, those wrappings—they mocked, damn them!

In her long black dinner dress Hung crossed her legs: functionally and prim (great calf muscles). But she was folding-in upon herself—she had begun to look porous. Then came, plainly, "I am not a virgin."

Still at a loss, Arthur went and volunteered: "Oh Hung, who is."

He'd meant that as minimization of course, nonchalant schlep wizardry.

It did not work: Hung wore a look of puzzlement and of resignation.

Are the Chinese as humor-challenged as are the Germans?

Hung stared intently at Arthur but beyond him, through him, as if to some sanctuary not yet created.

" 'Who is?' " she quoted him as a question. "*I. I should* be a virgin—for Mick-ah-yell. . . Although, Herr Becker, I still do love that other."

She's honest. She came right out and proclaimed it.

No American girl would reveal such a thing to her fiance's father. No German girl either—I don't think.

He tried: "Oh, Hung: We all still love our first. In a way, we do. That's just how we are. I think it's impossible to not be that way, and I guess we shouldn't *not* be that way. It shows we feel that first intimacy, that warmth that we had known about and then let ourselves go to be within, and feel the other's—"

You imbecile, shut-up.

Hung gathered herself to say, "Your Jutta?"

"Yes, Jutta. Mick's mother."

But actually he had been thinking more of Annetta Baron. Yes, Jutta was wonderful, the perfect girl for him when he had picked her up by the Andronico's cheese bin – or was it the vegetable stand? – and come to learn her equanimity (though never to absorb it), but Jutta had come about when Arthur was twenty-two. Annetta Baron and he had been seventeen. Smartest girl in junior year at Berkeley High—smartest kid, probably. Annetta and Arthur had been of the generation, the first generation in America, to make love—not as rebellion, not as philosophy, not as nothing-much-hook-up, just as culmination. They had sensed and known each other. Annetta had even had a girl-hunch that she could, at the right emotional times, ride pony Arthur on his back and make him come. You don't forget such profound-savvy-smartass teenage love.

In any case, Arthur had no more lessons to give here to Hung—and he could see that Hung could see that, and that he was quite uneasy with it all. His bullshit did not sound like bullshit because it wasn't bullshit, and yet it was bullshit, and it sounded like bullshit. It was like most things.

Tiny ripples had been curdling along Hung's throat as she'd gripped for emotion—or against emotion.

Becker had seen the same agitations form when Hung had struggled with Tschaikovsky before her demanding father.

He wanted to touch those lines along Hung's neck, as he had wanted at the family lineage hall. But of course before paterfamilias Jin Jianxin that had been impossible. What horrors would have happened!

Now, he could walk to Hung and touch her troubled neck. She had come to him. At least, to his room. He *could* hold her.

He didn't.

Arthur returned (retreated) to his accustomed position on his bed, his fingers again interlocked under his occiput on the cushions. By now his left shoulder ached pretty good, so he quick-changed to a perch-up on his bed's edge, his arms struts and straining. He tried to look like the most alert adult possible.

Hung said: "It *should* be necessary, my virginness. I hear such voice within. It is strong. And so I had to tell you, sir, tell you of it all."

"This is very honorable of you, Hung."

She's never called me Sir before.

"You are the *father*."

He said not a word.

"You do not wish for me to marry Mick-ah-yell?"

It seemed to him that he did wish it.

"I am not against it."

Wrong answer: Her eyes shot about, as if she'd spotted a mouse shooting across the floor. Or as if her eyes were racing about for words. She said:

164

"I am not a wildish girl—though some might think so of me, as if it is my duty, my being the daughter of freedom liberal Jin Jianxin."

"If you were a wildish girl, from what I hear of China, the New China, you would want to stay single like so many liberated now. And—excuse me—enjoy it."

An instant had her stiffening, as if she'd been slapped, as by that poor woman in the restaurant. But this was not a sagacious rigidity; rather a resistance:

"I wish to *break* from my father, Herr Mister Becker. He is too much anti-China, but he is in the *Chinese* way 'anti'. And I love Mick, and with Mick I can break from Jin Jianxin and also be not wild. And—well, I can from China rise above."

Sad familiar sadness. Hadn't I done the same with Jutta. But joining China was not for me social climbing—hardly—though Hung seems to have just said that about joining German Mick. Or American Mick. She loves Nyemo, that's the truth.

Prod a bit, as unsadistic as you can be: "Nyemo did tell to me your story."

At the mention of The Tibetan, Hung went neither rigid nor pale. She simply maintained her stiffened relaxation; her legs did not flutter, but they did manage to cross. Hung's calf muscles were so perfectly of the sort Western men conjure-with when observing dress-store mannequins or imagining flawless females who do not exist. Hung said—

"You have discoursed with Nyemo?"

"He came to me."

"Ah. I did think he might do so. But in any case, I do not wish to be mocked in our new free-girl land as what we call a 'leftover woman', an eat-aloner in a restaurant."

"You are very young to be so mocked."

"You do not know China."

He nodded his 'I know'.

"China, we catch an idea and we make of it a goal. An unflawed thing. We do anything, we think, to attain that goal. It is the ultimate. It is childish. Even as we hurt ourselves."

Arthur thought of that boy, Kuan, her nephew, who was being allowed free reign at the family lineage hall, destructive jangling little kid thundersqualls, this so as to be brought up in the fashionable "free-reign" way of The Fortune School, modeled on the "progressive" Swiss Waldorf Schools begun by Rudolph Steiner.

As if it were about to tilt over Hung leaned forward for balance in the giant chair. Yet even in that lurch, as with her small quick steps on entering the shoddy hotel room, there was that impelled grace, unavoidable; dance-in-all, dance natural and inescapable, it was in everything, it was libidinal, yes that—and Arthur felt a loss he had often felt, even from the first with Jutta: This girl was no Jutta, who was no dancer, who moved in chops of clockwork—she had no syncopation, what could you do. Jutta's grace was so large, enormous, all help for all folks (almost all), but it was always, always, not in her movement but in her character—and Arthur must you blame yourself for wanting one more chance, one more chance in life, life's dance—for young Annetta Baron's motions, those swaytaps way way back in decades—oh you'd love one more chance, just one, to touch such ways, oh just *wouldn't* you? to glide through—call them the sailing woman waters? At forty-six you are not so old, Hung would not see you as in your begun-sunset, she is too kind, she is too perceptive of your yearning, she could not be intimidated, she ...—*but what in the world, man? what are you thinking about?!—you are gliding, sliding, into the ethers, gone! You fantasizing schmuck* . . . Hung's huge dark eyes now went into a kind of gulp, a swallowing—call these her way of dancing too. Becker decided that if he wished he could interpret Hung's eyes as just Chinese eyes, woman-Chinese eyes, as on all those sex billboards he had witnessed on first bussing into town (what had that cocky-ironic young Brit beside him said: "This is the Year of the Woman in China; Beware the vagina which resideth in China"), or Becker could see Hung's eyes as a lure, a lure for *him*? Becker could decide to decide that Hung saw some similarity between he and she, some searching, even some violence, as ridiculous as that seemed—and that meant. . . *Oh you lunatic. You moron!* . . . Well, stranger things have happened. But what Hung said was—

"I am a *whore*. No other way to say. I have not told it to my Mick, but I must tell my Mick."

"No. Hung, no."

Come to your senses, girl!

You're going to tell Mick that Nyemo gave it to you you-know-where?

"No, yes I must tell it all to Mick."

"Please, Hung, no."

She folded her hands in her lap, a good obedient student—this was a bit surprising. She sighed, a sweet and reedy sound. Then silence—and the Beijing sounds outside could not fill it, not all those grindings and clangs, all that metal striking metal. . . She said—

"I have thought on it and I have so thought on it. Were China a freer land, an equalish land, and I am being honest with you, I would have linked with Nyemo for long and good and I would never have looked at Mick. I am sorry, but it is the truth."

No, she can't tell the kid, he's love's second best, the runner-up as winner; she can't tell my kid, not with Mick's just now admitted frangibilities down below. No call to burgeon Those substantial macho woes.

"Hung," he said, "if you have had relations, well, that is your—"

She again pulled on her pearls, now as if she were working at breaking the string. Let those gems drop away and roll along the carpet, goodbye the gems of life. As if she did not deserve those shining heralds.

He'd bet Mick had given the pearls to her, from the Volksbank debit card he and Jutta had given him for earning his *Hochschule Abitur*.

"Nyemo," said Hung. "*He* told? He *told*?"

"No."

Of course she knows he did.

She might even be proud that he did. Part of her might well. Part, strangely, of her respect for him, his genuine truthfulness—the careless way she'd wanted to attach herself to him at that Tibetan Bar, even while Mick had watched. She had been impolite to Mick, her intended, then. Inconsiderate. Even, one might say, cruel.

That Brit on the bus, he had also said that Chinese women were shrews—just hear them shrieking in the streets. But Hung is not like that.

Is she?

Mick will be henpecked?

Tears once more. Rufflings in that easy chair, that stupid plastic cistern of a thing. Those deep full moon eyes of hers were strongly swelling. His impulse: Go to her, she's no shrew. Console.

Father-comforter or lusting elder?—damnit I still want her.

Damn me!

She said, "I do not deserve Mick-ah-yell."

Who deserves whoever. Life wisdom of a horny forty-six year old

She said, "Don't you hate Nyemo? He is after all from such lower . . . grouping?"

Of all people, did she really say that?

"Hung, you don't hate Nyemo."

Those tears from before advanced now to weeping. She reached to the nite-table, where sat a blue-white box of tissues labeled in (Mandarin?) characters. They were not pop-up, like Kleenex or the German Tempo. She mined for a tissue-clump and dabbed at her eyes her cheeks her lips. Women's tears often render women radiant—at least to every older generation. Such tears can make men better than they are, for moments. Momentarily he felt as if Hung were not the daughter of "great" Jin Jianxin but of Arthur Becker.

Not the most comfortable of feelings.

"He is an animal, Nyemo."

Nyemo had actually said "wanton debauchery"—a phrase he had read or looked-for, and no doubt looked and looked and looked.

"It was what we did"—Hung through her tissues—"a generosity."

I didn't have that impression, but I'll go with her depiction:

"So: You are *not* a whore."

"Nyemo was so lonely-lost in Beijing. I felt sorry. The sorriness confused me and with me it makes a magnet, and then I learned the inside Nyemo—and then I did learn love."

Unsure of his understanding, Becker said "I understand."

It appeared then as if she were eyeing Arthur over the edges of her tissues. She said—

"And it continued then, I must say—the love. In its way, its passion, it just grew."

Within himself Becker watched that "passion". He found himself substituting himself for Nyemo.

His soul squirmed.

Hung said: "It was, I think, like leaping out of who I am, with Nymeo, while *being* who I am. To become who I am. A larger person, who I am. Does that make a sense to you?"

"Yes, Hung. I believe so. It does."

He decided to add, "I've done that."

"You have? How so?"

He shook it off.

Christ, there he'd been leaping out of himself and onto old Herr Strobel. He would never have done that, *being-who-he-was*; but he *did* do that, *being-who-he-was*. He'd even pretty much by now blamed his dad Moe for the whole lethal misfortune—while knowing that Moe had not had one molecule of blame. Moe had never killed a soul.

Unless that happened to be My soul—Arthur Becker's.

And, oh yes, Moe had killed his own. Body and its soul—or vice-versa.

Thus, despite Hung's so visible discomfort, and Arthur Becker's discomfort about that, all her reasons coming-up against all his reasons (some being the same reasons), he had to press: "You said Nyemo was an animal. . ."

She stiffened in the chair, which had her seeming not larger but smaller in that beige-red floral (plasticized-crinkly) oversized pouch. It appeared as if she were resisting someone's—Becker's—tugging her out of her private safety nest. She did not answer about Nyemo's animalistic manner.

"Mick," she said, "he is not an animal."

Don't I know that.

He had already seen Hung's regret for his son's benignity, especially at the Tibetan Bar. Despite her attempt to not show it, she couldn't but: her empathy showed pale, a sudden make-up dabbed-on by an invisible stagehand.

And that regret of hers hurt him—dad Becker.

Role model?

Still, Nyemo had said this whole shebang had begun months BEFORE Mick's arrival in Beijing. No betrayals here.

She began to weep again. This time Becker reached clumsily for the Mandarin non-pop tissues and handed her a clump. And as she received them from his hand she looked quizzical. Because he held onto her hand.

Because I held onto her hand?

He knew he was doing that, and he was surprised he was.

"I got . . . ," she said.

You got?

"I got so . . ."—she looked down at the cheap green-black hotel carpet—"wet," she said; "I got so . . ."—her eyes closed, as if the carpet were just too ugly, too unbearable to keep looking at—"I got . . . swollen?"

It took him a few moments to realize that she was talking, not about his holding her hand but about Nyemo's fucking her the way he had (and at the same time seeming to ask if 'swollen' were the appropriate English word).

How could she bring herself to admit this intimacy to her prospective in-law? China was so different. . . No, not China: Her.

Her voice had not been remorseful—as why should it have been. Her tone was simply flat. She took her hand away from his—not by any resolute yanking or determined drawing-away, but by a kind of wobbled lurching, as if she did not deserve to be held.

She stood and straightened her long dark dress, and her shoulders were slumping, so that one strap looped forward, as if trying to fall away from her, to detach, and she again seemed smaller than she was.

He stood because she had. He did not wish to stand before her, she seemed so small already.

And he, "mature Arthur," he didn't deserve their intimacy, this confession.

What he did receive was this plaint-weighted "Shouldn't I tell Mick-ah-yell?"

"I said *No!* I *meant* it, Hung. I *mean* it. *No!*"

He realized just then that if he sounded like anyone it was paterfamilias Jin Jianxin, a man with far more social emotions, societal concerns, than anything so petty as to be personal. The very opposite of his own father who only wanted to make the Majors, and about anything else—blacks voting, miners unpaid, sick street homeless, whatever—Moe couldn't have given a good-goddamn (and it wasn't until years later that Arthur had realized all this).

Hung now went and leaned on Arthur, her pearls pressed into his forearm, an apologetic branding which again kicked-off his fantasies, sad fantasies so desired, of oldster-he and girl-she. No, not sad fantasies—sorry ones.

"Before Mick came," she now said, "I would marry Nyemo."

That Tibetan sorehead with the thievery-rebellion and the ill-placed rantings and the underground paper "June 4"? Sure, I like him—but she'd considered marriage?

"Your father would not have approved."

"Yes. He would." Her roaming eyes said she did not mean it.

Her liberal-freedom father, all human rights, he would not have sanctioned such a liberal marriage. A freedom-marriage. No way.

I can't believe he would have. That posturing Jin, he's too conflicted, he's too ambivalent, he's too Han superior, foreigners beneath him. I could see that at their dinner.

"And now, I love your Mick. I do."

She's convincing herself.

It just happened to us—in a different way." She smiled distantly, eyes risen, as if recollecting a special instant. "Mick is from the West, and the West is better—all Chinese know that—although they do not admit. But it is not why I love Mick, I swear it. Mick and I, we are so the similar—Nyemo is so the wrong: Nyemo he will be dead."

Mick similarity, that I don't see at all. Blind as I am, benighted, protectively benighted—I admit it—but I'm not that blind.

And Hung, it struck—it finally struck: she had not uttered one word about Mick's admitted "problem".

She might have asked things about it. What it was. Was it normal? What it meant if it was not normal—or, worse, if it was. Mick's fence-straddlings? His racism? Pathologies even more perverse?

Maybe she had checked it out. Ten seconds on the Internet—*Impotence, Male*. (Maybe she'd have had to earmark it by modifying it with *Western*). In the old days she'd have had to go to the University of Peking Library, slunk the stacks, flipped pages while covering-up those pages so that no one else in the stacks would see what was her strange keen interest. . . And, maybe, eventually, in either case, she'd have given-up.

So why did she not pursue it now, The Big I, here while face-to-face with Mick's father, just venture-out Mick's "problem" with (you could say) the blood-progenitor of The Big I? Her grace here held her back?—her kindness, her not wishing to shame the father who had created the strange-performing son?

But smiling, she was *smiling* now?—and brightly—youth and their super-speed transformations, their volatility even when worried—that got him to smiling too. Damned if they didn't seem to reflect each other, he and she, Art and Hung (that was certainly untrue, but he repeated the couplet to himself—for the fun of its linkage and its sound? it could be nothing else but that.). By now her dinner dress had become not unlike her flesh—it had eased down smoothly and lost its wrinkles. She looked satisfied—Lord knew why—and she looked beautiful. So beautiful that an air in which they both were enwrapped played and lied to him that, indeed, they were lovers. . . Lovers that he and his wife Jutta never could be, never had been—not even from the first, this was true. He remembered how Jutta had never thought *Seinfeld* was funny, or any American politicians intelligent and moral, and how frustrating that void had gotten as it grew, though seemingly one might consider it such a nothing thing: Example: There sat Jerry and Kramer in a sauna, both men sweating profusely, and Kramer coming out with, "Whew, it's like a *sauna* in here"—and Arthur laughing and looking over to his young Jutta-wife who was just staring, as after all *a sauna is a sauna*, of course it's like a sauna in a sauna—what's so comical? Even Hung would have laughed at that, that Jewish humor, Becker felt sure of it, Becker so intoxicated with the Chinese girl—oh come on, damnit, you sanguine schmuck, Hung wouldn't have gotten that sauna bit either—and Becker did know that. But, hell, his knowing did not diminish his problem with Jutta, which, acknowledge it, which over the years you've seldom faced, that problem that had grown and grown: grown as he *needed* his wife, he *relied* on her—repairmen seeking, good doctor finding, insurances, friends, whatnot—in Germany. *In Germany!* And even as he respected Jutta, and admired her, he resented her abilities, her energies, you bet he did, more and more, as 'needing' was not love, and 'needings growing', that could wither real love's living with the years, it could further your seeing that once sexy German voice, that Dietrich guttural going spongey, going phlegmy (and never mind your own more fluted voice). And a man with his love diminished and seeping further, he could rage—*do NOT forget why you've just escaped Germany, why you'v HAD to*—and, well, maybe the the same thing would happen in China with Mick and Hung, he could see that, it would be even worse.

She now said, "Nyemo, I fear it, he is dead."

Metaphoric talk?

But what the hell do you know about the bluntness of the Chinese psyche? It seems closer to neither the direct German nor the voluble American.

Not ten minutes after Hung had gone from Arthur's room—and much more uplifted than when she had arrived—that was true—she was walking more on her toes than heels (what would she say to Mick-ah-yell?)—there was a knock on the hotel room door. It was polite, it was mild, yet it was heavy-fisted, a boxer consciously laying-out not a haymaker but a love-tap: that muffled rapping yet managed to exhibit insistence (the door resonated and it echoed—was it hollow?); nonetheless, the knuckling also said authority, undeniable, sheer firmness. Having not quite yet stripped-back-down to his comfy old Hanes (slightly torn at the elastic, so there was a gash that partially showed his pelvic notch, some stretch marks, and the edges of some longer pubic hairs) Becker had been busy pacing, stopping, staring, reviewing: he'd betrayed his son?—surely this was inadvertent and internal, he hadn't undercut Mick in any way, and considering Hung's confusion and her poignant uniqueness his behavior was, if not "chaste as morning dew", proper. *And anyway, why do you believe that you might have betrayed your son? as you DIDN'T betray your son, Mister Guilty Conscience.* So—Becker more than expected this intransigent door-knock, this solid-mellow klumpfing, to be by the couple, together now, in need of another go round, this time sweeter, more understanding, more familial, with all secretive hands finally on-deck. . . . He walked to the door, fully opened it. Two men, one sporting a swagger cane—or swaggering a sporting cane (multi-carved)? These men were fitted into rather attractively tailored suits (one was Dunhillish double-breasted: were these back in style?), wide ties (one was green with what looked to be garnishings of moons or ping-pong ball images—I Ching mishigas?) and broad lapels (which sported inch-diameter red-gold seals)—one wore wide horn-rims and carried a briefcase—no, an attaché, spiffy two-tone and unmetallic; the other wielded a brush mustache. The men were Chinese, they had buzz-cuts, definitely hi-price work by fashion parlor; but one had an ill-fitting (slanted) set of dentures (they implied eternal wiseass cackling, silly yet sinister). Having seen Mick and then Hung enter Arthur's room, and being operatives of some sort who might not wish to be interrupted, they must have patiently awaited their turn—Oriental forbearance with a portentous touch. The deviated denturite was speaking into his iPhone, a wrist model (which made him look as if he were licking the back of his hand); and he was conferring by way of a gravel-gravity, which might have been an acted tactic. He finished-up, disattached the plastic component and plunged it into his coat's side pocket. As if accompaniment, a squadron of jets roared over the Hotel Prince Gong—but this air-scrum had happened many times in the past three days. Both men were shorter than Arthur by two or three inches, but broader, considerably so, like wrestlers—side-by-side they shaped the lethal perfection of a leaden foursome. One had a boiled-red-lobster face, but it was not an angry face—maybe it was a drunk's. The other had scimitar-sickle sideburns which made it appear that he was running, or speeding, while not moving. Arthur had at first assumed that they were hotel employees, perhaps inquiring if he was enjoying his stay at The Hotel Prince Gong; perhaps apologizing for the lack of a TV and explaining that this was but a temporary absence, transitional ('Please, bear with us')—a new slimscreen plasma was on its way. But one of them said that they were sent by Chen Gang, which Arthur first heard as "chain gang" until they clarified that Chen Gang was Beijing Deputy Mayor, and they were, more specifically, from UMSEB; and because Arthur's expression still showed that he'd drawn a blank, the lobster-face spelled it out: the Urban Management Security Enforcement Bureau. Some kind of utilities or materials check was Arthur's immediate expectation then, he having become accustomed to such these last twenty-two years in thoroughly bureaucratic Germany (fireplace, chimney, heating, attic, roof tiles, driveway drainage, doors, door-locks, etc.). But this routine notion dispelled itself after approximately one stretched second—their smiles were too demanding, there was more than a whiff of overwhelming in how they'd come to plant themselves like football linemen (American football) and one kept clenching, harrowing one hand with the other as if savoring his next anticipated effort: These hubristic UMSEB boys intimated 'We are not schleps—*you, you schlep, You* are the schlep.' They did not flash badges or ID cards, nor did they ask if they might enter Arthur's room— they just entered as if they owned it—and Arthur felt his heart do a few staccato atrial fibs. He held out his hand to shake, and both men did take his hand in turn, and without exhibiting their obvious strength. (But— weird—they shook hands by contriving to stand to Arthur's left, so that Arthur had to balance uncomfortably, and beseechingly reach across his unstable body to make contact, while they came off sturdy-relaxed). Actually their grips were not only unmenacing but soft, surprisingly so, even as you felt the latent power, pincers bolted, clamped. Both UMSEB men wore Rolex-type watches (yes, until the crooked-dentured one had jettisoned his modish Walkie-Talkie he'd been sporting double-banded wristers), these Rolexy timepieces had glittery metal bands and overthick faceheads that implied excellent pro knockoffs (these care-made copies might well have been expensive in themselves, and they reminded Arthur of a joke he'd been told by that ironic Brit on the arrival limo: "A Mercedes swings by a Chinese man on a Beijing streetcorner, tearing-off his arm, and the now one-armed man shouts out, "Hey, my *watch*!"). Both UMSEB men had nostrils with strangely extending and bright platinum hairs (*that* was *very* weird: they bleached their *nostril* hair?), and both smelled of cologne—overabundantly: they were walking eau de toilette emporiums with muscles (like grapplers, Arthur thought, trying to look like brokers). One—the non- gnarled-dentured—was endowed with a cluster of gold-

179

capped teeth, which he exhibited recurrently, even with his unsmile-smiles. Oh he had practiced this. The three men stood before Arthur's bed—Arthur relieved that he had not already stripped down to his wretched shabby Hanes. The first hand-shaker, that same lobster-red face, said, "Sir, Becker, (*He knows me*) You supported Nyemo the Tibetan's 'terror-protest incident' in the Tian'An Men."

" 'Supported?' I . . ." Becker halted his squinted denial: he saw himself as a television character whose next line would be 'There must be some mistake'. He stood and waited. That seemed most normal, most manly.

"You traveled to Tian'An Men *with* the Tibetan, in the same Xiali car. This Nyemo, he was with *you* talking a great time in *this* room. You attended The Tibetan Bar. This Nyemo was of gravity concert."

'Grave concern': Arthur got the Chinesed-up cliché.

A moment later their past-tense-reference to what Nyemo was came to him: that *"was"*.

Without his directing them his wise shoulders hunched-in protectively.

Not his prerogative to *ask*, but his prerogative to remember Hung's fear that Nyemo was dead.

"Nyemo, he insulted the founder of the Chinese people, the Yellow Emperor. In many locusts in Beijing. You know that, no? Nyemo, he protested as well before, as at the pass of the Olympy torch when we, all China, we hosted The Big *Games*."

Both natty hulks eagle-eyed Arthur to make sure he comprehended "The Big *Games*"—for which, as Arthur knew, China had busted its total ass.

For terrified reasons, Arthur Becker said flat, "I'm

sorry."

Rather, he heard himself say it.

The men did not look surprised. Nor appeased. They did not look anything.

In a way Arthur Becker *did* feel The Tibetan a projection of himself. And despite the dangers—obvious now—he'd liked that feeling. It elevated him, a man who needed elevating—and importance. Still, to set things straight, and, face it, to save his own skin: "Nyemo is a fellow student of my son, from Germany. That is why we were together. We are foreigners, I and my son. That is all."

Coward—even if it's the truth.

In any case, his explanation seemed to not compute. Smirks were exchanged, those thick jaws and bermlike necks arching towards each other like those of wolves nuzzling, this in conspired and pleased success. . . But with, for some reason, a touch of self-mockery: they were too official machioso for any fool affection, for any boyish brotherhood.

"Nyemo," spoke the front man, "he had no *ganqing*."

"What . . . .?"

Why bother to ask! They knew he didn't know the word—he could see this. They were having fun with the Western idiot, like tossing a ball over his head and making him jump for it. This made their jobs worthwhile, fucking with a Eurodolt.

"No *wen*, no *wu*," added the brush mustache. "True feelings."

If anything, Nyemo has (had?) true feelings. Truer than had these two functionary assholes.

Arthur fought-off any sniggerings. He waited for

what was to be, evidently, wrongly, unfairly, inevitably?—his own fate. *What?—I'll be more lectured to? Blue-in-the-face. They've memorized their insipid script.*

Becker's fate: which when it came it couldn't have come, could it? because all he'd been doing was talking with these men, nodding, listening, student obeisance, coward obsequy, expressing no dissent, when his vision was suddenly taken up grainily by bits of lightning bugs to accompany the pains in his thorax, and his mind was reacting Run, Getaway—and *don't you goddamn move!*

'Don't move' was easy, as he'd been half-pushed half-thrown (and about an inch upraised) against the wall of his room where it faced the bed, and where that thinline plasma TV ought indeed have been situated. "Your warning," said the air (one man, the thrower, or the other—who could tell in the midst of such dislocation?). This happened so quickly that Becker had had no time to feel fear, only this strange bewilderment, this magnesium-lit not-rightness, a not-happening, an *I'm-not-here.* True he was not thrown full force, no— just enough thrust by a practiced strong-hand, forearm and wrist (the glittery Rolex band did clip his left earlobe) to let the weaker person, him, know that he had been thrown and he could be thrown once again, like a pitcher hurls a baseball—plus more and more. "Those distorts of Nyemo," said that main man (the lobster-boiled face, the non-thrower), "they can be convince, if you do *not* know China—you should not *be* convince, you should *know* China. In Nyemo's team you become a traitor, to the Harmony of The Chinese People."

'That's ridiculous,' Arthur answered. 'Harmony-of-the-Chinese-*people*?' Are you kidding? I haven't seen too much of that.'

No, he did not answer in that mind-bulging way—nor in any way.

Except, when the lobster asked him as he was still up against the wall, released but feeling like a standing fresco, "Are you okay?" he replied, "Oh, shoulder. Fine, fine, good, better, pretty good"—as if he did not wish to bother his body-thrower.

Did I actually just say Fine fine good!?

He saw that there was nothing malicious in the thrower's eyes, nothing, no abysmal rage, nor did such exist in the eyes of the other man, the scimitar-scythe sideburner, who seemed contented to just watch the event, a stand-by. Within these men, about these men, there was an aura, an undertone, that said they did not care, not at all, they spoke what they spoke, that scripted baffleblabber, but they were voids, vacuums: they would just as soon hang laurels round Arthur's neck as hang him from his neck. Some form of distant essential, robotic and normal human materielle—that was what they two comprised. No hatred; no contempt. . . Such realization, when you are not being amused by it, was terrifying, the old Arendt evil-banal crappola; but it also allowed Arthur a distance—a permissiveness, as if he, like them, were not fully there:

He hesitated to say the following—then he said it:

"Nyemo did nothing. All he did was holler insults. That's nothing."

And that was all that Professor Herr Strobel had done—no? You are like these guys.

"Nyemo, Tibetan, he sodomed a Han—and that is true."

Becker was stunned by their possession of that

knowledge.

How would they know what Nyemo did?: Jin Jianxin?

The thrower said: "You don't believe Tibetans do not rape and *kill* because they are 'good *Buddhists*'?" He stretched out his arms (the amateurish cut of his jacket forced it up at high mid-rib—it looked as if he had great bat wings, as if he were some flying monster hailing from some sixty million years before caveman days). "Ah," he went, "the *Mmmmmmmmm-Mmmmmmmmm-Mmmmmmmm.*"

The Mmmmmmm-Mmmmmmm-Mmmmmmm?

Arthur, still up against the wall, still a frightened fresco, hears those barbaric *goût* groans as pure relish: a cannibal in an Abbot and Costello movie about to toss mashed-Arthur-potato into the broth pot—they were going to beat him to a pulp. . .

No: The *Mmmmmmmmer* was mocking the deep-mellow moan-groan of the long Tibetan ground-horn. He enjoyed disabusing a USA schmuck of the finer points of fake Religion.

"Nyemo," said the thrower. "He was in Re-Education School."

I can imagine what that is. Plus, that 'was' again.
Jin Jianxin told!?

Arthur pictured what he could not picture. He had written once on German (and French) incarceration verses American. The German prisons, he remembered now, he could have tolerated as an inmate—for say a month. The American, a half-hour—tops. (The French would not allow him to inspect their insides).

"May I see Nyemo?" Arthur asked.

"See?"

Arthur nodded, by slow respectful fractions.

Both men smirked.

" 'See'. The Nyemo? That is impossible."

"I really would like to go and see him. I wouldn't cause any—"

"Nyemo, he can no longer be befouling the girl Hung. He was in the 'black jail'."

That *'was'*.

"Black jail? It means not a real jail?"

Once again the men exchanged amusement. "As India is to China," cracked the chaotically dentured, "the black jail is a real jail." Whatever that "witticism" meant, it was clear that these UMSEB boys were having a real fine time.[10] Their broad cheeks looked to be competing for comic stretchability. The brush mustache man clicked open his ugly-tasteless attaché. "Black jail," he announced, as he extracted a tablet with screen, a Chinese brand with only Chinese characters; he then pressed the one looming oversized dark button. Nyemo appeared on the screen. He was handcuffed and sitting crosslegged, wearing only dark-tight underpants, nothing else. He was caked in dirt, rings of filth curled round his neck, jagged lines of sludge streamed along his sides—old blood?—down to his already wasted-looking belly; pieces of colored rags lay by his now-thin thighs (rags for an unknown purpose but some easily imagined); the room was also caked in dirt, its walls wrecked and streaked with thick-dripped letterings, along which crawled a not-so-furry rat,

---

[10] As sadistically fine as the quip Arthur had often rendered about America's "waterboarding" of supposed terrorists: "We had a great time on our vacation in Hawaii; we surfed, we speedboated, we waterboarded."

licking at draining drops of water ("That is from the toilet upstairs," explained the teeth-challenged state official). Nyemo's head hung, as if he were staring at the concrete floor, which canted down to a pewter drain with a grayish paste floating on top of it, not draining. Even with his head hung, even through the spaces of the cell bars, one could see Nyemo's eyes, his big fatal-looking almond-shaped eyes, once so sensitive and decisive: they had gone so thickly sappy that they appeared like shreds and dollops of a rancid pudding—the gruesome silence made it all distant and immediate, you didn't hear but you smelled it, that dank-chill odor of murderous rot, of mold and of Nyemo shit—it was so hard to look and harder not to, so you looked and looked and looked. But who in the world wasn't accustomed to seeing such scenes and hearing of them?—old hat on UTube. No, you had to know the person congealed into this barbaric stew to feel anything—and Arthur Becker felt (and he realized that he felt more trenchantly than he ever had about his own people in Auschwitz or Dachau, etc.). He decided to not ask these flash-loving blinged-up palookas anything about it—is Nyemo given food? how is he allowed to pass waste? (if he is not dead) will he ever be released?—in condition to survive? No straight answer would come, only accomplished grins, this brutality joyous and indifferent, a reason-for-itself, you knew that.

The lobster said, "You are leaving China. We are here to advize."

"I am on the plane tomorrow. Lufthansa, you can check."

Absolutely this was the truth, spineless as it was.

A real man might cancel departure—or postpone.
Maybe I will.
I can't.

The thrower, that well-dressed accomplished bruiser, began whisking up-back with one hand Arthur's upper body, as if to wipe away the cocksure-filth involved in his having thrown him. Arthur accepted the mocking sweep like a punch, he took it. This had him feeling as if he were Nyemo in black jail, and it had him feeling sickly ashamed for the lame and false comparison. He stood there and he took those mocking bruiser whisks across his chest, as if his chest had fleas.

Okay, gather courage, ask:

"Is Nyemo dead?"

They exchanged their glances, as if How many ways did they have to explain the obvious to this naïve Western pinhead writer who knew zero about real life? The swagger-cane UMSEBer now reached into the vest pocket of his sweet-sharp sportscoat and brought out a folded newspaper page; he opened it and absorbed it with a punishing sort of watchful grin; he stared at his comrade, as if for a final okay, then he showed it to Arthur: the newspaper was in Chinese characters, but it displayed a half page wirephoto of severed male heads on spikes—five of them; the heads-on-spikes must have been Tibetan—Arthur guessed that; they yet looked alive; the background was not a cell's sickly walls but an expansive country plain with distant peaks—it might have comprised a painting on the Jiang ancestral lineage hall walls; or perhaps that vacant redoubt where The Wall had crumbled, the famous ancient Wall. The head-spiked men were still adorned in colorful woolen Tibetan caps that came down around their ears and necks in twists like a girl's pigtails. Each might have been for sale as a doodad (*a conversation piece?*) in some brokendown Hutong district alleyway. Perhaps Ricky Rubalcava owned one and used it as a lure out front of Havana Heaven, his America Fifties Auto Lot.

Irony never ends.

What would this poor world be without rich irony?

The wirephoto might have been years old. Or from yesterday. . . And no, from the shrinkage of the heads and the wrinkledness of the newspaper you could not tell if one of the doodad-spiked Tibetans was Nyemo.

Satisfied, fright-mission accomplished, the men from UMSEB had cruisingly taken off, like U.S. congressmen escaping a seniors tour from, say, South Dakota, and leaving Arthur hollower than even his sorrow, an impossible pining for the heart's born core. Just like him, Mister Mobius, he wanted just now to have appear his wife Jutta, who, tell-the-truth, he had not really appreciated in quite a long time. Jutta with her many many school stressations, all that inevitable obsessive generous *work* of hers for others—a true Christian. Have Jutta now, huddle up with her in bed and maybe even just watch her assiduously reading PhD thesis submissions as if they meant The World's Cure; or, sure, sure, they'd watch a TV-streamed Netflick (*LoveFilm* in Germany), romantic ridiculous nothingmuch *Notting Hill* for the umpteenth time (their favorite—a nobody loved by a movie star [and for no conceivable reason but the nobody's just plain awkward *niceness*])—or, better, he should be with Jutta now in spirit on that first night they had slept together in his small bedroom on Cedar Street in Berkeley (November,

'89), after walking out of The Solano Theatre, after they had seen, what?—ah!—*The Fabulous Baker Boys* (two nobodies given-up becoming piano stars [one sourly, one caring not at all])—and with Jutta wearing her Berkeley couturier-costume of white Osh Koshes, carpenter-painter crisscross-strapped over her breasts (in black T-shirt, which had them appearing both larger and smaller at the same time), and they both discovering from shouts and cheers on Berkeley's Solano Avenue that The Berlin Wall had just been jackhammered and axed, screwdriver debricked and carried-off to History, and East German folks were pouring out, unafraid of guard-orders of being shot— and Jutta cheered (and Arthur was embarrassed: *East, West, they're all still goddamned GERMANS!*). . . In his crappy Prince Gong room now he happened to look out the window: there were the intimidating men from UMSEB, his attackers, and now they were lumbering, now they were like oldtime bulky Mafiosi—and sonofagun they went and entered and drove away in what appeared to be either a Chevvy Malibu or a Ford Fairlane from the Fifties—Becker didn't know his old cars *that* well, but he knew that those two crude (but snazzy-dressed) lummoxes had got their cars (or had had them bought for them by the government?) at Ricky Rubalcava's—it had to be from conning Ricky. Palm-greasing importer, happy-face hustler, that homesick Cuban, damned if he didn't know how to get-along to go-along (or was that the opposite?)—and Becker, down-at-the-mouth failure (or semi-failure) he was, you bet, envious. He then stripped down to his Hanes and slipped into bed, and stared, just stared, and he almost soppily believed, for a moment anyway, that

Jutta, good Jutta, might open the room door and come walking in to be beside him and to be that beloved woman (once again) who understand all or tried so very hard to—and that the UMSEB men with their tossing him, with their wirephotoed trophy of severed Tibetan heads on spikes, with their Nyemo-dying, they had not come through his door and warningly flattened him against the room wall, and they had never happened.

So, Mick and Hung would marry now.

And Becker pictured his kid Mick's Chinese kid or kids.

His Chinese grandkids—halfbreeds.

Like Mick.

And knowing of Hung's true genuine hot desires Becker might still have kiboshed that marriage deal, or tried.

But, knowing of Hung's other desires, which were also true, and knowing Hung, he could respect that marriage deal, he could approve this union or even relish it—he could try, and he would. Mick couldn't beat a Hung in Germany. No Hung-like Fräuleins brought-up there. *You kidding me!*

Okay, Jutta, the closest on that match.

Except, one of their kids could be Nyemo's.

A different kind of half-breed.

Becker and Hung's shared knowledge.

(Do Schwäbisch-Jew-Mandarin (Tibetan?) mixes turn out facially first-chop?)

But why, Chrissakes WHY?, would Nyemo have been so stupid as to have proclaimed his infidelity to this nation, his hatred of Empire China, at of all places Tian 'An Men?—the last sacred center in the Chinese world to shout out your sedition! Nyemo had known what would happen: Black Jail rather than daily nothing-much macherhood at the rebellious underground JUNE 4 and the Tibetan Bar. Enough of La Résistance underground fulminate and its pathetic truths that no one reads—the Jews in Germany had had these too. And in Poland. And in Hungary. American Commies too—no Black Jail for them, just the highfalutin Blacklist. Literacy, the last refuge of a humanist impotent who's read books. No, Nyemo would leave "his" Hung for "my" Mick, an acceptable substitute (once he understood good Mick's real good), and he would have achieved his martyrhood, to be lauded, worshipped even, in those subterranean-sunk-snuffoutable pages of JUNE 4; while no practicing Buddhist, he would be a canonized glory-soul sans the self-immolation. . . And for what though?—ain't that always The Big Question. Surely not for My Western benefit. Perhaps to embarrass this conquering Go West Young Man Eastern nation that had conquered his own native nation in its going. Yes, that. Of course, that— Going Going Gone! . . . . But Cynic Becker finally, ultimately, answered his own question in his own Cynic Becker mode: Nyemo was a martyr mostly for Nyemo— humans, they got the psycho-warts: humans cannot escape their being Human. And Becker the Pillow Strangler on the lam, he tried his best to believe that true lie and to not believe. Becker the lam a lamb.

So, call it a cadenza. If you will. But what you're contemplating now, lowlife as it is, un-natural-natural as it is, you're *driven* down to it, let-it-all-hang-out! (that's your excuse) (*that's your excuse?*), this foray you're about to be about, it runs counter to the exhortations of the human rights people, and also of the human health people, and also of clinical psychiatry, and the church—every church, and, so, morality. And the law—but which is probably the only one of those above six which lets it slide, the law being practical, being realist, all flex—and thus frequently a participant. It's normal though, no?—what you're contemplating now. Normal as is Death. As is fearing it and (admit it) craving it. And far more normal than what we wish it wouldn't be so more normal than—the NDE (Near Death Experience), with the tunnels and the floodlit confabs with (usually) Jesus—in English (Modern Idiom English too). What Becker was contemplating now was also a tourist tradition, a tourist disorder—the Traveler's Lust. Well, no reason to become a monk. Especially as just now you are done here in China, and you don't wish to be, while you do wish to be, and so you are feeling it, a splitting-tugging emptiness which becomes that old goat groan: The Alte Cocker Hooker Blues. Especially as now you are bereft of a man you have come to consider a brother—you find you have felt this (once you've realized that you've wished it all along, insipid as was that wish—*face it*), that weird Tibetan, a twin brother it occurs in brave act and vocalese?—and amazingly you really are feeling empty and deprived because you, Arthur Becker, have not had brave act and vocalese, but cowardice—and so "that old goat groan" may well be just now an-old-goat-purgative, a mourning hard-on, no pun intended. Or a punishment, for (somehow) not having helped that

Tibetan kid? Or a substitute for the patent non-possibility of Hung, of your having fancied being naked with her, hugging her that way, attached to her, making love to her. (And *he would have* had there seemed some possibility). He'd been to a hooker before, once, he wouldn't lie, especially not to himself on that conduct, like most guys did—just like they bullshit that they never get colds. One prostitute he'd met in, of all places, a Laundromat (well, maybe that wasn't so weird.). He'd already known Jutta, but they were not yet a full-fledged couple (because she had never really turned him on—truth is truth.). The black woman (what could you expect?) had lied that she was also a Dental Assistant, but told the truth that she was also a "bigtime" Forty-Niners fan. On a Sunday then they'd watched Joe Montana and the Niners on Becker's ancient TV, and this girl—he'd forgot her name—she was witty, natural-gift-sexy, bold, intelligent, ironed-straight hair (which yet somehow managed a softish flow)—she'd taken hold of his unready dick on a long-pass Niners score to Jerry Rice, applied a rubber, quipping that "You'll grow into it, my man." (Seeing that he was circumsized, she did say as well, "You're a Jew. How come there's no Jews bangin' heads in the NFL?" [He hadn't wanted to say "As a rule we're too small", or "We're too intelligent" [or cowardly?], so he'd shrugged and said "There's a few."—which there were.]). Although she'd never kissed him (he did try and try—he'd loved her full ironic lips), Becker thought this girl was great, better than any Berkeley girl he knew, so wise-loose, so unprincipled-principled, and so he asked her out, for a *real date*—dinner, whatnot; and she regarded him as if he were a pervert more demented than any crack-brained screwball she'd ever met in jail. A sado. A maso. And as perspicaciously as might any tenured sociologist at Cal she explained hooker-john fundamentals to him, Prostitution 101, re privacy's dignity and its rights, inalienable. Comic, bemused-grinning, even sensitive and sympathetic, she'd elucidated her Declaration of Independence. And for that lesson he loved her more—and, to follow through, out of respect, he never called her again; and Becker never did drive the streets like any low-souled John. Never! So, there was his sole prostitute experience all wrapped-up in one, and he'd always (kind of) relished it. But now, here in Beijing, he was, finally, as if a dare were involved, following-up. Maybe a girl great as the "Dental Assistant" might appear. . . In thick enticing numerals, Mandarin-shaped, there was the phone number on that card on the nite-table—the one slipped under his door almost moments after he had taken guest-occupancy of his "economy"-rate room in his Economy Hotel. The card that read CERTIFIED ADULT HEALTH PRODUCT. The sort of card, the sordid card, that at other times might have you washing your hands after touching, just touching with your fingertips, as if the ad might infect you (well, who's to say who was the door-sliding deliverer?): Chinese Sex Cooties . . . He called. The woman on the other end picked-up before he heard a ring; in a hoarse-raw voice (a woman of an extremely certain age, this madam) she spoke English—pidgin-broken but good enough for conducting any transactions. He made the inquiry. The woman corrected his "girl" request to, word-for-word, "Certified Health Product": The ADULT expunged, as ADULT must have meant filth possibilities. The woman asked "Girl or Boy?" Just about kneejerk, he inquired after a Tibetan. Tibetan had not been a forethought.

"Girl or *boy*?" she insisted, as if boys were a delicacy little, but ought be better, given a shot. An acquired taste.

Becker could just see her kimono smirk, tired and sarcastic.

"Girl! *Girl!*" *No, be nice, don't exhibit your insecurities—which, damnit, plague Everyman.* "Girl. I want a girl."

Laughter. Cackles of ambiguity. Not so different from the sniggering mirth of the two UMSEB rumproasts who'd just left him—job well done. He heard the madam utter words to others nearby, and they laughed. Some of the indolent laughers in the background had various, itchyish, male voices.

He deduced:"You have no Tibetan girls?"

"Extra yuan, Tibetan."

"Yuan? What?"

He'd been so taken-care-of by Mick and Hung that he'd had no need to learn what all tourists learn: simple currency. That lack of exchange knowledge, weirdly, had had him feeling superior.

"Meiyuan," said the madam. "Dollars. More for Tibetan girl. She only one in house. Rare fillet. Loin tendersome. Special good too for peters sleepy. For healthy misters too."

Again the peripheral chorus of muffled mixed-sex laughter.

He didn't lower himself by insisting that his penis was *not* slumbersome. *(I'm gonna get in a dick-mass dispute with a Chinese hooker CEO?!).* Edgy, he obsessively pictured the bordello headquarters—and in degenerate detail: a narrow low-ceilinged corridor in unsteady polluted light, opaque and leading by multi-eroded floor to a crooked shabbily slatted door with a smudged and misty chicken-wired window, behind which could be red velvet draperies all tattered, crappy shag rug and beaded curtain, chlorine stench, then a floor-length TV (for "operatives" on temp-hiatus) showing, what? a Bruce Lee kickapoo. . . He and the madam agreed on the price for the rental of the somnambulant schlong-prescriptive Tibetan girl.

He waited, in his habitual posture on the bed (fingers clasped at nape or testicles) thinking of nothing but sending the girl back upon her arrival—or just preempting that unpleasant scene by decamping *now* and walking the streets. After all, he still had seen only a fragment of Beijing. Reclining on the bed, he did become aware that his back did hurt, just at the thoracic, from that wall-slambang by the well-dressed UMSEB man. A Beijing walk would certainly make it hurt more, but then again sex with a Beijing hooker would have it hurting far more than that.

When the girl arrived, as if it mattered in the least, he pridefully told her he was not plagued by a sleepy penis.

She wrinkled-up her brow (her eyebrow-penciled line jagged-up-down like a moderate graph and then near disappeared), and she answered, "Sorry so?"

He replied, "Forget it."

She came back with a multo forte, "*Sorry* so?"

At her delicate door knock he had quickly thrown on jeans and T-shirt (well aware of the ludicrous nature of one's clothing-*up* for a hooker); nonetheless he found the girl staring discerningly, and disconcertingly, at his groin. She giggled a shy tee-hee and (for some reason) rattled her fuchsia cosmetics (and sex toy?) bag as if it were a piñata: Private joke? What had the madam told her?

She introduced herself as "Cherry-Cherry". What could have been a more loopy pun for a call girl?—especially a Chinese one, since the name sounded-out to Arthur as if it could be quite legitimate Chinese—in her tambourinish voice it resonated like "Chay-Chay". How many Cherries, or Chays, had been sitting around at the prostitutional roundtable of the Certified Adult Health Product Headquarters? Cherries Galore, hardeharhar. Cherries Jubilee. Cherry was a shade darker than Nyemo had been, and she had a broadened face, but only slightly; and of course dark eyes—which were unnecessarily, roundly, shadowed-up and lusterless, as if she had only moments before emerged wide-eyed from the thickened soot of a long-abandoned cellar or coal mine: she was, weirdly, pointlessly, impossibly, quite startled looking, as if she had come to quick-turn the usual nerdy trick and, as per instructions, make a quick getaway—but found herself facing the likes of George Clooney (Arthur hardeharhared himself again on that impossible notion). No, this shock-eye drill must have been part of her usual naïve presentation: Do What You Will to Me, Great Sir. She would have shown the same soft vulnerability to hunched-bald forthright but unprepossessingly sexless Bernie Sanders. Cherry's full cheekbones, needing no emphasis whatsoever, were emphasized by a brownish paste and chandelier earrings, and her lips were blindingly emblazoned with the sharpest red lipstick handleable by the human iris. Still, one could say she was attractive, her pug-nose (one-nostril-jewelled) seeming not punched-in but adorably intrigued upwards, like a good eager girl-student's nostrils might tilt in a classroom's front row—*teach me! teach me!*—it was as if that nose was in perpetual retreat from her slender upper lip. Her getup was what Arthur Becker thought of (thinking himself clever) as hooker-tricky couturier: bargain secretarial (mid-knee longish yellow dress with one wide stitched pocket lengthily efficient); multi-fluted Errol Flynn Robin Hood blouse, buttoned-up in *haut*-prim all the way, but see-through to stark black lacy bra; moderate heeled pointy-toed brown shoes and light ochre stockings to match her complexion. In a way she looked as if, after the polishing-off of Mister Becker she might be en-route back to her row-desk at the lowest-level government office job. But what was most endearing about Cherry Cherry, or Chay-Chay, was that enunciation of her mousy English, so light and so so tentative, a frightened-fragile crackbrained screwball, her speech reminiscent to Becker of no one but the "transplendent" stoned hippie in *Annie Hall* portrayed years ago by Shelley Duval.

But—"You are *cleanly*?" This, Cherry's requisite question, did ring with no-monkey-business admonishment.

"Spic'n'Span."

"Sorry so?"

He said, "You know, on cleanliness, I might ask you the same question."

This time she did not apologize, not with any words. She simply stood there, dark eyes balancing on her cheekbones like bowling balls, tentative boulders. There was even a bit of challenge now in her stance.

Sure he'd known there hadn't been a snowball's chance she'd have grasped his smartipants Spic'n'Span, but her fringe phonemes—which were of course far more ample than were his zero Mandarin ones—coupled with her requisite subjection—had transformed him into a smug-spined Laurence Harvey.

"I am clean," he amended. "Are you clean?"

"Very very clean." Cherry grinned, which raised her cheeks and momentarily shut her eyes. "Clean girl. Spicaspank. Sorry my English."

Admirable nymphet, she'd quick-picked-up on foreign idiom. Well, necessity in her employment—or her (it occurred to him) slavery. . . And again, certainly more than he could do in Mandarin.

"How do you know?" he asked. "I mean, you're spicaspank."

"How I? Lookover needle test: one week."

"*In* one week? Coming *in* one week?"

Meaning the previous blood test must have been back, what? six months?

"*Out* one week, it done. I am proved."

She cringed playfully while rubbing her bicep where the testing needle had been injected. But her widespread nostrils had begun to say indignation: You arrogant spoiled Western pig.

The pig made his calculations. Seven days or so; even *that* was not optimal, especially with all the chicken viruses that the world newspapers had reported were beginning their lives in China despite the megaton cullings—and all the penises from all over the globe that may well have ended their working lives within this sweet displaced (and likely maltreated?) girl, *within* the seven days in which she had been "proved". Let's see: seven times what?—say five per day in big popular Beijing. Thirty five. Odds hardly A-1. He had read up in the complimentary *Frankfurter Allgemeine Zeitung* on the Lufthansa plane: AIDS; Hepatitis A and B; Cholera—and hot out of Africa, Ebola. Plus the usual syphilis (*usual?*) and the garden-variety drip—and the not yet fully known sexually-transmitteds. *Der Schlong siegt über den Kopf* (the peter triumphs over the brain)—but that is when you routine-hat-trick-whack-off in a frat house or movie theatre (or psych class?) and are not forty-six years old. Already Becker's "instrument" was losing it *("already"!?)*—about to hibernate as had son Mick's for other, decent, reasons: why had he even considered this adventure? A zillion reasons, no? He wasn't even certain that sex was the main factor here in the sex. Of course it wasn't. There was that mourning for a Chinese German-Jew, i.e. a Beijing-Tibetan; there was homesickness (for *Germany?—god the world is weird!*); there was guilt over Nyemo—and guilt's confusion for guilt's guiltlessness (especially over that Fritz Strobel murder). And masochism, mustn't leave that dullish gem out, fella. Come on, hadn't there been some other way for Mister Herr Becker to have diverted himself? A productive way? . . . Curiously however, he was also determined here with Cherry Cherry, as if he were about to do a good deed for this girl, who being Tibetan was thus a stand-in for her dead countryman, a sister. Having been requested especially, this Tibetan girl might earn extra. Lotsaluck there, you're not *that* naive—and anyway, pity-screwing a prostitute? Shame to think this as any more than a symptom of, well, shame—self-punishment. . . Of course he knew full well she'd not get any extra pay—just as he doubted she really was Tibetan.

"Would you," he asked, "say something in Tibetan?"

"No under," she said.

Meaning she doesn't understand?

"Tibet—talk," he said.

"Yes," she said. "They talk, Tibeters. Yes yes."

"No," he said, becoming more than a tad impatient. "Words, in Tibetan. You. Say."

He pointed at her with his right index finger, as politely as he could—which meant he bent it: Which made his finger less potent.

She grinned and nodded; then she mumbled syllables, vowels; fluent Asian gibberish he was sure.

"Do you care," he asked slowly, "about the free-dom of your count-ry?"

"Cunt? You call me? *Cunt!?*"

"No. No-no." *Give it up.* "I'm sorry. Very."

She turned and knocked on his door, as if there were a doorman or guard outside who could let her out.

He heard light rumblings outside his room's inferior hollow door.

"What *is* that?"

The outside rumbles pealed into Becker's room like evil spirits, like sepulchral smoke.

"That the man," she explained in her coy Shelley Duval voice, as if a man outside your door while you are engaged in prostitution was pro-forma, a sine-que-non—the law. "For protect," she advised, "like prophylactic rubber."

A man like a condom.

Well, why not?

Had whoever lingered now outside his door (and was likely ear to that door) passed by the two men who had just "visited" from the Urban Management Security Enforcement Bureau? Was there acknowledgment? Humorous glances of knowing-corrupt indifference?: *Your* turn, good monster buddy.

Irony said 'Terrific'.

Cherry stared at Becker, scrutinizing his face as might a fatigued job interviewer facing the day's final 6PM applicant. Her eyes did not ascend from their angry world weariness, and suddenly she appeared no gamin but dense as steel. The Steel Gamin. She licked a middle finger and slipped her right hand beneath the waistband of her skirt and scratched, abstractedly, her behind. This was hardly alluring or beckoning. She was obviously waiting for her money. Becker asked how much.

"Yuan, two hundred."

Pliantly she cupped her hand and held it out, as if he were about to deposit a major heap of coinage, as if from his precious boyhood piggybank.

He said, "I have only dollars."

Aware that U.S. currency was standard, coin-of-the-world, he had exchanged some euros at the Frankfurt airport. He might have changed to yuan, but not knowing those monies he'd figured he'd be cheated.

"Dollars accept."

"How much?"

"Two hundred, same as yuan."

"Yuan equals dollars?"

"Eee-*kwall*."

He expected he'd be losing pretty good on such

exchange.

But why quibble.

Again: As he had been taken round and paid for during his four days by Mick and Hung he really had not the slightest conception of the monetary ratio, so again expecting that he was being swindled, and not caring all that much, he paid, handing over the dollars—ten crisp twenties. Which Cherry took to the door, slightly opening it, and handing the bills out to— well, Becker couldn't see—likely that door-guard man who was "prophylactic as a rubber".

A returning hand reached through the ajar door. In exchange for the dollars came colored pills. Cherry gulped no few and offered Arthur: M&Ms. They did look like M&Ms—the ununiform longish peanut kind.

He shook his head No. Paradoxically the candy offering had rendered this commercial transaction of theirs even more mercantile. Becker was losing it further, further. No, he had lost it. He just wanted out— he wanted *her* out.

As Cherry began to undress, slipping out of her Errol Flynn blouse, showing a silver bra strap and the low arch of the bra's laced cup, he said, "I can't do this."

"Do what do can't?"

"This."

His 'this' explanation was comprised of pointing at her person, straight-fingered too—this time at about stomach level. Which he instantly discerned as exceptionally impolite; but he could think of no corrective.

"I not pregnant."

"No, I didn't mean pregnant. I just meant, you know, 'do'. I cannot."

It was no picnic now for him to decide if he were more a frightened child or a Solomon-wise granddad.

"*Me?*" She said, "Oh you must *do*." Cherry pointed to his room door, where doubtlessly that outside enforcer-man was cooling his heels and chomping-on his M&Ms—or whatever drug their shape imitated.

Weakly, Becker advised: "You may keep the money."

Even though I do nothing. But <u>She</u> doesn't have the money!

Cherry advised: "You must *do*. Satisfact. Our *by-*word."

'By-word' yet: She's been drilled good on their motto.

She'll pay for subverting the reputation of the Certified Health Product outfit?

Cherry's eyes went blinking a few times, twinkling, as if a smart thought were grinding its stone-obstructed way up through the meagerest of tunnels. This looked as scrupulous and honest as it looked painful, and he felt a tremor of pity which he was sure she caught sight of. "I not dumb," she said.

He said: "I didn't mean . . . "

She then took hold of her hang-down straight hair, bunched it in her fingers and pulled it up, as if about to pin it. "Tibet women," she avowed, "up hair show they like you lot. It's flirt. You want it stay up top high for betterest love while you up top?"

He repeated with an anguished shrug, "I just can't *do* this."

He felt a bit that he was acting—while thoroughly serious. Which was certainly what she was doing, what she had to do. That similar shit, *Them was Them*, it unnerved him.

In obvious waiting-annoyance, with nowhere else to go, her small hands took to her hips, which tough-girl picture looked thoroughly out-of-place. Her glaring frustration had Cherry slowly shake her head. She repeated, "I not dumb."

He really did feel bad for her, and that sadness was getting worse. He said—

"By what you call 'dumb', Cherry, I didn't mean ..."

"I pick-up Tibet language, here-there, I mean I *am* Tibet but I forget. Songs, I do—did?—Tibet songs at their place, *our* place, The Tibet Bar, *you* cannot go. I do karaoke there one time and they told me—tell me?—me to come sing more. They know what I do for money-living and they don't not care, some say it is rightful in my place. You believe?"

Her bleak eyes surveyed up at him.

"I believe. But, still, Cherry, I can't—"

"You learn from me, not mere the sex, okay? I not dumb."

"I just really didn't mean—"

"Yes, I the only girl can do to be Tibet, so good so *you* become Tibet."

He was lost. What's all this mean decrypted? She's the only Tibetan at The Certified or she's the only girl there who can act Tibetan? And so goes to The Tibetan Bar, which maybe the other hookers at The Certified haven't even heard of, or . . . Does all this brain-flipflop matter in the least? . . . But, a brilliancy:

"Cherry, do you know Nyemo?"

"Many name Nyemo."

"At the Tibetan Bar, I mean."

Cherry frowned: "Many *name* Nyemo."

"Yes, I know, but—"

"I no know no Nyemo." Her huge eyes rose northwest:

Too bad I'm not a psycho-biologist: Eyes northwest might mean lying. And so what if she does—or did— know Nyemo? She might know if he truly loves (loved) Hung or had done what he did to many girls infatuated with Tibetans. Western girls as well as Eastern. She might know if Hung was being "played", reasons obvious: favors from ombudsman Jin Jianxin (who might well be a Xi agent himself). Favors to help Nyemo? Or The Boys of The Tibetan Bar? The Tibetan Fuck the Ass Society.

You're going crazy, Becker!

Cherry asked, "You tourist. How *you* know a Nyemo?"

"Many," he answered wiseass, "name Nyemo."

She showed nothing. She did not let-on that she got his false irony.

She may now have suspected Arthur Becker, the least likely undercover agent in the universe for Beijing president Xi, to be precisely that, and she was being hoodwinked, for she simply, tightly, said—"I do my job." She said it like righteous duty, right enunciation. A hooker is a good girl in a bad world who does what is right.

The inscrutable East?

Oh come on, you shmageggy. You got railroaded into this by your confused railroading self, now your limbic system says you're off your rails, but hell, fight yourself, you make the best of it.

Cherry had by now, again, taken hold of, then let go of, her hand-whip-upped hair, which fell round her cheekbones; she grinned—a true trooper with a difficult barbaric nincompoop schlemiel who might be more than he lets on, he might be cagey with his Nyemo questions—so this is an untrustworthy assignment which must be fulfilled so as for her to not end up in the old-town gutters, or worse; she pointed genially to Becker's penis, still holed-up like a high-strung turtle within his pants, and she said, "You watch." She climbed slowly out of her long yellow skirt—this looked so painfully poignant, a tired girl home from some hoped-for exciting festivities in rural China where she was cruelly excluded and cast down because her father was a drunken clod who had escorted her into the demeaning "service" of . . .—oh stop it. Her bending caused the lacy bra to point downwards, which she observed Becker's assessing, and she graciously undid it (for in instance Becker saw her as an indifferently indulgent airline hostess). Her breasts were lovely, so youngish round, so beautiful, her nipples large as saucers, those nipples a roseate brown—but she had a large birthmark, like a flame or torch, which reached from her right hip to the base of her ribcage, with a tattoo of a human head atop it: one might feel, if of such a mind, that she was about to be burned up, maybe sacrificed—or already had been. Her panties were of the same silver-black material as her bra, but she did not climb out of her panties. Instead, she walked crisply to the room closet and careful as a servant (a Tibetan?) she took down two hangers and hung up her skirt and blouse, smoothing them tenderly with her palms. She returned upright, a convex-concave-spirit of undulance—there was nothing flatly utilitarian about her body. She pointed lazily for him to undress—this looked like a schoolmarm explaining an ancient principle to a special backward class. When Becker did not undress, she twiddled her schoolmistressy pointing finger—but, again, lazily.

She was trying her damndest to be unthreateningly threatening, for of course men liked both. Craved both.

"Just take off clothes. No basic teach."

Now what does that mean?

It sounded as if she were referring to an introductory class at college: John-Trick Fundamentals 101, from which he would be excused: Becker straight on to 201.

"To please her—or to not displease her—and perhaps whatever beefcake meathead might still loiter on the other side of the door but a few feet from them and polishing-off his "M&Ms", Becker disrobed, or rather disLevided. Unlike tidy Cherry, however, he indifferently let his vestments drop into a shirt-pants puddle on the crappy hotel rug—and in her observation of his slapdash disrobing he discerned a disdain: amiable, tired; but it said what it said: PIG. He was pretty sure of the disdain.

He did have a mildish case of pot belly, no doubt about that; but it had never much bothered him till now. (Dad Moe'd had one, even up-there on the pitcher's mound—he'd even fucking *bragged* that he could hurl with that unbalancing breadbasket). And sure Jutta had commented on Becker's *Bäuchlein*, but in a way that was sisterly—too sisterly. Good-natured Jutta: She ought have chided him.

"Good enough?" Nervous, he could think of nothing else to say—and he did definitely feel the need for words. "I look okay?"

Cherry Cherry answered "You look you look." With

her diffident shrug.

Which irked him: It sounded like—if there were any—a "working mādella"

in some bordello in some shtetl in The Pale of Settlement in the previous century, who might well have asseverated: 'So you got a schvanze, vahtayavant? a medal?—a schvance is a schvance is a schvance.' A callous-listless ironic Yiddische Mae West in Kiev carping "Do-your-business already, I got mine boiling *knädlich* on the stove."

Cherry's 'You look you look' really did bug him bad.

Conscientiously not observing Arthur, Cherry bent over his bed, now like a hotel cleaning lady drawing down the sheets. She then hotfooted it in her stockinged feet to the bathroom, where she retrieved a bath towel, and next lay it on the bottom sheet not beneath where her rear end or her pudenda would rest but at a point approximately twenty-four inches southwards.

What the hell was this!? Certainly she didn't expect that Becker's penis would plant itself way down there—and then elongate. The Penis of Pinocchio.

She now did turn to him, her eyes wheeling slow with implication, and oh he got it alright: The towel was to absorb the semen which she was sure would ejaculate (sooner if not sooner), however not within the walls of her (off limits?) vagina—where his *mouth* was to be planted? Cherry lay down on the bed, she arched up using one athletic hand to slip and flip away her panties; she then spread her legs at approximately two feet north of the lain towel; her thighs were very thin and pallid and her crotch bore scant but silken hair. A dainty golden ring was attached to one of her vagina's quite extruded lips (Had she borne a child?).

The ring did have a kind of eye-appeal in that carnal setting—it said (to Becker anyway) sinister romance beyond his wan-worn ken of middle-age, and he now could see that Cherry's vaginal lips were prolapsed quite markedly: likely she'd borne a brood.

Poor Tibetan (*if* Tibetan?) girl with a golden (and riddle-distorted) opening.

"*Chi*," she said, softly, a winsome witch?

"*Chi*? Huh?"

"It mean eat. Eat," she said. "You come *chi*."

Eat?!—as if, by the southernmost spot where she had carefully lain the bath towel for his coming-on-terrycloth it hadn't occurred to him by now that pussy-lapping was the target goal in mind.

Was she kidding!? Was it that he had brought up Nyemo and thus all his identity possibilities?

Eat!? Christ, the Yiddishe bubbie redux—except that the *Oma* would have gone with *"fress, fress"*. And meant real food, like the *knädlich*.

Here he was in truth softened-up like a moistening sponge by more than a tinge of tenderness for this burdened immigrant from an imprisoned land, this "Jew" of years back—even if she was a fake Tibetan he couldn't help but see her as a Tibetan—and she's ordering him to go down on *her*. Sure this vaginal-worship might have been intended as a warmup, a prep, a prelude to greater things, and sure he did experience an instance of interest, a drawing-in, but it was more like an act of ministering—his eros was not kindled (not sufficiently.).

Tian," said Cherry. "Sweet. Mine is."

On the bed, on her back, Cherry was smiling up at a

still standing Becker. What in the world had the madam *told* this girl? Did Tibetan hookers (ersatz or no) really prefer to be preliminarily *eaten*? Did Cherry see—or had the madam on the phone perceived—a skittish tourist silhouette of submissiveness?

Do I project that?

NO!

Well, I did just learn of a (kind of) brother's death.

The submissive suggestion also downright angered Becker—and by way of protestation he considered doing a Nyemo, which even the Tibetan boy had been at first loathe to do on Hung: Fuck this paid bitch up her ass—which, when she'd raised herself up on the bed, had appeared to be strangely short-clefted. (That was weird too: She'd had surgery?).

He pictured the procedure. Directing himself up the rear of this poor girl from the provinces, perhaps she was an orphan. He knew that millions of Chinese girls were orphans—even the ones who weren't official orphans and did have parents—they'd come to Beijing from province dereliction to "survive". Far more girls than the hitchhiker "Minnesotta Greyhounders" to Port Authority Building New York. Hung had told him how many arrived daily. Thousands. Thousands. An infinite swarm of orphans, pimps at the gates, assaying the pageantry. Be a hooker or end up, what?, in "black jail", like Nyemo. Better a live hooker than a dying orphan in a city of fifteen million which didn't give a good goddamn. This Cherry had certainly been done up the ass before—who knew? a thousand times?

Which apparition made him sick—a quickened bloat beneath the heart. *Mir ist krank.* The German way of describing nausea.

The held-back tears again—and that was it, the ballgame.

Gently, whispering, almost ushering, he told her it was best if she just leave.

Her bloated eyes lied that no one had ever told her this before.

He bent down, picked his slacks up off the floor, fished into his money pocket and extracted another hundred.

"Please," he said, "keep this for yourself. Don't give it to the man outside."

He knew, first thing, she would give it over.

Or, well, "black jail".

He'd have bet anything that she was not Tibetan—as if he knew anything. As if that non-Tibetanishness mattered regarding his behavior, or its lack. Apparently it did.

She was a schicksa acting like a non-schicksa.

A Fräulein acting like a Jew (perversely, there'd been, from *Schwarzwald* to Berlin, a bleeding sweetheart heart).

He simply stood silent and stared at nothing, before she left—and after.

His back still hurt from that UMSEB civil-servant (with the fashion-Fifties American auto) throwing him up-against-the-wall.

Bizarrely he felt that he had, somehow, failed.

Failed what?

VIII

JIN

Who's good, who's bad?—bad guys believe they're good, better in fact than good guys. Who weighs the butcher's weights?—who has the heaviest finger? Next day, before his red-eye flight to Frankfurt, Arthur Becker entertained the inchoate notion that he ought face once again his likely in-law: the man blessed with that complex dramatic voice and convoluted conscience—a murderer in effect, if only by a directional zigzag; the man with that flexible narrative rhythm, necessary wheelabouts in a country quickly changing wheels: Jin Jianxin, a good Macbeth with necessary witches for determined good Macduffs. How else even try to understand the guy? (Or yourself.). . . Arthur sought out ambiguous Jin Jianxin at his NGO offices in what was called "The Historic Drum Tower District." He passed a sign that read Picking Flowers Temple, Ming; but there was no temple; only other signs, in English over Chinese characters: Nianhua Printing Press; Qing Welding, Guo 5 Minute Oil Change Lube Plus Super Extra Multi. Underwear hung out to dry on lines in front of the press (which was strangely supported shoulder-high on cement stilts) and the shed-splintered welding works; and under the underwear, like tumbleweed (in a Fifties cowboy movie) a single windblown large beige plastic bag. Into Arthur's head popped, "The Sagebrush Rebellion"—as outside his head thundered with a tremendous explosion, as if a war had just begun. Despite his self-concern he walked towards the boom—about three blocks: A building had collapsed, whatever structure it must once have been it was not now, now it was rubble dustcloud pancake, with a crowd forming and dispersing. It turned out that this was not a controlled implosion, for a new skyscraper—*the* Beijing thing. It was an uncontrolled implosion of an old building, uncared-for, a leftover from old poor Beijing: it had just given-up under its own old weight. Apparently imminent collapse had not been unexpected, as with many other Beijing oldtime structures: no one seemed to have been within. . . Skin dries and flakes and drops off. Comes new skin, smooth. With built-in the old skin's fate.

Jin's building was peripheral and utilitarian, and still-standing: a concrete cube refuge from street noise with a guard rail tippy-pawed along by a super suspicious calicoe cat (which meowed its unsure 'Hello?—friend or foe?'); otherwise the structure floated in eery calm. Jin's office was at linoleum floor level (drab almond?); it was modestly named *Xinfang* (Chinese characters over English phonetics [i.e. Pinyin] over English wordage block-painted on frosted glass): two rooms, one for the receptionist, the other for Jin, who was visible on one's entry: The talismanic "saint" sat in a checkered sportsjacket (the white sleeves of his shirt were rolled-up over the jacket's sleeves: ready-ready-ready, work-work-work), such behind a rather scuff-worn oaken desk piled high with two columns of papers. The receptionist faced three dull yellow plastic molded chairs; she had an Apple laptop open before her, next to an I ♥ New York coffee mug; Jin did not have an Apple—he had no laptop at all—not one visible—just papers; the only decoration was a fineline drawing on the wall of a landscape with a sharp mountainous ridge jutting into clouds and vanishing. Jin Jianxin's office indicated that he was either very modest (which Arthur already knew he was not) or he was not so very important as his daughter (and Arthur's son) had declared. . . When Arthur arrived, an egghead-bald man was leaving, gingerish complexion, in an oldtimey honey-yellow Mao outfit (these total button-ups were still worn?—maybe in the boonies?). Jin leaned forward in his chair, eyebrows arched, accentuating his near two-dimensional face with its dot-dot nose; this confidentialish pose told Arthur that the exiting oldish man had been seeking Jin's crucial help—in vain: Jin told Arthur that the man was a paper maker from the Yellow Mountain district; he had complained that "electronics and screens" were destroying his business. Jin had said that he would see what he could do, but he confided to Arthur that progress was progress, and aside from the man's producing special paper for artists, little would be accomplished. The man would soon need public assistance, and although public assistance was being raised ("I have helped in work for that," said Jin) it would still not be near enough for the man's family.

Placing his hands together, then wobbling them as if struggling to pull them apart, he exhibited sad helplessness trapped within life's prison of tight wrappings: Life is life, progress builds and progress destroys. Jin told Arthur that he hadn't given that financial bad news to the man.

"Onwards and upwards." Arthur's ironic shrug.

He was sorry he'd said that—it came off so indifferent—but he'd had to come up with something.

Jin said, "Well, we are yet working hard to restore Beijing's soul."

"I hope," said Arthur, "you succeed."

So, Beijing had had a soul. Well, of course it had. Everyplace had once had a soul. Germany had once had a super soul. Just ask the historians of music and philosophy, and architecture (and even some arschlochs *of Hitler)...*

Jin, for some reason, was looking offended. Had Arthur implied that Beijing-soul would not succeed, could not? Jin said: "You know, Mister Becker, I pride myself that I know men, even across our cultures. And I, I have to be honest: You look like a lonely man, a one so hemmed-in. . . in soul. Offensive I hope I am not being. No, I think presumptive is the word. But I should be honest."

Despite Jin's forced syntax Becker forced a dismissive friend-laugh. He certainly wasn't going to tell this human-rights mavin that he had murdered a man, an important man, and that a hospital bigshot investigator was on his trail.

"You are leaving today," Jin now said. "I am sorry. You have seen so little."

Easily offended Becker was offended. He

answered—

"Actually, I've seen interesting things." *Be nice*: "I loved your family lineage home."

Jin nodded with a patronizing smile to that polite patronization.

"And," led Arthur, with caution—"Tian'An Men Square."

He needed to see Jin's response:

"Yes, Tian, yes." Jin seemed to consider for a moment. Nodding obliquely, he echoed, "Tian'An Men Square."

Okay Becker, you came here: take your stab:

"Poor Nyemo, at Tian'An Men, that poor kid."

"Ah, poor many Chinese. I was you know of the age of the involved."

But I said 'Nyemo', not 'many Chinese', you fucking artful dodger: Arthur pictured Jin now as that anonymous rebel kid who had stood his ground before the Chinese army's tanks—a shot seen all round the world, except in China. Arthur couldn't complete his picturing of Jin before the tank, that was impossible: Jin forcing that iron megalith to divert itself around him. Jin would have been off behind the scene.

What Arthur Becker did confront now however was the solemnity of a reflective face and voice which he had not observed at the family dinner.

"So you do know," said Jin Jianxin, "those old Tian'An Men events—you know of them?"

"Yes. Of course."

"That 'of course'." Barely parting his lips, Jin allowed himself a momentary slender grin. "More in the West know of Tian'An Men than are knowing here. Do you know that? We here have the News controlled."

"Yeah, I have read that."

"In 'your' *un*-controlled News."

Is he being ironic? I can't tell with him.

"Jin Jianxin—"

"Jin. Just Jin."

"Jin." Becker ducked his head, as if Moe were throwing a baseball at him. "When I brought up Tian 'An Men I didn't mean to—"

"Criticize? Be superior? Well, Tian'An Men, it still has its presence—and not just for Japanese cameras and American."

"I understand."

Looking at Jin's new-projected gravity, that hybrid slant of it. Being the object of this difficult man's variations was like wobbling on cliff's edge.

"The Tian: When we were young. It was a point-of-definition in our lives, you know; many of us who remain in our lives with it. A search for the deeper meaning, deeper vision. Far or near. Which *does* exist in our society."

"This is why you work to improve society."

"Oh, you now indulge."

"No. I—"

Jin's glare stopped Arthur's words; Jin's thin face now seemed to pin-point accusation: "You are taunting. Please don't taunt, that is insult."

Jin's heft seemed held now by a forearm he had placed over his leaning chest, so he had developed a kind of floating potency. A wetness appeared now in Jin's eyes, a sort of humorous bitterness.

Which brought silence, a forcing pressure of deep water, which further discomposed.

"Nyemo. . ." Discomposed Arthur couldn't but

finally go for it—he had to: "Nyemo, he went crazy at Tian'An Men, you know."

"Oh I know, I know." Jin swiveled in his chair, as if to look out his one office window, as if to survey Tian'An Men, which was not nearby. Or he'd turned to think without Arthur in plain sight—or to allow a tear without embarrassment? "A reforming by way of remembering Tian'An Men would surely help Nyemo."

He doesn't know that Nyemo is beyond help? Dead is beyond help.

Maybe Nyemo isn't?

Jin doesn't want to let me in on Nyemo's black jail demise? Most likely that.

"Nyemo," he said, "at Tian'An Men, "and his other actions. They are so ego."

Defend the kid, defend—you have to: "But that's not all they are. Patriotism, that has ego in it, sure, but—"

"All Tibetans," Jin said, "they are not like Nyemo."

"Maybe more should be."

Jin's fist raised—it might come down hard on his desk.

But it didn't.

"You, Mister Becker, forgive me, you do not know nothing."

From within—no, from outside—came this raw insistent zing and flash, likely from Qing Welding. Arthur jolted for a moment, as if stung. He was out of this dungeon mirror that was showing him to himself as nobody else but Jin. Both men waited until the welding faded—it never completely passed.

Jin said: "Nyemo, he pushes. Nationalism and religion, these are bones and blood. This is true of all people, it is genes I think. But it is moreso for some people than for others. At least some people, they act on it far less, and they should. It is the only way when you are so outnumbered—by the millions. Something else is needed. Many Tibetans, most, they are placid. They are nice. They accept. Not that that any is all so good. Again, something else is needed. Do you know, Mister Becker, that Chinese mourning, it is not in black but in white?—like porcelain."

Now what the hell did this mean?

"But Nyemo—" Jin just shook his head, and his fist opened-up.

With more mention of Nyemo the atmosphere in Jin's office kept-up its inflation and constriction; it loaded and it veered. Nyemo, his very name, had become a loaded weapon, perhaps it was not even Nyemo: it was more a substitute: the hidden antag-onisms built-into the upcoming marriage of Mick and Hung, maybe Jin did *not* even wish this union—the very air in this office seemed conspiring now to just push Arthur out. He heard too many clanking sounds from outside—Jin likely did not even hear these, he was too used to them—there were too many air-brakes of Beijing trucks and buses, too many shouts, too much chaotic Easternness—which created its own heavy silence too. Transparent porcelain.

Wise Jin dropped-away from that Nyemo name: "It is an insoluble solution, Tibetans. They are a different race. Really I must say."

This from the great local moralist?

He added: "There are many insoluble solutions."

An oxymoron, sure. But true—quite possibly. Arthur could not fault Jin for that life-observation, as much as he wanted to, as so many times he had thought it too.

Knowing there was no need to ask, he asked: "Why not just freedom? China, you know, letting Tibet go."

"Those people, they would not survive. Not in these times. If you traveled there you would see. They are not built for survival—I'm sorry. Only for mountains they are built. And the mountain era"—like a balloon's helium, humor filled Jin's narrow face and swelled it—"the mountain times, these are done."

Jin then made these lunatic floating strokes with his arms, high and sidewise, watching Arthur's reaction to this nuts absurdity that made the Chinese "saint" look like Marcel Marceau. Jin said: "It is outmoded, Tibet, and comical, like our Chinese Tai Chi."

"I thought Tai Chi still helped."

Jin grunted, and Arthur said—

"So, China is helping Tibet, by possessing it?"

"Ah, you are irony-taunting once again. You cannot help yourself."

"I did not mean to—taunt."

Like hell I didn't.

"We are a face-culture," Jin said. "I admit it. China just does not let Tibet go, even though its face is different."

Jin Jianxin forced a hoarse throat-raking—it did not seem quite authentic. He laughed at face-culture? He laughed at Tai Chi? He laughed at the absurdities of folkways in general—face-cultures, ass-cultures, mountain-cultures, sea cultures, whatnot. This wry cackler might well have sacrificed Nyemo, sabotaged him while yet trying to somehow help the kid.

Arthur debated, then he ventured despite himself—almost in an undertone: "But I heard something."

"You heard? What have you heard?"

Jin leaned again toward his large desk, as if Arthur were about to whisper. Jin's forearms held his head; those forearms were measly, as if he had never in his life hammered one nail. Jin's face was now framed by those two chaotic paper columns before him, bookends for his domelike cheeks. Because his head was so slender and his nose so small he appeared to be a mini-sculpturing, even a shrunken head; or just a living paperweight.

Arthur fought himself and hesitantly brought back that edge-sharp weapon of the Nyemo name: "Do you know, have any idea, what has happened to Nyemo?"

Jin did not hesitate:

"Yes. It is no secret."

"You do know?"

"It is no *secret*."

Jin is implying that I am implying that he has special knowledge—and that it is not good?

Leaning back from his cluttered desk like a bored but ever-tolerating boss, Jin said: "Nyemo was reported, although it was not necessary, since he was well-known. *I* reported him, yes—as a 'separatist'. I had to do. I admit. This pained me, you cannot conceive—there are those above me, who make decisions, decisions on *me* too, my state, my position. My future—in doing what I do. The good things."

"I understand."

"You do not."

Jin's head was shaking, firm, intense and slow.

Becker shrugged and he nodded; he was quite willing to accept his ignorance, his lack of Chinese understanding, even his sympathy for Jin in his position between the government and those left underneath it.

"And about our Nyemo I took no *xingzai lehuo*." Jin saw Arthur's confusion at the phrase, but he merely shrugged once more: he did not know the English, which Arthur guessed really was closer to German: *Schadenfreude*.[11]

"But I meant," said Arthur, "what, finally, happened—to Nyemo."

"Finally?"

"He's dead."

"He is not dead. He is in jail, yes, for the moment. That is all. It will not last. He is, as you say, 'on soul, ice'."

Arthur doubted that Jin had read Eldridge Cleaver. He bolstered himself: "You're wrong."

Jin 's face went energetic, supple snaps-jerks-pulses, the face of a man about to tear a room apart—he did not appreciate being labeled as wrong, if that branding were not administered by a government superior: "How *dare* you!—Herr Becker! I am *not* wrong. We here have reduced the death penalty by *half*. I *myself* have contributed to that, and it was not *easy*. Didn't you know *that*? Nyemo, he is only to be *held*."

"The UMSEB men, they—"

"The UMSEB, *yes*?! They came to you?"

"In their Fifties American cars, yes."

"What? In their what?"

Jin appeared genuinely to have not a clue as to Ricky Rubalcava and his thriving oldtime import trade of The New World, the eensy China-Cuba Axis. He stared at Arthur as if the American-German were beyond cognition. Beyond help. And beyond discourse.

"The UMSEB," Arthur said, "they first only implied

---

[11] Joy at another's misfortune.

that Nyemo was dead in black jail. Then they came out with it."

"They have lied. They lie a great deal. To frighten you. They are practiced."

Jin observed Arthur's disbelief, at which he sneered.

"Something is wrong?" he said with a dab of vinegar.

"I'm sorry, but I think it may be. Wrong."

Jin efforted another thought-activating half-spin round of his desk chair. "Perhaps, well, it is possible. I don't think so. But, to relax you, I will, I will do check-up."

Now's your time. He's unsure, he's wobbled, if only slightly. As muchso anyway as he's likely to get. Your words are scrambling to your throat, clawing. Before they choke, take to your advantage:

"Sometimes," Arthur ventured, "I saw—I thought I saw a—how do I say this?—a . . . 'relationship', between Hung and Nyemo."

"Re-lation-ship?" Jin muted his grin of likely secret knowledge. "A relationship, of course. They are fellow students. They do live at our house."

"A . . . closeness. . . Like . . . knowing one another's thoughts and—"

"Oh, that—they *did* have that, Hung and Nyemo, and from the first. It is why I allowed Nyemo to live with us. I can attest to their closeness. It was nice to see, so much with a Tibetan, oh so nice. But your Mick-ah-yell, he had with Hung the same re-lationshipping. He had as you know so more."

"Different."

"And 'different' I should hope."

Damnit, GO!

224

"Sometimes, I thought, forgive me, with Hung and Nyemo it was even"—the squeamish Becker shrug, the apologetic hoodlike brow, the hands overturing wide—help my helpless—"sexual."

"Sexual!?"

Jin's rout-out bark at a burgeoning dog pack.

Think quick—try!

"You understand, I'm coming from the . . . Western . . . where we . . . assume and . . . no scandal—we . . . "

Limp shrug of the lamest schmuck.

"*Sex*-ual? You allow *that*? You, the father of our *Mick*."

Our Mick?

"Well. It's not that I allow it. Indeed, I . . . question—I . . . "

"China, Herr Becker, we are not America. We are not Germany. There was no *your*-way '*relationship*'. Not with Nyemo and my Hung."

Jin Jianxin once again leaned-in over his desk between the paper columns, creating a wind-sliver that brushed away some papers from both piles. Some sheets butterfly-flapped to the floor. He gazed at them as if they might be pets, annoying adorables. He didn't bother to bend for them. He said—

"I, Herr Becker, now please, what exactly have you heard?"

Absurdly, pointlessly, cowardly, divertingly, stupidly, Becker went with an "Excuse me?"

"You are questioning. You have heard, or you have 'decided'—I can see it—that *I* had abetts to do with the Hung-and-Nyemo re-*lay*. If you *have* heard, that is the poor Tibetan boy's distorts. Lies, I have to say—it is a Tibetan way, I'm sorry—they *lie* because they are *down*. They *do* that. Lies are all they have, Tibetans. They and their dalais."

What's he now going to lay out?—'the only good dalai is a dead dalai'? . . . Come on, stop it. Stop Him. You're as bad as him. You're worse.

Jin went on: "And I too have heard of what Nyemo has said, so ugly-ugly—and I must admit that I am *amazed* that you allow them their credibles. And that *I directed* them, he has said that, has he not? Yes, Tibetans *do* lie, you know—even your *pure* Tibetans. . . But *you*, sir, you are the *West* again, eh, the *'just'*." Jin performed his actor cackle. "Your West *'just'*—I *love* it: All voices heard from, all having hearings—the underdog. Lies are not lies, lies are the truth, until the lies just die, or are killed, by truth. Which no one proves is truth."

Huh?

This the great civil libertarian? The ultimate Chinese egalitarian? Mandarin of Mandarins of suburban Beijing. Just observe Jin, his dented certainty, his now-unforced spurts of curtness, his thin sharp face in that near-knife narrowness increasing further with its narrowing. Was he much different from old Professor Strobel in his deep Germanic guttural, Strobel—Jutta's *hero* yet—Strobel, Arthur's victim? Substitute Tibet for Jew and Jin equals Fritz?

"I love Nyemo," Jin Jianxin now said. "I loved him from the first. I *saw* the potential."

Arthur Becker affirmed that he did too, although of course he didn't, how could he? He hadn't even cared.

"But this charge of separatist on Nyemo, of troublemaking to revolt, it *had* to be made. By me, by anyone. But no one would. Not Hung, not your Mick.

Yes, I made it, the charge. It was a sacrifice for our own patriotic hopes—China's, what Nyemo was about—I don't regret that duty. . . But *sex*—you said *sex*!?"

At a loss, off-track—Arthur didn't care about "troublemaking to revolt", what was that to troublemaking-to-sex?—he ended-up giving-out with a weakly, "I suppose."

At this point he was not even sure of what he'd meant.

"Nyemo's activities," said Jin, "his ravings, they can facilitate much turmoil, they endanger the lives of thousands, you know?—no, you don't, you cannot. Many Tibetans too, their lives, the guilt-by-the-associates. Those Tibetans, they work in the factories here and all over China, they commit suicide. With Nyemo's diatribings they could be identified and then let go from their jobs, unjustly, thence to their nothingness, their crawl-wormings in the mud, their suicides. Yes to even starving slow, for Tibetans—which is not so rare." From between his stacks of papers Jin took a pen, a fountain pen, and tapped its cap imperiously on the table, as an ordering judge might in court, a silencing judge—or a dictator: "I must think of everyone, you know. I must protect *those* people, Nyemo's people, and so I must weigh."

"So you reported him."

"I *said* I did, I am proud and I am not proud. And I do not have to explain to *you*, Mister Becker from Germany."

"And America."

Jin smiled, seeing neither division nor discrepancy. He said—

"This I did is too *also* Tian'An Men and its mix of

memory, all for what it stands."

This too? This too, Arthur realized, was how *he* had changed the picture of his murdering Fritz Strobel. On the plane coming here, the endless plane over long EurAsia: his turning the story round: making it *Strobel's* fault. So obvious: Strobel had courted his punishment—he'd wished it, he was waiting for it, waiting. Arthur was like Great Moralist Jin Jianxin. . . . Maybe without the morals. Maybe with the morals—he wasn't sure. On a long long flight you can turn round anything.

Our absolving ways of looking at unabsolving things.

"So, Nyemo *has* been killed."

"*Ny—!*"

Clamping down on whatever assault was forming within the grip of his mouth and about to be propelled Jin said no words but stood, as if his chair had suddenly become an amusement park trickspring seat lurching-up off the floor and shoving him up. The pupils of his eyes had gone strangely small and empty, shrunken to barely there, and for an instance a tremor took hold of his jaw, which he actually grabbed and stopped. As if surprised at himself, at his stark blind standing, he as quickly sat, almost in a fall: "Herr Becker," he said, "do you think this is *easy* for me? *all* of this, choosing and teaching and sacrificing, people's *lives*, like Nyemo; *deceiving* with lies, yes, I admit that, *deceiving*, and *deciding*—do you think this is my *natural, any* of this? Do you think I *live* for it and I *love* it, and it *increases* me? *Do* you? . . ."—but he'd stopped; and you could not tell sorrow's tear from tear's rage, red-faced rage, nor distinguish these from his humiliation—which was also there—as was, yet, his fighting steadiness, his fortitude, all increasing each other and decreasing, truth and lie and in-between. All of which crushed. All of which was Him.

His overwhelming honesty locked-down on any Arthur Becker words.

"I did not want to say," said Jin, "of Nyemo's death—if so. And it is a mistake—if so. If, as we say, that angry boy in jail is *qisile*: angered-to-death. By his own anger, from his insides." A poor poker player—and admitted self-excuser too—Jin went scratching scratching at his ear, weirdly inserting his right index finger too. "Otherwise, Nyemo is alive. We have reduced the death penalty, as I said. As *I* have helped the bargain for. *As* I said."

"You did say."

"It is *Nyemo's qisile*, if he is—"

Nyemo's fault, if dead? Not Jin's.

No, Jin's fault, not Nyemo's.

Faults?—none. Not in China nor in the ether of the world.

"I so do hope not," said Jin. "Nyemo's death."

"You don't know, for sure?"

"I do-not."

What more to be said? Jin looked about, Othello angling for the stagehand's mislain knife, the Moor-actor split-off momentarily from the true fervent Moor, but reaching tight for both selves. And at that moment, emboldened by Jin's outburst of moments ago, and drawn intimate by it, Becker the Outburster thought to tell "The Great Man" what *he* had done to old Strobel—and why: Jewish history; Western history; people history; moral history—these fitting into the cavities and crevices it shared with The East, Inquisition to Inquisition, Nanking Rape to Holo—it could become a child's jump-rope game. He imagined Jin's reaction. Bewilderment? Perfect Understanding? Respect in a mirrored (or mirror-avoiding) way? . . . Like that (likely) black-faced actor of Othello, Arthur Becker held his tongue, it seemed artificial, it couldn't but. . . And Jin reached behind him to a short, stubby bookcase, chock-full; he found what he wanted; he held up a red-blue can that had been resting on the top shelf. It looked like a soda product—it bore the image of a smiling man, a smiling *Western* man. "This," said Jin, "it is Beijing air; it is canned. And, well, it is not *my* likeness on it, you see, although we did consider that." Arthur leaned to the can. Yup, there was a version, deviative, of The Marlboro Man, who might have been Jin Jianxin. "We are promoting this can," said Jin," as a promotion—*for* environment: There are millions of cans now in Beijing and Shanghai, we are promoting that they should be recycled, for the *shame, for* clean air."

Yeah, real nice, your almost *image on the can— you're good Jin, real good; you change our death subject on a dime—to a different death subject, from a one-person end to a safety of fifteen billions, fifty billions: you do good things; but what about that one person, that Nyemo? Dead horse: nothing more to be asked or said.*

Arthur asked: "So what then about your Hung?"

"What then what? What do you mean? She will marry your Mick-ah-yell. No?"

Jin apparently did wish such union. Honestly. In modern China the young were in no hurry to marry, everyone knew that. The richer young, in any case. They were now as in the West. Yet Jin Jianxin, great liberator, free-thinker, free sacrificer, he wished for his young daughter to be Euro-*wed*?

Arthur asked: "You don't prefer for your daughter to marry a Han?"

"I wish her wish." Sincere soft eyes had now appeared. "This, might I say, this is the New Chinese. No more one-child policy, as from the old god Mao— that had made parents' one-child their all, not good, the child builds to resent. And the parents, they resent that resenting. And all fails."

I sure saw that at the piano at their lineage hall: Jin ordering Hung's playing, just about: Hung doing her deliberate dissection of Tschaikovsky, just about.

Becker had momentarily forgotten that he too was the father of an only child—and that *he too was an only child.*

Jin said: "Thus now it can follow no more marry-limit, with only a Mandarin. Such provincialness."

Brainstorm brought its bravery: "So: For . . . worldliness?—you ordered Nyemo to—?"

"Nyemo. *Again* Nyemo!"

"I'm sorry. But you ordered him to . . . well . . . "

"*Say* it."

"To 'taint' your daughter. The experience? Give an only child a tougher skin, as if she weren't an 'only'. The school-of-hard knocks, for . . . success . . . ?"

"*Insanity!*" Jin's hands, again tethered to the table, had closed to fists and locked. Angry animals with their own autonomous brains. "Nyemo *told* to you *that!?* Hung told to you *that*!?"

Eyes closed, Arthur nodded. Then: "Hung didn't say

that exactly."

Some solace there, some appeasement: These allowed Jin a constricted breath.

"Well, Nyemo," he said. "Again, Nyemo lied—*again*! *again*! And could you believe I would *do* such a thing as what you seem believing?"

Actually the answer was Yes. But Arthur gave-out his No.

"Yet Nyemo, I come back to him, *you* come back to him: Still, all he does—dead or if alive. *So smart* a boy. But I insist: Nyemo is *not* dead."

Jin's face bubbled, small pops small lumps, as once before, as if he were rigorously gargling-rinsing—or were turning sick. He sneered, which lifted his mid-lips. Obviously embarrassed now to be holding it suspended, he returned the can of polluted-Beijing air to its shelf. From habit, or from ego? (and were these different?) he faced front his ironic non-image on that can. . . When he turned back to Arthur he had, like that, composed himself. It was like a comedian's swift swipe expression change.

"Well," said Jin. "Herr Becker I forgive you for your suspicions. You seem to have to have them so you have them—I understand. I have told you of our problems with our offspring—and I say again: I have tried to explain why I find it would be wonderful if Hung and Mick who love did marry, one foot for Hung outside the Han world, that is good. Even one-half foot. This is honesty. This is not easy to admit, in China. These explainings I have made, they were *not* to say I told Nyemo to do anything—in the real world. Nothing. With my Hung."

Arthur said, "I'm sorry."

"You are sorry?"

Becker still did not trust Jin's disclaimer.

Only to recollect Nyemo's hurt drained face was full enough.

Because it was necessary, pro forma—*and natural*—they both smiled. Or they found themselves smiling. It was really difficult to see why they were trapped now in this mutual pleasantry, this quick discovery, this settled awkwardness out of nowhere. But there they were. Identity, thought Arthur, what else? Arthur the man, isolated, who endlessly searched for brotherhood, especially, firstoff, with his father Moe, only to then jettison that brother-crap as crap. . . The two men knew that they were finished-up here. Business uncompleted as far as business could go. They stood, they shook hands across the cluttered desk of the ambiguous ombudsman; Jin's hands were velvet-smooth—less marred than even Arthur's. Arthur told Jin Jianxin that his wife Jutta would come with him to Beijing in June when the Heidelberg semester ended. Jin said that that was wonderful. Madame Becker he would love "eagerly" to meet. He had heard so much of her. He added too that he was sorry that earlier he had called Arthur a lonely man.

But that statement-of-lonely, even in its rescinding with apologetic smile, it still echoed bleak, as it was not rescinding, was it?—it was just "Sorry". Yet Arthur, the brotherhood seeker, he wished to embrace Jin for even that human proferring, that recognition of Arthur's sentiments—and his hauntings.

But Arthur didn't broach any huggings: too many resonations here, conflicting elements, like the continuing scraping welding noise outside.

Standing, waiting for what? Their eyes met—an endurance contest or an emotion? Jin had to live with himself as much as Arthur did. . . Arthur, who again might just now have told Jin of his own depriving of a man of life. A man, Herr Professor Fritz Strobel, not so unlike Jin Jianxin. Perhaps Arthur might have hugged the man this time, hugged and confessed, had not the suspicion jumped—as it would inevitably with an Arthur Becker—that Jin Jianxin was just patronizing him—withal, with all that he had admitted: This man knew the ropes, he had to in China, all the persona-jockeyings. This man was hardly *lonely*.

Everyone is not like you, Arthur. Not remotely. And why the hell do you keep on with wishing such a thing?!

Arthur had not bothered to correct The Great Man this time for his having called Arthur's wife the Jewish Madame Becker; not the proper Deutsche Frau Koenig, which name she had never changed. . . Which had had Mick so often, too often, being called, at school, at *Fussball* (and in those anti-Semitic *Pirates*?), and at church with Jutta—Mick-ah-yell *Koenig*. . . . Which the boy had corrected, yes. But less and less and less. Until no, enough, not at all. . . The name Mick-ah-yell *Koenig*—electro-shock treatment! For Arthur Becker.

So would Hung be known as Hung Becker or Hung Koenig?

Arthur would remonstrate with Mick—to avoid The Saddest Story Ever Told.

Hardly would he order—Jin style—but hardly would he beg.

Arthur turned to leave, but his departure was prevented by a rail-thin man opening Jin's office door, whack, as a cop might, and half-hurtling in in what was also a semi-stumble, with Jin's receptionist close behind him and pulling back on his gray jacket (old-time Mao-collarless, which did make her earnest collaring difficult), she yanking as if the worn jacket were a leash and the man was some mythical animal. "I am *Norbu* from *Tibet*," the man announced, "the father of Nyemo who lived in your home, sir, and I am grateful—until Norbu is now imprisoned." Although he was presumptuous to rush in, bumptious, bold, his voice was weak, apologetic. Drawing a gray hankie from his slender coat and wiping away what considerable sweat he could wipe he said he had just arrived aboard the Qinghai-Tibet Railroad, where the speakers played endlessly the song "Riding the Train to Lhasa" (he clamped his ears and rocked with this complaint) and where paramilitaries kept checking him at every stop.

Jin said, "I am sorry for that." He motioned to his receptionist to release the man's jacket; and she left.

This Norbu held a wide-brim ochre cowboy hat in his right hand and he kept nervously slapping his thigh with it, a bit of Beijing dust taking flight throughout the small office. It looked silly, the entire picture, it looked as if a misplaced movie were being filmed here. And this skeleton torso Norbu was no bronco buster, he appeared barely capable of manhandling a squirrel. He had curly orange-brown hair going gray, widespread bat-wing ears, a broad nose like a long-ago-time boxer's with many burst capillaries, and a tight chin that swore directness.

"Please, Mister Jin Jianxin," said this harried Norbu, the man who had laboriously carved out the wooden nations of Africa for his young students, until Han manufacturers had taken his idea and run with it by mass production. "Please, can you help my son?—to be released. I have so *do chag*[12] for him. He is in what they name the 'black jail'."

Such watery sorrow in his voice, such confusion, as his eyelids closed in what appeared to be a strong-gripped prayer—then shot open.

Jin answered him with the matter-of-fact "There are many black jails, my Norbu."

'His' Norbu!?

"There is no *the* black jail."

"There is no *the* black jail?"

Norbu's eyes seemed now streaked, stabbed by that supposed truth, so damned overwhelming.

"So, as you can see, it would be very difficult, impossible for me, to locate the location of your Nyemo. Some even say the black jail is a myth. And it does not exist."

Must you lie to him? And in front of me, making me complicit. Must you be so flat with him, so unstirred by this old sad man!

Arthur saw an image of himself strutting to Jin and ploughing his fist straight through the chin and nose of the ombudsman for "the people". A pitcher throwing his fastball at the face of the innocent batter—all a-part-of-the-game.

Arthur simply stood-by and watched that roughneck image fade.

Norbu went staring about the office, even the ceiling, a medieval astronomer searching the multitudes of strange galaxies for what conceivable *what* they

---

[12] Sticky desire. Attachment.

could tell without reducing him, the searcher, to an ant, a microbe, a little nothing. To Arthur he appeared a kind of Ptolemy obsessed not by dark universal riddles but by far and wide black jails.

Arthur ought have left the office then, but he couldn't bring himself to do that. And Jin had not motioned such departure to him. Embarrassed, he turned his attention to that one fineline drawing on Jin's office wall: the ridge portrayed was so long and narrow it seemed as if it might be the endless-imagined China spine that twisted about the globe.

Jin simply said to Norbu, "Oh, but nothing does please me more than to help your son. Nothing would please me more, and I will try."

NOTHING could please him MORE?!

Come now.

"Please then?" said Norbu.

He eyed the chair beside the one in which Athur had been sitting, but the subservient man understood presumption, and he did not sit.

"I have been trying for your Nyemo," said Jin. "I should tell you that. All along I have been trying."

"You have so?"

"Yes. I have."

Arthur could barely restrain himself from announcing, 'No, he has *not!*'

He restrained himself.

Jin came round his desk and, as an uncle might do but not a father, he placed a lightly cajoling arm about Norbu. "I have been trying, and I continue."

"Oh thank you, my sir." Norbu bent slightly.

Why disillusion the poor man? Because you are so notable, so renowned, so famous, *and* so safely obscure—and you wish to remain that way.

Simply put, with all the unbalanced ambiguities at Jin's disposal, Arthur wished he were as multi-equipped as that callous-sympathetic man.

"But," allowed Jin, "it is not so easy, what to do for Nyemo. There are so so many steps. After all, I cannot go to Parliament."

A joke, meretricious at this time. Uncalled-for. Or perhaps most-called-for.

Unsophisticated provincial Norbu did not know enough to laugh.

Jin added: "We just need patience here in this case."

"Nyemo," said Norbu, "he is a good boy. It is natural for him. He is very passionate and he is trust unstained. If he did wrong, he did not do wrong. It was his passions."

"I understand," said Jin Jianxin. And if one might imagine a molasses drawl in Mandarin, one would understand his "understanding".

Eyes moist, eyes buoyant, Norbu then told of Nyemo's helping him with his African nation carvings, how good and determined the boy was, how he'd learned to use expertly so many shaping tools—chisels, knives, awls, planes, sandpapers, acrylics, small brushes more—mythic Jin did not exhibit bored— Norbu's hands on their own making motions you made with those tools, he didn't even know he was miming from beloved memory, he didn't know his voice had become more muscular, more ethereal, less intimidated. And oh how fine the work was too, how demanding, how his son Nyemo had looked up and back at that map of Africa, the boy's nose at that continent pinned to the school-shack wall, like a leg of lamb it was, Africa—

and the boy could tell a Nigeria from a Chad, which he, Norbu, could not do, could never do. Nyemo was just a genius. And how Nyemo had even worked hard to store the tools by making shelving, drawers, and *two* pegboards—"and these even still *exist*."

Jin curiously, but expectedly, said, "I know."

He might have worn a weary face of sympathy, but he did not. He'd managed such a face at first, but he had lost it with Norbu's draining pain.

Did this piteous-to-observe heart-to-(sham)-heart continue on much longer? This shrunken-down charade. Did the two men further share their affections for Nyemo?—and their praise. What with all his "multi-tasking", his China-saving of the poor, well, some of the poor, and the justice-broken, did Jin have time for compassion that was true, simple, real, as it was so close to home?—or was the multi-saving, the multi-compassion really a compassion wall?—a strong concealment of self. Arthur couldn't know, of course, and at this point, unable to bear any more of the painful drama—feeling himself in conspiracy not so much with Jin Jianxin as with the Arthur Becker who had himself killed a man, he left the office, knowing that Jin's professed attempts to have Nyemo freed were no more than a magician's misdirection, a lie. No, worse than a lie—a perversion. And knowing as well that Jin had little choice: Why tell Norbu what was was: That trying to have his son freed would be hopeless, and it would only endanger himself, and so forestall what good he might do for others?—even other Tibetans. These were the rules weren't they?—life rules, politics rules, existence rules—all that tainted balance—and rules were such necessary things, they had to be. Even the unjust ones unjustly made up.

Why tell Norbu then the truth of his son's death?

Sure Arthur still believed that was that, that was what it was—death.

The father would find out soon enough—when Jin would not have to be around to deal with distraut's distractions. *C'est la vie.*

The men had spoken in Mandarin, of course.

Arthur Becker had heard the words and watched the men, the novelist heeding their eyes and hands especially; what the writer imagined must have been, had to have been. What else could the words have signified? And that 'what-else' infuriated with gut sorrow: The soul-sickness of holding out false hope.

Oh yeah?—and what would *you* have done, Herr Becker? How would *you* have operated?

What a lie truth was. . . But it did not work in the opposite.

Outside Jin's offices, outside Jin's building, Arthur Becker heard a tolling bell, not so distant. Of course, this city, this country, so large it had many Christians,[13] more than did Iceland. More than Belgium. Etc. Even being Jewish, Becker appreciated the Christian bells, their wind, disturbed and resonant; their air carried their familiarity, as when he had poked his head within the

---

[13] Hey, wasn't this was why the Pope had refused to grant an audience to the Dalai Lama. Lord knew what burdens the Chinese, Confucian or Communist or "Lenin-Capitalist", would lay on their Christians in residence. Protestants or Catholics, they wouldn't differentiate in retaliation's fair play. So, you, the Pope, you weigh you balance. You sacrifice. Sacrifice is a lie too. Ask the sacrificed. Morality is morality.

gap of the ajar doors of that Heidelberg synagogue, Chizuk Amuno (what had those Hebrew words meant?—ah yes, Strengthen the Faith), and he had seen what he—never a joiner—had never seen: German Jews. German Jews ajabbering, German Jews at home. *At home!?*. . . As much as, in Beijing, Nyemo of The Green Brain People was *at home*! . . . But the Beijing belling stopped now, and then did its echo, quite the potent echo too; and then crashed-in anew the Beijing realities: the metallic whining-in-the-shed beneath Jin's office: that searing sparklight of welding's joining necessary contracted-for whatevers, the smell of wood smoke now too, as if the workers here were burning and fusing together not only functioning metal but also the very inner protective walls of their surroundings and (who knows?) their souls; the operators' faces were enclosed in pulled-down tinted visors, which accentuated intensity, isolation, specialness (if you will), alienation, protection and danger; and there nearby were the huddles of untalking laborers rushing through their oil change-lubes to meet the advertised five minutes (or be fired?—probably), they working in what was essentially a carport unequipped with even a pneumatic lift. The lube-men must have crawled and slid beneath the cars, when called-for, hidden at least then from that insuperable up-above, the well-smokened-coal-skeins of Beijing sky ramped-out from The Great Beijing Dumptruck of fifteen million souls (*twenty* million?) arching-back overhead under heaven, or not, just forgeddaboutit (as how did this air-mud-up-and-*happen*!?) and having no clue as to what to do—as China grew and grew. And grew. Number Four, Number Three, Number Two in the world. Then, *watch-it America!—but don't let the Koch Republicans in competition muddier-up YOUR skies.*

And the tumbleweed, that was still there, that large bulky-awkward plastic bag; it hadn't tumbled far from beneath the dangling washline of pale underwear. It was as if the cotton panties getting sooted by the city was a roof protecting that manmade wounded tumbleweed. Priorities reversed. And Arthur walked to the tumbleweed and bent to it, and tore it, that Jewish ritual of mourning when a family sat its *shiva* for its dead soul. The sound its tearing made was like a whinge, quite human. And you could see the close-packed, huddled stuff within, as if maybe you'd torn-open large intestines—good god. And it did not occur to the mawkish tearing man, this Jew-German who had just seen the smog, The Great Beijing Dumptruck, to consider whether or not there actually *was* the smog—just now—or how thick it was. Thick as Greenland-snow? You simply trundled along and became Beijing, a Beijinger. You had such other problems.

Becker the mawkish man returned to himself and left himself and returned again. He not being a man who could escape himself for long. Becker the volleyball.

IX

A 380 TURNING TALE (no sic)

And what, for whatever manifold jittery reasons, as the jet smoothly groaned its way up up up, and gloomy Beijing fell away like a scuffed-spiked-shrivelled shoeprint, did Arthur Becker find himself picturing on his Lufthansa return? First, foremost: The Fat Man Problem. While not fully revealing his true colors (too cagey for that) Jin Jianxin had thrown The Fat Man (Nyemo) off and over the infamous trestle onto the equally infamous train tracks in order to save the dozens of people tied to the tracks farther on down the line.[14] Ethics 101. What can you do with that? Especially as you, Arthur, you have no Fat Man Problem of your own: You were saving no one when you smothered old "Fritzey" Strobel, that self-relishing

---

[14] Rare mention in philosophy courses of the thousands killed or injured on the derailed train, as such would take place with either alternative. Thus, comes the *ceteribus paribus* assumption ("all other things being equal")—equally infamous, equally necessary too, and equally unrealistic. *No other things are equal.* Ever. So what could be the point?

and scheming anti-Semite.

So on that plane, Arthur couldn't sleep (but he never could on planes), and he saw Jin Jianxin sleeping badly, he decided to see that: Jin held within a night's sweat of guilt and nausea and ear pain (the plane did that to Arthur—always did), Jin sleepwalking with his dominations and his decisions and his well-distributed Marlboro Man substitution face-praise even on a *vercochta* can of guiltifying bad Beijing air. Was it satisfying to see ego-Jin tormented this way? Yes, sure—but the real Jin was fine, you knew it. Slept like a baby, no doubt about it. Jin was no Chinese Communist (that joke), nor no Chinese capitalist (which was no joke). Jin was a Confucian—confusing to Westerners, but pardon that pun. Jin lived by an order that was old and was rational and made its decision on The Fat Man Problem rather than just posing it for students: if he sacrificed a person or a principle, a Nyemo, this was for more persons and for greater principles. No ceteribus no paribus. (But who determined the principles?—a principled man?—but who determined therefore who was the principled man? etc etc etc). Jin was how the world worked. THE (vulgar-dumb) HARMONY on those big Beijing billboards—it was not so vulgar-dumb. . . . And Now: With its row upon row of composite-plastified window shades up, down, and fractionways, creating searing crisscrossed light shafts on shielding shadow, Arthur looked about Economy's steerage, and forced a laugh (half-assed); and his immediate rowmate turned to him, and he laughed too. Shared forced laughter for no reason beyond that shared cocoon of intimacy, enforced. Shared forced laughter, better than a handshake. "Temujin", said Arthur's seatmate, extending an extremely adipose hand; he turned out to be a Mongolian-Kirgistani who happened to be a wrestler. He was short, hair close-cropped (nothing on the sides but skin and bone and ears, tiny pit-bull ears), maybe five/seven, eight, with a bulging belly—his Hawaiian shirt buttons kept popping open (just as had Nyemo's shirt-belly buttons) and got unembarrassingly rebuttoned (and then repopped)—and barrel chest and those hands as worn and calloused—and wraparound—as a catcher's mit. And this Temujin was smelly (the Chinese, owned Temujin, called his people "Stinkies"—which word they'd got from Westerners.). Temujin told Arthur that he had just come from a wrestling match in South Beijing (for some reason he made a point of its being *South* Beijing), a match between his people, his team, and the Chinese—and his boys had won: "The Chinese, they now these days, they try to wrestle the *Western* way (" 'Holds', ha—they call them '*holds*'!"). We, we Mongols and we Kirgis, we are 'primitive', *they* call it—we *throw* them down to the ground, so too with our bellies too we throw, and when they hit the ground, they don't bounce, bounce-back, like in the Bruce Leeses; they stay lay-down, flat from no air-breathing and *we* win, that is the rules—the Mongol-Kirgi rules." Tamujin then illustrated for Arthur his "earthquake thunder and sky lightning", his "body-grab-methodical", by close onto squeezing the daylights out of the frail (well, relatively) American who still (face it) saw himself as an American Jew, a narrow-shouldered intellectual. "And that's it?" wheezed Arthur (condescending by acting more huff-puff breath-squeezed-out even than he was—although he sure *was*), Arthur who did imagine that the

Western way was better, prettier, more analytic-strategic-conceptual-talented, more 'scientific'. "That is *it*, *our* way, because *we*, *we* are not *art*, we are not imitate or complicate, we are power and *belief,* no trick-lies—We *ground* them to the *ground!*—*and* because we dislike the Chinese, oh *do* we, they try to overpower us in every *other* way—they killed one *million* of us, you know." Arthur didn't know. Arthur pictured these calloused and fatbellied thick-chesters like Temujin beating the *kishkes* out of the two Han Chinese who had assaulted him in his room, those men from UMSEB, the "Urban Management Security Enforcement Bureau", them with their Ricky Rubalcava America-Fifties cars. Arthur laughed again, along with this wrestler Temujin, who was now on his way to matches in—where-else?—Germany (and England and Turkey), where, he said, he was sure his men (who he pointed out on the plane, those who he could locate), his men would win against the "civilized"—a word the Mongolian slavered-out as if that very word had barbarized the world. "I am sure too," Arthur said. (And then he lied that he would attend the match in Berlin, although that city was six train hours from 'his' Heidelberg). Arthur had been rendered lighthearted by a superficial thing, a wrestle-victory by the life-losers, for surely the Mongol-Kirgis would go on losing out to the life-winner Han-Mandariners in every other "civilized" aspect. Hell, they already had been. With that wrestling victory story for Arthur Becker had come the clearest-imagined witnessing of it—Mongols belly-bouncing and hurling Han! Mongols victory-dancing over grounded beaten Han—and then some pain-remission for him, which he sat with as they flew over Kazakhstan—orange dust, hills and Islam. "They are free, Kazakhstan," said Tamujin, "They are not *under* China—but they are *Russia's* poodle." "Can they defeat the Russians at wrestling?" Arthur asked as a joke. "Yes," said Tamujin. "And they do and do." . . . And there was a pause, in which vacuum they both laughed again, at nothing really, and this Tamujin raised his hands, and he stared straight about Economy and then he stared and stared straight ahead into his large hands, as if they were Something. "My only worry," he said, "is that the Westers, like you, you will make fun out of us Mongols, as do the Chinese."

"They won't," Arthur lied. "We won't."

So: Talk about your desecration of dignity, will you—and its relished bounceback (if only The Fat Man could fly; if only Nyemo could have broken out of black jail [except then he'd have done some new Tibetan-rebel thing and been hustled straight back to "The Black Death"]). Well, desecration, that was where all this ricocheting began: There was that desecration of dignity that had been baked into every slander-slogan that old Fritz Strobel had bought and then brickworked onto Arthur Becker's brain for years, really for the fun of it, for *his,* Strobel's, amusement, his silent *laughter*— he *needed* that?! "Man's inhumanity to man"—kneejerk or planned or justified—as normal as a fart, a loud-crack or a puffer, as every man misunderstands his self and misunderstands every other man, while believing that he *understands*. (Poor Temujin-pride if, say, the *Germans,* they defeat his poor Mongols.). And so thus the true miracle was (is) Morality; that we humans, immoral mothers from Jump (from "God's" intention?) have worked-up such a concept *as* Morality. That we have created The Fat Man and Ethics 101.

Because we are *not* immoral mothers from Jump.

We've got these goodness glimpses.

So Arthur Becker was now glad for his Mick-ah-yell—he told himself and he told himself. Married to Hung Huang: young marriage, yes (as had been Arthur Becker's), and to a good woman, a girl-woman who felt for others and who would work for others—a girl-woman who had discovered, pre-Mick-ah-yell, her powerful sex essentials and credentials and their gravity (*with Jin's help!?—her taking Nyemo up her ass, pleasure or not, it was Life, Life's Way, and, side issue, it built up Nyemo, No?—it was a Fat Man thing*). And did Mick know his powers equal to Hung's knowing hers? Good bet No—and maybe he suspected all this, and thus that impotence?

So Mick would come to learn that . . .that *what?*—the pleasure-pain principle.

Stop THINKING. Lufthansa Economy is hardly a think tank, it's a cramped delusion tank.

Scores of TV screens about him on seat-backs, and he watched not a one. No Woody Allens, no George Clooneys, none of the newer American guys whose names he didn't know—he'd been away too long, and anyway he could never enjoy a shrunk-down movie on a plane. Arthur closed his eyes, and what he watched now was not what he intended to watch (which was nothing), but She came nonetheless: She with her strong brown eyes and her pursed appraising lips, and that explicitly fixed but fragile avian structure that women often refer to as "good bones". No, not his wife Jutta, but his mother Eva: *She* who'd mattered before Jutta (and like Jutta, so like Jutta a helpmate, as when

dad Moe was off busting his balls trying for the
Majors), she and her quiet pain at Moe's suicide, she
hermitting it for some years, two years. Arthur Becker
had lived with that wide heart-hole, as if his soul were
one of those bundle-gathered Conestoga wagons of
good-folk surrounded by Apaches, those attacking
barbarian Injuns good folk too; Christ he lived with that
Eva misery as a young man watching in sympathy his
mourning-dismal mother just glomming-onto TV re-
runs as soon as she awoke (*All in the Family*—what
else?—as Sammy Davis came on to rap with funny-
bigot Archie Bunker, and then kissed him, just planted
one, hahahahaha); just as he watched as a younger man
his beshamed "loser" father—yet seeing his father too
as that hero-man-with-the-big-hook-curve, a Jew guy
winner who could hang with hillbillies and niggers
(though he bigot-badmouthed them) and who had
forearms bulging with manly (goyische) outgrowth
"weedy-beany" veins (Arthur had spent some years
doing free-weight curls to develop such "man-veins",
but they never came—must've been mom Eva's
smoother forearm genes). Murdering Strobel was,
basically, Temujin's "thunder and lightning", Nyemo's
rants (and ass-fucks), Arthur's forearm curls: Moe
Becker's Big Hook Forearms Wrist and Curve. . . For
Arthur Becker it was America! . . . It was the World.

It was also invisible: Old Strobel had no face—not
any longer. Going going gone. Except for, say, when
for some reason or no reason at all the Nazi's features
might find quick focus, sharp, acute, large as a night
flare, as when that bigot's atrial fibrillation had once
come on him at dinner in Heidelberg (and Arthur had,

at that time, *tried to help!)*—or it, the man's face, had manifested as a resonant vibrating jumping thing—*in yo'face*! Time a tranquilizer coming equipped with (or disguised as) an ice pick.

EPI

LIMBO'S BEAUTEOUS REWARD?

And so once home *(Home?—"Ah, the consoling normalcy of Germany!?")* you embrace an embracing Jutta, her forehead in tender fall onto your grimey traveled forehead, you caressing, raking, Jutta's short-cut hair; which gesture Jutta's right shoe ratifies by pressing on your left—an awkward instinct of hers, which has evolved over the years to a cute (albeit slightly annoying) code. Five-sevenths of a week (almost six) and you've missed Jutta's words, Jutta's love—so the crush-embrace is long, even though the missed days are trifling in their number; and after all there is that possible (probable?) Forever China—Tschaikovsky's "Till the End of Time"—for their Mick there is that. So disarray does fortify this hug. . . Along with, now—Jutta has had these few days to vex—Jutta's own guilt, for not having gone along. Couldn't she have taken *"eine blöd"* week off?—She says this!—*She should have taken one week off!* Arthur doesn't second this, he never did before he left, nor had he expressed letdown with a displeased face, no kind of disparaged face. Other professors—and not just of Business Admin/Econ—they would have jumped to go. Hell, The World's Fast Rising Superpower, this New China, with the heavy-duty racing GDP. Other Heidelberg profs would have located (scrounged-for) some *schlumpf* class-teach-substitute eager for adjunct laurels to earn a later full-time gig. But Jutta? Frau Conscientious?—two-time winner of Heidelberg U's prestigious University Award?—You kidding? But now the one Jutta-Morality leaps and tackles at the other.

"I'm sorry," she says now, "that I didn't go."

"I understood, you know that. I didn't expect you'd go. That you'd have been able to."

"Arthur, I know you did understand. But did *I*?"

Good question, honest-honor question, modesty question, a question she might have asked so many times and for so many things, and a question he might have forced her to ask or *asked* her to ask—while now after late dinner they've made it to early bed. Arthur expects that Jutta will continue now with her China regrets. But—

"There is a note here for you," she says, "from this Doktor Schiffer. From Heidelberg Krankenhaus."

My life's over.

"What'd it say?"

"You know I wouldn't read your mail. He didn't send it email, so it's private, personal, I do imagine. I didn't know that you knew any physicians at the hospital."

"I don't. I don't know the man."

Jutta's eyes loom and fall, forcing Arthur to create

*her thoughts: Is Arthur covering-up some sickness?—
one so serious it bypasses email? Has Arthur been in
constant contact with this* Arzt? *Not merely a doctor
with a street office but a man at the big Krankenhaus. Is
Arthur protecting me? Doesn't he trust me enough to
tell me?—he knows I can handle anything, whatever
sickness he has I will be within as well, fighting it. . . .
He does not wish for me to know that I will be alone,
with a son in China.*

"Arthur, you have a health worry?" She touches his
chest, nuzzling there what in their youth-days she'd
once tabbed "Your Jewish Black Forest—I love it."
Now she lightly caresses it.

He holds her hand there, it has become a quick
palliative against the dangerous intrusions of the
investigator *Überarzt* Schiffer—her hand must stay and
stay.

"I have no health worry. Jutta, I don't."

Only murder. Prison.

She's seeing his worried eyes worrying, but about
the wrong thing. It pains him to be covering up the
truth. *But what truth! Was it in any way possible that
my first suffering and finally suffocating that old racist
bastard Strobel actually proved my love for Jutta?—my
anger at that man's influence over her? Can I convince
myself of this?—even if it does hold a trace of truth.*

*Would Germany convict a Jew of murdering an old-
time Nazi, even a professor? That wouldn't look so
good for the now Champion of Europe, Chrissakes
they're even now allowing in a million refugee Syrians
while no other Euro-land is even coming close. Still . . .*

Still, you see Nyemo, and you keep seeing: Nyemo
hanging from iron meathook-clasps in his black jail

cell, the boy's face rigid with Morality and Right and Sad Vengeance that is Impotent, the boy sewn into a black shawl, sealed, a votive body bag. Becker's brain had seen this image all along on the plane, as folks watched Woody and Clooney go through their patented quirks and singularities, and as Becker and Tamujin the Mongol had, at crappy Chinese wrestling, enjoyed underdog therapeutic laughs.

"Anyway, the note is in an envelope. Sealed, as it did come through the post."

Jutta's questioning eyes have not diminished in the slightest. They even seem to be pulsating.

"Where is it?"

"I put it on your desk. On your laptoptop top. You want to go up and see?"

He does, you bet he does. But of course he doesn't go. He says he'll check it out later, or tomorrow. No biggie (is this super-biggie), that's the message to the worried wife who wants for him to go up and see—and then *tell her!* Mister "Unworried" Casual imagines Doctor Schiffer's chosen formal words. He pictures trial and then that *Deutsche* prison—so much more clean and well-ordered than an American or a French.

Maintaining her hand on his chest, now keeping it still, Jutta returns to her own issue: "*Quatsch*," she says, "I just should have gone."

So seldom, so seldom, is his wife remorseful—but perhaps that is not the best word. Jutta rarely questions her decisions. She always has reasons, her reasons. Always spontaneous, out of a pop-open box, Jokerless, and always For The Best—the best inherently found, and don't you argue. The Best is the pedestrian form of the Jutta Libidinal.

Arthur does not kiss his wife. He reaches for her shortcut hair, his palm holding onto her cheek. He's saying I understand you, my wife. I love you.

By elbow-liftoff from her pillow (large-ass *German* pillows, large as oat feedbags: *Why*?) Jutta is now looking down at him, determinedly shaking-shaking her head. Stopping. Shaking once again. She puts him in mind of—he can't help it—himself lumbering over Strobel on his huge thera-pillow in the *Krankenhaus*. To kill the Nazi bastard or not to kill?! Hamletskovitchsky. Once again he sees poor belligerent Nyemo the Tibetan. Ingrate Nyemo (after all, the Han did give him a scholarship!—they didn't give son Mick-ah-yell yuan-one), Nyemo underneath the big bigot China heel and hopelessly fighting back—air-swings, air roundhouses, the Impotence of Forced Sparring. . . Jutta's face over Arthur Becker's: Some puff-hangings at the cheeks, dewlaps not-quite-but-threatening, a lapse under the chin begun: so thus from two decades of life's gravity with Arthur, Mick, and university; Jutta's neck's crinkles—no, mostly he feels it's *he*, he-and-his-shtick, Arthur-Nyemo shtick, Arthur-Moe shtick, which has created this decay—*decay!?* (*Christ, call it breakup? call it crimps, call it flounces!*)—it all might not have begun for another decade with some other husband, some calm and cocky kraut, some straight-upper; but it's *Arthur* now who would *also* think these Jutta scrunchups are luxurious—just now he *would*—and damned if he doesn't *love* her neck. Jutta-molecules. These markings of so many years, he could almost name them, the events responsible. . . He kisses them, some of them, and she studies him, but smiling. She's not embarrassed—she's too *her* for that. And, she knows him.

They have had a weird pre-nup—not written-down, implied: If their son grew up in Germany rather than in America, the mom had heftier obligations, weighty work, headaches. She has always known this. Arthur has always known this. She has always been torn by this—he too. She has never regarded it as any sort of victory. . . But he has, his loss. So the headaches she was supposed to have, *he* had. . . As much as she did, anyway.

She touch-taps his nose: The Sweet Hostility of Affection.

He starts in telling her of Jin Jianxin, of Hung. Estimable people, couldn't be better. He's never met better. Despite his Jin-reservations he actually believes what he says as he says it—and then he realizes that he truly *does* believe it—why not! He also believes that she, Jutta, would have been a better emissary with Jin— two big civil libertarians sharing implored civil liberties, conflicts, decisions, letdowns and their created schisms and even required evils. . . He mentions neither Nyemo nor Tibet.

As if her sight can sigh she closes her lids to lashes and says, "I just really should have gone. I would have learned. That opportunity is foregone. There is nothing that can change that. I can be so stubborn."

He decides to say, "It's not stubbornness."

She begins to smile in a kind of love-gratitude, but there is that old quiver-quake about the Jutta mouth that no one outside the family has ever been witness to—he is so sure of that. Intimacy's whole bouquet.

"We *will* be at the wedding," Jutta says. "You *and* I. Full-stop."

"Yup, full-stop."

Yes she'd meant 'Period'. She can be as guilty as a Herr High-tone of those poor German-*faux*-Oxfordisms too.

He hadn't intended to, but he now does mention Nyemo. Low-voiced as a hum, a solemnity, an Amen—the Tibetan's name does make such aspiration easy, unavoidable—but Arthur's leaving out now the deepest Hung-involvement (but which he can't help picturing [and picturing]), he tells the poor tale of the Tibetan-in-Beijing.

"This Nyemo," Jutta says, "he is like The White Rose."

"Those Munich kids in the Thirties who rebelled against Hitler."

"They were killed."

"Not that China is Nazi Germany."

"Not that China is Nazi Germany."

Jutta's arms are strong, her supporting elbow must be painless: he's aware that he could not support himself over her in this way she has held herself above him, not for so long. To brace her, although she sure doesn't seem to need his buttress, he fastens his right hand round her elbow, and her grin at his unnecessary effort is adoring.

"Did our Mick bring himself to be involved? To help this Nyemo?"

"With revolutionary Tibetans, you mean?—their underground? No. They are some scary cats."

" 'Cats'." One of those Americanisms of which he's got aplenty and she loves—or pretends to, for she so often mocks them.

Damnit, he has just excused Mick and his passivi-

257

ty—which he'd not done when he was in Beijing.

A worrisome turn of her neck to him, her eyes promising that they, she, can divine any protective lies. Not that he needs such reminder.

"Mick is more involved in becoming Han Chinese—in the normal way."

"Normal? Such a wide doorway is that word."

Mick is not even 'normal' here in Germany. So he lets his 'normal' slide away.

Jutta's outward stillness—Arthur knows it, he has faced it so often: She is relieved that her son will not be killed while helping "scary" Tibetans. Mick is not on *that* tenure track. *And*, she is disappointed that her son has not helped "scary" Nyemo and "poor" Tibet by being an Asian White Rose Boy. Her other self *would* like Mick *on that* tenure track. . .

It's The Fat Man Problem rearing its protean head.

Who in the world is not ambiguous? Dangerous people with no qualms. Ambiguity the humanity of the world.

"China," says Jutta, "it will progress itself to democracy."

She's nodding as she speaks. She does this often. Her affirmation of her voice which has not yet reached full unambiguous opinion or belief. Becker knows this is how she teaches. It is not the worst way to be an example to a class.

Her right hand has fallen to his balls. It is like asking a question: 'I know you've had a hard long tiring trip, but.'

He covers her hand with his.

This is—what can you say?—nice.

His penis is not hard, nor does he expect that it is

headed along that route.

He doubts really that she even expected it.

He does expect however that she expected he might expect that she might, well, expect. Or offer.

Marriage—The Fat Man Problem.

A thought has never left him, it's honkered in, a lead implant: this Doctor Schiffer, *Oberarzt*. A hospital bigshot hot on his ass: *Don't forget who you are and what you've done!*

They lay on their backs in bed. Arthur had long ago learned to sleep that way, as Jutta had picked-it-up way longer before. And it wasn't easy, this alertish sleeping at-the-ready: the flat lay implied keep your eyes keen, ears too, leap-if-called-upon; or just read—and it hurt his back, the lumbar. He has never seen advertised on German TV the Sleep Number Bed. Were such available he would talk Jutta into one—she'd lay out at 90 and he at 10 or so, or was it the other way? Perhaps Jutta had learned to sleep on her back naturally, since childhood—just as he had. Her reasons would have been different—imagining the good, possible and impossible, a little White Rose Girl. . . Ah, CHILDHOOD: Ah, Mick's kid, Becker's grandkid—a Wu? a Ju? (*haha—I just can't resist.*)—he/she might be crawling into bed with Mick and Hung in a few years and wondering why his/her eyes are more moony and his/her lips less overbit and his/her height this and skin that and and and and? Different from who?—Mick or Hung?—or was there a Nyemo in the woodpile? Arthur on his back was amazed at how, well not exactly proud, but receptive he was to such a prospect. Life can be nothing without its fantasies, its ambiguities—and,

well, its cruelties calling forth, begging for its good. . .
And speaking of good, or amazing, it was always that,
it was wondrous, a sublime thing really, when in the
morning they, Art and Jutta, awoke hands held. It did
happen—what? once-in-ten? Times were though, when
in night's middle Arthur had had to get up to pee, he
had had to softly separate then return from the toilet and
reattach their hands—it could seem prosaic as
electricity, a plug-in; or call it a quiet religious act, a
sacrament in the dark; and/or a medical act, like a
surgeon retiming an off-beating heart. Jutta felt it, sure
she did, but really she knew to conceal her knowing
was best, and that even within her self (Arthur would
swear to that) Jutta would assist in the rejoining (again,
subtle, concealed even within her self), dear volition
alive in the secret chamber of one's hand—a bit, well,
like their marriage. . . What Arthur knew was that,
before Mick-ah-yell he and Jutta had lived together
more easily in Germany, she reading his writing, she
offering her kind intelligence (based on the European
novel: "More *writing*, darling, less *dialogue!*"), he
attending her economics classes (at times), happily
amazed at what a befuddled dope he was with the
calculus—for that made Jutta a genius—even if she
wasn't one. Truth was that for young Arthur then it
hadn't been so bad, that German thing. That Jutta thing
that did not dance as, say, young Annetta Barron had,
or even Hung might. Be honest, you bigot: Arthur's
Heidelberg street-ambivalence (or antipathy) could in
those days be turned-round by a random German's
smile. . . Now, Mick gone, Mick's duality, that struggle
so unwanted by Mick, Arthur could hope for such
virginal return? Hope, yes. But, come on. . . .

Doctor Schiffer was there, the Hospital *Oberarzt*. That probable disaster of that waiting letter.

Might Arthur try going to Chizuk Amuno once again? Talk to the Rabbi. Explain what he could not explain.

Like a lifebuoy, hold onto Jutta once again. Fully hold.

But the jet lag: on his back, holding hands with his wife, leaving the Schiffer letter for the morning, and being a writer, he couldn't help but create its payload:

Ich bin ein Deutscher Patriot
Nichts wird passieren.

Appeased then, hoping he might have created the right appeasement, he was already gone gone gone— and was that marrow-sounding that he heard full praying? *God, You Understand: Our Goods Can Be Our Bads: Forgive Me.*

FOR COMMENTS TO THE AUTHOR
PLEASE CONTACT:

americaneditions@aol.com

www.ingramcontent.com/pod-product-compliance
Lightning Source LLC
Chambersburg PA
CBHW022153170626
46807CB00005B/2195